Secrets of a D-List Supervillain

by

Jim Bernheimer

Visit the author's website at www.JimBernheimer.com

First Printing: January 2015

Print ISBN: 1507540604

Print ISBN-13: 978-1507540602

Dedication and Acknowledgements

There is something special when an author finishes a third book in a series. I've officially made it to the land of trilogy. Shockingly enough, I've written three books in a series and people are still reading it. Pretty amazing stuff if you ask me! Thanks to the fans for coming on this trip with me. You folks keep coming back and I'll keep writing.

As always, I want to thank Kim, Laura, and Marissa. You are the reason I keep at this.

My group of advanced readers (Flora "Crazy Cat Lady" Demuth, David "42" Bagini, Graham "Frat Boy" Adzima, and Todd "No Filter Ever" Osborne) deserve special thanks for being a sounding board and helping me to navigate the treacherous backwaters of this ever evolving story. My hope is to one day be successful enough to visit all of you except for Todd. I see his ass at work every day. So, I actually hope I will be successful enough to only see Todd occasionally. That would be cool.

David Wood and Janine Spendlove (Garner) have both taught me lessons in being a published author that go far beyond writing. David is a master of productivity and every time I am fortunate enough to be in the presence of Janine and her husband, Ron, I am reminded of the power of positive thinking and how people who are kind and gracious can get ahead in this business.

Janet Bessesy at Dragonfly Editing takes a bow for hammering out my plethora of grammatical errors and I certainly keep her busy. I'll go ahead and thank Jeffrey Kafer for what will once again be the incredible audiobook he creates.

There's a whole bunch of other people I thanked with cameos – Patrice, Jeannie, Larry Hitt (well a little bit more than a cameo there), Dave Evans, Amanda Rae Westfal, and fellow authors Megan Bostic and Joe Ducie. Thank you for your participation.

Special thanks to Jay Herbig for post Kindle release corrections.

Secrets of a D-List Supervillain

Chapter One

The Present is Prologue

"Guess I'll need to change the sheets," I observe, and wipe some of the chocolate syrup onto the pillowcase. I'm exhausted, but in a good way. The reduced lighting in my bedroom does me a favor by disguising the horrible mess we made in the names of science and make up sex.

Beside me, Stacy Mitchell smiles and tugs at the sticky clumps of her hair. "I'd expected something more from what everyone says about it. Maybe we did it wrong?"

Considering the way I feel, I need to refute her statement. "I don't think there's a 'doing it wrong' when you're involved, Stacy. Maybe you just can't get any more awesome than you already are? You're kind of like a peanut butter cup."

"What?"

"You know, perfect. Don't make it bigger, don't change the type of chocolate, and for God's sake don't put the peanut butter on the outside!"

The avatar of Aphrodite rolls her eyes and says, "That's sweet, Cal. I see you haven't changed at all. I'm still amazed that I'm talking to you and you're not actually dead!"

"It turns out the one thing; maybe the only thing that I'm really good at is being a survivor. I'm not a real good superhero and even worse as a villain. Being a survivor is the one thing I'm good at. I sucked at being a hero and the sad thing is that I was a better hero than a villain."

She rests her chin on her palm. "I think you're exaggerating. You weren't so bad."

Arching an eyebrow, I say, "Remember Mardi Gras?"

She frowns before replying, "Even so, you're selling yourself short again, Cal. You built a powersuit by yourself that outclassed Ultraweapon. I bet I could name a couple of more things you're good at. For starters, you're a bestselling author."

Technically, she's right. The book sold way better than I ever imagined. "Wendy mentioned you'd been taking a lot of heat over it—sorry."

Also, I decide not to say that Wendy seemed rather pleased about that fact. *Then again, the tiny tornado queen received a more favorable treatment.* In her interviews, most people dance around that whole *second level* part. Others just jump in and start talking about it and there have been at least three pornos made on the topic. Naturally, I watched them all—just to be certain they were close to the source material, of course.

On a related note, Stacy doesn't do nearly as many interviews as she used to.

She chooses her reply with care. "I'd be more upset, but unfortunately, your portrayal of me was probably closer to truth than I liked."

"Maybe for Mindwiped Stacy, but not for you," I say, with the hope of building up some brownie points. "So, what now, beautiful?"

My reward is a smile. "Why don't we shower, and then I want to hear all the details."

Her question baffles me and I respond, "Didn't I tell you when you first got here? It was all pretty straightforward."

Aphrodite gives me a piercing gaze and says, "Oh, really? Forgive me if I say that you glossed over several important parts in your book. We haven't been together in over a year and that two minute explanation just isn't going to cut it."

"You really want to hear all that?" I ask, slightly taken back. Yeah, I'm being a hypocrite. I went out and published the edited version of my life. In doing so, I managed to polish away most of the *suck* that seems to follow me around like a shadow.

"Actually, I do," she says while standing; her bare flesh defiled by streaks of chocolate. "Two questions. Is the shower still in the same spot and do you want to join me?"

"Yes to both," I reply. "Give me five to try and straighten up in here."

"Don't keep me waiting, Cal."

Doing my best to commit the motion of her ass to memory, I tackle the messy sheets and try to decide whether to scrub the whipped cream off the ceiling or just let it fall. The antigravity generator gave out after two hours—pretty shoddy work on my part. In my defense, I was very distracted during the assembly.

With a shrug, I start balling up the sheets up and mutter, "I'll just retask one of the maintenance bots into a janitor for the rest of this disaster area. What's the point in having robots if I'm not going to use them?"

Pushing the comm button I say, "Andrew, my good friend, could you send a janitor in here in... oh I don't know, thirty minutes. Pay attention to the ceiling, it's pretty jacked up."

"You seem especially happy this morning, Calvin. I see copulation with the female of your choice has improved your disposition. I will do as you request, my friend."

"Thanks, bud," I reply. Under Andydroid's direction, I won't have to spend three hours programming a robot to do forty-five minutes of work, because I would seriously do that. I'm that rare kind of lazy that will go to extraordinary lengths to avoid doing something I don't want to.

There's a copy of my book on the nightstand with a glob of whipped cream smearing the cover. Stacy doesn't seem to be holding it against me... at least for now. One person I probably owe an apology to, if it ever gets out that I'm alive, is Chain Charmer. Jin can't go anywhere without people asking, or even demanding, to try on his magic necklace. The necklaces grants people powers, like Charmer's ability to control all those unbreakable chains like extra limbs. The other one is presumed destroyed, along with me, a few miles west of Los Angeles. In truth, it is under Larry Hitt's costume. On a person with superpowers, it actually cuts their abilities in half. Without it, Larry was Imaginary Larry, a telekinetic titan who is so strong that his mind couldn't handle it, and he ended up reliving his high school days over and over. With the necklace, he's no longer insane and unbelievably powerful, just mostly sane and incredibly powerful.

Rounding my three minutes of introspection and half-assed cleanup up, I figure I've kept the lovely woman without a shower buddy for long enough. I'm not sure where this is headed. My track record for relationships isn't exactly stellar, and the Olympian and I have already crashed and burned once before, but it's comical that I've made it this far in life, so why stop to think of what could go wrong.

"Damn," I say with a grunt. "Probably just jinxed myself!"

• • •

"Your coveralls still don't fit," Stacy comments, while wrestling with the material as we walked down the short corridor to Central Command.

"Guess we weren't thinking about the possible mishaps when we disrobed," I answer. "Andy will get your clothes clean in a jiffy. As for the coveralls, both Larry and Bobby are bigger than I am. I'd be tempted to let you rifle through the things Wendy keeps in her room, but that would be more amusing for me than you."

3

"Cal, you're also forgetting the fact that I would kick your ass," a different female voice replies. "Hello, Aphrodite."

The diminutive Italian powerhouse doesn't look especially happy. Larry and Bobby are both decidedly interested in the unfolding events. I wouldn't be surprised if there is some kind of wager in place.

"Morning, Wen," I say, and plaster a smile on my face, and ponder how I can get in on any action related to this encounter. "Where's the munchkin?"

"Playing in her playpen in my room. I'd have left Gabby with Mom if I knew you were entertaining."

I shrug. "Came as a surprise to me as well, besides I'm always entertaining, aren't I?"

"Maybe in your dreams, Strings," WhirlWendy says, and rolls her eyes. Gesturing between me and the Olympian she continues, "Does this present any kind of conflict of interest to the team?"

"No boss, I don't think so."

"Don't let it become a problem, then," the mother of my child states in her thick New Yorker accent.

"Interesting team you have here, Wendy," Stacy tries to break the ice. She seems slightly miffed that Wendy is talking "around" her like she's just another object in the room. As Aphrodite, she's not used to being ignored.

Which is probably why Wendy is doing it.

"That's a word for it," Wendy answers. "I could think of several others off the top of my head."

I just showered, so the stench of hostility must be coming from her. Instead of voicing my opinion, I look at Andydroid and ask, "Anything going on? Where's the Megasuit?"

"Your armor is currently in southern California combatting wildfires. Our retention pond has been reduced to thirty percent capacity. As a result of that, I have switched to pulse cannons and am creating a fire break, at this moment in time."

"Cool, I guess," I acknowledge him, and look at Stacy. "Andy runs the suit when I'm not in it. Part of the reason everyone keeps thinking Mega is a robot, because it is always out in the field. They think it's helping our public image. Me? I think it's a waste of time. When's the last time I cared about my image?"

"I thought you're set on calling yourself Ultraweapon now, Cal?"

"I still might," I reply. "But Ultraweapon turned out to be a loser. Why would I want a loser name?"

Bobby coughs something that sounds suspiciously like "ManaCALes" and Larry gets in on the act by smacking his chest with his palm and choking out "Mechani-CAL."

"Go eff yourselves," I say to the dipshit duo.

"You know something? That's one thing that's always bugged me 'bout you Cal," Bobby states. "You never say 'fuck.' You've been to prison. Hell! You've killed people, but in all the time I've been around you, I can't remember ever hearing you say the 'F' word."

Now everyone is looking at me expectantly, like I'm supposed to reveal some great mystery.

"I don't know!" I protest. "Why do some people say soda and others say pop? I just don't like the word."

"Mommy issues," Bobby says, while looking at Larry.

Exasperated, I look to Wendy. Her response, "Your hang ups are not my fucking problem. Can we get down to business now?"

"That would be nice. Anything stirring on VillainNet?"

"You're on VillainNet? How? No one has been able to stay on it very long." Stacy stammers as Wendy shoots me a dirty look. I guess I wasn't supposed to bring that up.

I point at Bobby. "He's a criminal and keeps telling anyone who will listen that this is *his* base."

"It is," Bobby states.

"Might as well take advantage of it, and what the Wireless Wizard doesn't know won't hurt us one bit. We run all of our Internet traffic elsewhere. Best anyone can tell, it's just Bobby here."

The Wizard runs a pretty tight ship and so far we've been able to keep him suspecting that Bobby is really a mole. After all, who'd ever suspect Hillbilly Bobby of being a spy, or a regular bather for that matter?

"Oh," she says, unable to come up with anything for a second.

"That reminds me," Bobby says. "Apostle wants to hire me for extra muscle. Want me to take it or turn it down?"

Wendy nods, but I have reservations. "I dunno. Apostle is pretty well-connected, but he's notorious for taking out failures on his underlings. He's definitely the Old Testament fire and brimstone."

"Getting soft on me, Cal? Ain't nothing Mr. Bible thumper can do to me that I can't take!"

Except, oh I don't know—maybe killing you. "What's the job?"

"Won't know 'til I show up."

"How about the money?"

"Fifty up front another fifty on the back end."

A hundred for Bobby? "Sounds suspicious. No offense pal, but you don't usually rate that much, and if you get bagged during the job we'll have to help you escape custody again."

Out of the corner of my eye, I notice Stacy's sideways glance. *Guess I shouldn't have brought that up either. She probably doesn't approve.*

"I'm sure all of you have taken into account the risks of running an unsanctioned superteam? It's not exactly a friendly environment out there these days."

"I'm a dead guy with a pardon... finally," I say, and point at each of the members of The Reinforcements. "Larry's been declared mentally incompetent, Bobby is an unrepentant criminal and, Andy has been replaced by his creator. The only one with anything to lose is the one giving the orders, and she's America's darling."

Stacy turns to Wendy and says, "Don't you think this is hurting your father's chances at becoming President?"

With a pained look on her face, the team leader replies, "Do you think my dad would actually make a good President? I'm his daughter and I'm convinced he wouldn't!"

Bobby opens his mouth—no doubt ready to say, "Daddy issues." I give him a look that says he's on his own if he's dumb enough to blurt that out.

He wisely reconsiders.

I voice my thoughts on the matter. "I wouldn't be voting for him because I'm supposed to be dead and all that, but even so, he seems to be the one leading the charge to get all the supers firmly under Uncle Sam's thumb. Thankfully, they know they can't push too hard. I think Hera did a good job putting Senator LaGuardia in his place."

Stacy seems somewhat mollified when I point out that her current team leader has recently endured a testy senate hearing, which culminated in her pointing out that the Olympians had a duty to the world and not just America. They could easily relocate to some place like The Hague if the US Government is no longer interested in their services.

Superhero community 1—Power mongering politicians 0, well at least for the time being. Even I'm not daft enough to think there won't be a rematch.

"Ah, to hell with it!" Stacy declares and spreads her hands out. "I didn't come here to fight. You five seem like you've got the angles covered. If it wasn't for your unsanctioned team, Lazarus would have killed me in San Fran. That gives you a pass in my books. Let me know if you need my help and we can probably do something on the sly."

Wendy pauses for a moment and then nods. "Thank you, Aphrodite. We can probably do a limited amount of information sharing. We're monitoring VillainNet through the jobs Bobby is being offered, but we don't really care how many banks E.M. Pulsive has robbed this month. We're more interested in stopping the next World Domination scheme. That brings me back to my earlier point. The Apostle isn't going to be the next one trying to take over the world, but he's going to be someone that The Evil Overlord, or whomever else, will need, in order to do it. Getting Bobby's foot in that door might get us closer to the big fishes. It's really up to you in the end, Bobby. Think it over today and get back to us tomorrow morning. I don't have anything else for anyone, so let's call it a day."

"Fair enough," Bobby says and stands up. "With the water in the pond so low, there oughtta be some good fishing. Wanna come, Larry?"

The telekinetic shakes his head and goes to grab a six-pack from the fridge. "Used to cut school and go down to the fishing hole all the..." Larry trails off, stopping for a second before finishing, "Nah, I guess that shit never happened. Damn memories! All right, Bobby let's go catch some fish."

There is no chance in hell of me being confused for humanitarian of the year, but I did feel bad for the poor lunk. The loss of over 20 years of his life to his guilt and powers, as his mind continuously forced Larry to relive his high school years, over and over again. Helping him out is one of the items on the short list of things I've done that the world at large might support.

On the plus side, he can play every instrument taught in both orchestra and band. With me on the drums, Bobby playing the guitar, and Larry on the violin, we can give you a pretty good rendition of *Point of No Return* by Kansas. Andy does the lead vocals until we locate a singer, but he's too perfect. To a wannabe musician like me, it's a greater transgression than auto-tune.

I just can't tell him that!

"Are you leaving Gab-Gab?"

"Assuming you can watch her, Cal. Are you capable of that?"

Before replying, I muse, *I definitely made her sound too nice in the book.* "Of course I can, Wendy. Quit being nasty. Why don't you go see that Paper Tiger guy you're so into?"

"Maybe I will," Wendy says. "Maybe I'll start bringing him around here, too."

Yeah, I've about had it with her attitude. "Look, I didn't know Stacy would get her memories back. She could've shown up here with her entire team in tow, but she didn't, because she came to see me."

My leader gives me a death glare worthy of Blazing She-Clops and says, "I'm out! I'll be back tomorrow afternoon."

A forceful jet of air carries her over to the recently built secondary entrance shaft while scattering papers, empty beer cans, and everything else all over the place. An updraft propels her out of sight and forces me to open and close my mouth a couple of times to adjust to the sudden pressure change.

"I don't think America's sweetheart likes me," the remaining female says, after the air current dies down. "Are you sure Wendy isn't hung up on you?"

"That's just the wishful thinking of all those people who read the book. It's an unintended consequence of me being too nice to her when I wrote it. In my defense, she did have my bun in her oven at the time. If I had to guess what was behind that outburst, it would be that she thinks I'll start being less of a father to Gabby if you're back in my life."

"Because that's one of the traits I really look for in a guy," Stacy says, her voice dripping with sarcasm. "Do people really think I'm that shallow?"

I'm already picking up everything Wendy's exit kicked up. "Probably comes with the territory of being the Love Goddess. However, it was more directed at me and how shallow she thinks *I am.* Mind giving me a hand, and then I'll introduce you to the most important girl in my life."

As Stacy starts to help, I reflect that while I'm not nearly as superficial as Wendy fears, I'm also not nearly as deep as I pretend to be. My heart of gold is closer to pyrite than the real thing, but now I'm going to make damn sure I'm a great father if, for no other reason, than to rub Wendy's nose in it.

After all, she keeps saying how she's the most mature member of this team. I shouldn't disappoint her.

• • •

"She's adorable," Stacy says with my one year old bouncing on her knee. Gabby seems to be at ease with the Olympian... or she has gas. It could be both.

Reaching over, I run my fingers through the young one's fine black hair. "Her looks are from Wendy. Best I can tell is that she got her digestive tract from me. The girl can really fill a diaper."

"Any signs of powers?" She goes straight for the million dollar question.

"Nothing yet, but Wendy's didn't show until she was eight."

"So, what's going on with her and Paper Tiger?"

Paper Tiger is a sketch artist with the power to possess and animate his sketches, so long as they are of a tiger. They can be Flying Tigers, Ninja Tigers, or even Robotigers. He has sketches in places all over the world and can be on any continent in seconds.

"When her mother hired Paper Tiger to be Wendy's bodyguard during the final months of her pregnancy, people started talking. Wendy was going to go ahead and quit the Gulf Coast Guardians, but changed her mind when Paper Tiger joined that team and she just went to being a reserve member. I'm pretty sure there's more going on than just talk between them. Wendy knows his real identity and has gone to see him, wherever he lives. Actually, he's a helluva a scout, and I wouldn't mind him on this squad eventually."

"I don't know much about the man," Stacy says, fishing the pacifier from the folds of her coveralls and putting it back in Gabby's mouth. I could see the gleam in my daughter's eyes as she immediately spit it out again. "We have one of his drawings in Mount Olympus, and he went out with us a couple of times as backup. Not exactly a heavy hitter, but pretty good in his own right."

She echoes my opinion of the dude. Of course, I'm not that far removed from the D-List where I'd be looking down at a guy on the B-List. Wendy likes him and that makes her less interested in getting all up in my business. I consider that a win for both of us. "Yeah, so you really want to know how all this happened? It's better as a mystery, trust me."

Aphrodite laughs and plays the pacifier game again. "Well, you're not planning on writing another book are you?"

Grimacing, I shake my head. "No. I'm hanging up my pen."

"Well then, I'm the only one you're revealing this to, so spill."

"All right then, let's see. Where should I begin? I guess I should start right after my armor got turned to stone."

Chapter Two

Everyone's Naked, so Pass the Eye Bleach

Kicking the dinosaur's body didn't serve any real purpose; it was pretty obvious that thing was dead, but it did make me feel slightly better, because he'd turned my armor to stone. Hell! If there was more left of Tyrannosorcerer Rex's head, I'd have been sorely tempted to cut it off and mount it on a wall at the headquarters. Given the current state of my team, I actually didn't think they'd mind.

In the dirt, near where second base would normally go, was Kimodo's body—no more alive than this piece of shit. A hunk of flesh roughly the size of the grapefruit was missing from the area where her heart would normally be. Everyone, including me, had assumed she was another Manglermal. Instead, Kim Lemoine turned out to be a grad student from LSU who'd been transformed into a human reptile hybrid by the same magic that almost did us in. Truth be told, I didn't like her and thought she wasn't cut out for this line of work. In retrospect, I had been partially right and equally wrong at the same time.

That's the story of my life; I thought and kicked old Rexxie one last time. The few people who'd shaken off the effects of the transformation flitted like hummingbirds from one patient to the next while waiting for emergency responders to arrive. My desperation tactic had saved the day, but left at least one death and numerous injuries in its wake. In the old "villain" days, there'd be a press release and I'd jump up on the most wanted list. Now that I was a "hero," there would still be a press release, but the spin would say how hard the team worked to minimize all the suffering. Two sides of the same coin, if you asked me.

Instead of heading to the outfield with my limited first aid skills, I left it to the others and walked toward the foul ball area between first base and the dugout, looking for the wreckage from my hoverdrone. I moved cautiously, taking care to avoid any of the fragments of the destroyed portal that killed both the dinosaur and Kimodo—no telling what that magic would do to any part of me that touched it. After She-Dozer ripped me out of the statue that my armor had turned into, I was left barefoot and wearing a pair of shorts that I'd recently pissed in. Not exactly fearsome superhero attire.

My other robot, Roller, was now nothing more than a smoking crater where the chain-link backstop and a section of the bleachers used to be, but I still might be able to salvage something from floater.

"Hey," a voice called from inside the darkened dugout. "Cal Stringel? Is that you?"

I wasn't exactly a household face just yet, so the fact that someone called me out piqued my curiosity.

"Yeah," I replied. "It's me. Now who are you?"

The guy leaned out of the dugout and I could see the long blond hair and the moonlight reflecting off of the Minotaur carrying a battle ax tattoo on his chest. I knew that tattoo! He didn't have any clothes on. That meant he'd been one of the transformed dinosaurs. Since the T-Rex went down over in this area, I had a pretty good idea what happened to him.

"Holy shit! Bobby!"

"Small world ain't it?" he said. "Sure didn't expect to see you here, especially with a few of those heroes around. I saw little Sheila and that guy with the chains."

Sure enough, Bobby Walton didn't look that much different from what I remembered. I hadn't seen my old roommate since we fought the previous incarnation of the Gulf Coast Guardians and lost. Hillbilly Bobby was dragged off to prison as soon as he had been treated for his injuries.

"Stringel? What the hell is going on? Why are we on a baseball field in the middle of the night and why am I naked? I can't remember a damned thing! Some freaky shit must've went down."

"We're in Louisiana. Some magic-using dinosaur turned you into a T-Rex. My team got lucky and killed him, but it cost me my armor."

"You went and got yourself a team? Who's on it?"

"I'm part of the Gulf Coast Guardians now, but don't give me any shit about it, either! If it wasn't for me, you and She-Dozer would be hatching little baby dinosaurs together."

"With my cuz? That's nasty!"

"Wait! Sheila is your cousin?"

"Well, yeah," Bobby replied. "She's Leonard's sister. You didn't know that?"

"No," I said, and tried to figure out how I'd never put that together. That meant she'd been the one in the pond with him the day they got their powers.

"And here I thought you were the smart one. Sometimes you amaze me, Stringel."

He has me there! "Yeah, it's a gift. All right, Sheila's running around trying to salvage this mess, so you'd better go on and get out of here before she gets back and recognizes you."

Bobby looked puzzled and says, "If you're supposed to be a *hero* now, aren't you going to try and take me in?"

The way he said the word hero made it sound like some kind of vile and disgusting word.

"I'm just getting a paycheck and a pardon, Bobby. Don't read too much into it." I was almost tempted to make some kind of illiteracy joke, but without my armor I wouldn't stand a snowball's chance in hell against him.

"Fair enough," Bobby said, and slipped out of the dugout. "I'm kinda naked though."

"There's a lot of that going around right now. Not really as cool as I thought it would be either. I think there's a thrift store two streets over; probably something in there that'll fit you. Get to our base in Alabama and sit tight. I'll meet up with you when I can. The code for the elevator is 8675309, just like the song. It might take me awhile because I have to try and cobble together a new suit, but there's plenty of food and beer."

Actually, I was kind of low on beer and most of the food was still frozen waffles, but he didn't need to know that.

• • •

"Heya, Cal," a man's voice said from behind me. "I thought that was you. Saw you handling Bobby and figured I'd wait until he was gone."

Shocked to be recognized for a second time tonight, I turned away from the useless wreckage of floater, the putrid smell of rancid eggs assaulted my sense of smell. The cloud of vapor rushed together and coalesced into yet another naked man. This one had white hair and a scruffy salt-and-pepper beard that brought the familiar banjo tones of *Deliverance* to mind. I didn't know his real name, but his nickname was Hooch.

Did I mention that the fifty-something year old was naked? It seemed to be a theme.

"Swamp Lord," I called him by the name most knew him by. "I could've used your help about an hour ago."

"My memories are kind of fuzzy, but I think we were fighting each other."

"You were the Triceratops?"

"Maybe. I think so. It's slowly coming back to me. I... I sensed some kind of disturbance in the bayou. Hillbilly Bobby and I went to check it out and we found some kind of monster. It attacked us and things got hazy after that."

Part of me was stunned that Rex had taken out Swamp Lord in his element. In his prime, Swamp Lord had fought two teams of Guardians to a standstill when they'd tried to arrest him. A smidge of panic crept into the back of my throat over how fortunate I'd been.

Then again, the Dinowizard had magic on his side. Swamp Lord's gaseous form and elemental powers might have no defense for that.

"Sorry, I never made it to your hideout when that bug shit happened. I got attacked by the Olympians in New Orleans."

"T'ain't nothing," he answered. "The kid I had working the shortwave rolled over on you as soon as he had a bug on him, so, if anything, it's me who outta be apologizing."

"So, the Olympians didn't get you?"

"They tried, but I was too slick for 'em. I saw the Biloxi Bugler and Chain Charmer over yonder. Don't tell me you done up and went all hero on us?"

"Just a job, Hooch. Nothing to it, but to do it. Used to come with better perks. Besides, you've worked with the heroes before."

"Yeah, I reckon you're right, but I don't trust 'em one bit. Most of them are slipperier than a greased pig, and hide behind the power of the man when it suits 'em. If'n you ask me, crooks at least don't try and fool people into thinking how good they are."

I managed a smile at the older man, who didn't seem bothered by his nudity. Then again, he can't carry anything, including clothes when he turns into vapor, so this was familiar territory for him. Hooch had a folksy kind of common sense that can't be denied. Considering all the dirty deals I'd seen in my limited stint on this side of the law, I wasn't in any position to refute his claims, even if I wanted to.

"Yeah, I'm keeping my eyes open. The grass is greener over here, but that's just because they use a different brand of fertilizer. Any idea who the Stegosaurus really is?"

"Unless I miss my guess, that's Susan Voss, the captain of the fire department in this parish."

"She a super, too?"

"Yup," he responds. "Can lift about a ton and can't be burnt. People call her Fireproof, but she always jokes that if she had an official hero name it'd be something like Asbestos."

"Oh, I think the Guardians tried to get her as a reserve member, but she turned it down."

Hooch shrugged. "Smart lady."

"Stringel," a far off voice bellowed. It belongs to She-Dozer. "Get your ass over here and help!"

"Mind pitching in?" I ask.

Hooch begins to turn into mist. "These folks are my people too. I know where they keep the keys to the emergency vehicles at the firehouse. I'll grab an ambulance or something and bring it back."

"Thanks, Swamp Lord. I owe you one."

"Don't mention it, Cal. Come to think of it, I'll probably want some new weapons from you sometime."

"I think that can be arranged, provided you don't go telling anyone who your supplier is."

In the old days, I'd have wanted him to shout it from the rooftops, but these days, his status as an unsanctioned vigilante required discretion on both our parts.

As he began drifting away, I turned and headed to where Sheila was tending to a man with a head wound. At some point Dozer grabbed a spare costume from her hoversled. *Hooch and the rest of these chumps being naked was one thing. Sheila was at least nice to look at, even if she is a world class, anal retentive, bitch.*

"I know you're pretty useless without your armor, but I'm guessing you know some first aid. Grab the other kit off my sled and get to it."

The curvy amazon annoyed me more than the rest of the team put together... except for Kimodo, but she was a traitor, so it qualified my statement.

"Swamp Lord thinks the dinosaur you fought is the head of this parish's fire department, a super named Voss. Have you seen her? Swamp Lord should be rolling up here in an ambulance in a few minutes."

"What's he doing here?" Sheila asked, ignoring my question.

"He was turned into one of the dinosaurs we fought. The T-Rex you were going to end up mating with was none other than Bobby Walton. How come you never mentioned you were his cousin?"

It was a well-documented fact that my mouth has a tendency to get me in trouble. The look on her face told me that this was one of those times.

"Where is that no good piece of shit?"

"Gone," I answered. *Why do I even try talking to her?*

"You let him get away!"

"Just a second ago you were saying how useless I am without my armor. Exactly how was I supposed to detain someone like him? Tell him amusing stories? Dazzle him with witty banter?"

"You used to work with him," she growled, as I noted that if she pulled that gauze any tighter, it would either rip or crack her poor patient's skull.

"And now I work with you. The only difference I see is that Bobby never led me into a trap where I was almost killed. You, on the other hand, did it tonight, and don't think I haven't forgotten about your part in Patterson's little ambush, Sheila."

"You know damned well I didn't know anything about that!" Dozer was angry that her leadership skills almost killed us all tonight. It might be wrong to push that button, but the way I saw it was I could see her guilt and insecurity, and raise her three destroyed sets of custom crafted powered armor and a statue of Andydroid.

Poor Andy was petrified, just like my gear. Both the Bugler's legs were broken. Sanford's containment suit was in tatters after Rex transformed him into a velociraptor, and he was leaking his paralyzing juice all over the place.

Not exactly one of our most stellar outings, even if we did sort of win.

"Yeah, I know. I'm also looking around and seeing what happens when you do know something. Makes me think ignorance is actually bliss."

"Get out of my sight, Stringel! Don't let me catch you helping my cousin out, either."

"Nothing would make me happier, fearless leader. And don't worry, if I do help Bobby out, I'll be sure to make certain you can't catch me."

My statement might have been too harsh, but only because it was true.

My mom used to keep all my report cards; she probably burned them after our falling out, but I did recall reading my first grade one where it said I had problems "Playing well with others."

Not much had changed.

• • •

Wearing a borrowed set of coveralls from the ambulance Swamp Lord provided, I'd been pressed into EMT duty and my patient was none other than Bo Carr—the Biloxi Bugler. In my zeal to help the man with two broken legs, I might've given him a bit too much painkiller, because he became kind of giddy and chatty. In my pocket was the magic necklace that allowed Bo to assume a man-bat form. All the doohickey did for me was let me read and understand languages.

It was just another way to ruin my night.

"You should probably try and get some rest, Bugler," I said, and then asked the woman driving the ambulance how far we were from the nearest hospital.

Her answer didn't exactly fill me with joy.

"We'll get there when we get there," Bo said.

"Do you need anything?" I offered, and held up a small pillow. "This?"

"Nah," the older man said, and gave me the thumbs up gesture. "I'll bounce back in no time. It takes more than this to keep a good man down. Heck, I remember when you hurt me worse."

Naturally, he was right about me putting him in the hospital back in the day. I'd broken several of his ribs and forced him to hang up the spandex until the bugs showed up.

He yawned loudly and said, "Melinda is going to be ticked."

The Bugler's wife was his biggest supporter and critic. Given my track record with women, I couldn't comment on the matter with any authority.

Instead, I made my own assessment. "Maybe it's time to ride off into the sunset with her? If not, I can start building your mechanized assault wheelchair."

Exactly when did I start getting soft on the old coot?

"Nah, Calvin," he slurred. "Not my speed."

"Fair enough. It's going to take me time to get a new set of armor together."

"If you're so keen on putting me out to pasture, you could always become the next Biloxi Bugler."

What the...?

"That must be some serious happy juice you're on Bo. Thanks, but no thanks. I'm too much of an armor guy."

He could have told me that he was an alien or my real father at that moment and it would have been less shocking.

"You'd make a good Bugler," he proclaimed.

"I think you meant to say burglar."

Mr. Carr gave me a look of sincerity, the kind only the drunk or stoned are capable of, and said, "Nah, you're smart and think on your feet. There's more to you than just the tech. Maybe it's time you start realizing that."

When I didn't, or perhaps couldn't, reply. His head lolled to the other side and he muttered, "For all its power, your armor can be a crutch. Gotta learn to stand tall on your own. Say, did I ever tell you how I knew you'd be at that bank all those years ago?"

"No," I said, suddenly curious.

"I got a postcard a week before. One of those, 'Wish you were here' ones with a picture of the Grand Canyon on the front and a California postmark. On the back was the name of the bank, a date, and a time. I've heard other supers talk about getting messages like that from Prophiseer."

"It couldn't be," I protested. "The Overlord killed him years before that happened. And I've heard several occasions where villains have used that as a ruse to lure a hero into a trap."

"So, were you trying to lure me in to a trap?"

"Uh..."

"Yeah, didn't think so," Bo seems more than half asleep now. "Anyway, those cards supposedly show up when it's something important."

"I hardly think I rate that."

"Way I see it; you beat the bugs, and who knows how out of control things would have gotten tonight. Chew on that and get back to me."

Mercifully, he passed out shortly after that. I was left stunned, and wondering if I should inject some of the drugs he was on.

• • •

Stacy looks up from where she's using a cloth to wipe the applesauce dribbling from my daughter's mouth. "We've gotten those postcards before. Always the same thing, a date, time, and location. They're always important, too."

"Yeah, yeah, I know. I looked up all the instances in the Guardian's database after that. Still, it got me thinking about the mess that was HORDES. I heard the Overlord brag that before he killed Prophiseer, the fortuneteller said that Ultraweapon would die at the hands of another man in armor."

Frowning, Stacy wrestles with her feelings for me and the things that I'm capable of. Internally, I scold myself. I shouldn't bring things like that up if I want to avoid an argument.

Stacy finishes whatever internal debate she was having and says, "You know, I'm picturing you in a Bugler costume right now."

"Please, don't," I plead.

"I have to," she replies. "I'm so going to get you one."

"You're going to make me say a bunch of bad words in front of my daughter."

"Oh, come on, you dress up as the Bugler and I'll be, let's see, how about... Blazing She-Clops and you can capture me."

"...and try to bring you over to the side of righteousness? You'd totally rock the eye patch, but I don't think so."

The Love Goddess smiles and I wonder how she's going to talk me into playing dress up. As long as the costumes come off at some point I can deal with it, but then she frowns.

"What?" I ask.

"I think she needs a change." She hands me my daughter and the smell follows. It reminds me of Swamp Lord. "Maybe she got the super flatulence you wrote about."

"Cute," I say. "Why don't you go in the other room and relax? There's no need for both of us to suffer, and I might need you to send in a hazmat suit. Gabby usually goes down for her nap about now."

Stacy leaves, and I begin the time honored tradition of being amazed at the smell an offspring can produce. So far, the first full day of our reunion was going well. After Lazarus mindwiped her, I'd struggled to relate to her, and everything fell apart. I'm the same person and, quite frankly, it's difficult picturing me ever changing. So the real question becomes whether her recovered memories are enough to keep her interested in me.

"There are worse problems to have," I inform Gabby. She smiles at me and then scrunches her face.

"Again? Where do you put it all? Well, you are definitely my child. This is going to take longer than I thought."

Chapter Three

Louisiana Stringel and the Temple of Humiliation

"Sorry," I say, entering Central Command and addressing my guest. "Gab-Gab took longer than usual to fall asleep."

"Probably me," Stacy confesses. "My presence has been known to make children hyper. My sister hates it when I come around; her twins get so spun up. I always try to keep my visits short."

I notice she's looking around at the rather drab décor in the base. I stress usefulness over attractiveness, but could see where things were lacking.

Some plants would be nice and liven up the place, but I'd need grow lights and if I install grow lights, I have a good idea what type of vegetation Bobby would start farming. Better say something before it gets awkward!

"So you're better around kids than you are around their parents; good to know. Want to grab something to eat? We actually feature more things on the menu than frozen waffles. How about pancakes?"

This piques Ms. Mitchell's interest. "Made from scratch?"

"Hardly," I answer. "But if it will help the process, I'll scratch something while opening the box. I've managed to learn how to read directions and I'm told that most of the things I make are edible. Anything beyond that is not going to happen."

"In that case, I'll take the pancakes and you can skip the scratching part."

As I head for the kitchen and beckon her to follow, I say, "But I'm a guy. We're trained from birth to be scratchers. Chocolate chips in your pancakes, or are you a heathen?"

"Can a goddess even be a heathen? Normally, I'd go with the chocolate, but after last night, I will pass."

"Suit yourself. More for me."

"So, the other two are fishing and Wendy's gone, where's Andy?"

"Downstairs running the suit and running in-place upgrades. Two of the shield generators are showing wear and they need to be replaced. It's pretty simple when there's no one inside. Why? Are you intending to seduce me in the kitchen?"

The nice part about her baggy and ill-fitting coveralls is that they would come off really fast.

"No. I think we've tried mixing food and sex enough for the time being. Let's just stick to the bed, or I suppose I could be talked into the shower again. I was just surprised that you're not down there supervising," she comments, while I get a mixing bowl and a frying pan.

Looking over my shoulder at her, I reply, "Something more important came along. Andy's got this."

Her expression is worth the knowledge that I'm still going to double check those replacements at some point. Otherwise, I might have to turn in my Mega OCD membership card.

"Do you still want me to go on, or is it as boring as it sounds? Honestly, I'd rather not talk about what comes next."

"It's anything but boring, Cal," she says, leaning against the counter. "I'm all ears."

"While I do enjoy your lovely ears, I'm glad you're not all ears."

As she shakes her head, I decide that I'm on a roll. "Hey, if I ever do write another book, I should use that line and make me sound like a Casanova. Music, play Levert, Casanova."

We bob our heads to the opening beats as she says, "If you do write another book, not only are you getting in that Bugler outfit, but you'll have to make another sex tape."

She brought that up? Wow! If Stacy is joking about our taped escapades, I must be doing something right.

"You could call it 'Blow My Bugle.' We'd need to send a complimentary copy to Bo. That's most of the reason people are always trying to find this place, to find that video. It's become the modern day Holy Grail."

"You ever watch it?" she asks, as I watch the pancake batter bubble in the skillet.

"Once," I reply.

"Once a day is more like it," she accuses, before seeing whatever sour expression just crossed my face. "Oh, I guess so."

"Yeah," I confess. "Didn't want to torture myself like that."

We're stuck in an awkward moment for a few seconds before I change the subject. "Anyway, this place is going to become much more difficult to find soon enough."

"Why is that? I know you called it a pig farm and said it was by the Mobile River, but someone could still put it all together."

"Two weeks from now, the renovation begins up top. James and Flora are moving in. They're a couple of crazy kids who are getting out of the California rat race, and turning this old run down place into a rustic Bed and Breakfast."

"Actors hired by Wendy I assume?" she asks.

"Two modified Type A robots in costume," I correct her. "Andy wants to practice his 'pretending to be human' skills. Gives us a way to hide some guard bots in plain sight, and allows us to use the land up top. We can't really expand this base much more. Unless Andy is downright horrible, the locals will pass it off as a couple of crazy west coasters."

"Makes sense. Clever idea."

"I try," I smile, and flip the pair of flapjacks. "The silo is coming down and will be replaced by James' garage; the guy is a real car nut. The horse stables will house our Type B bots."

"Any real horses?"

I shrug. "I believe so. Andy was telling me that Flora wants to breed those miniature ponies or something like that. If you want to know what I think, Andy wasn't allowed to have pets before and now he's overcompensating, but it's cool he has hobbies. Just don't be surprised if it turns into a petting zoo up top. Wendy thinks Crabby Gabby will want to learn how to ride at some point. She even has this crazy idea of letting anyone stay here. I think we should just add more Type A bots as guests."

"Pool?"

"Off the chain," I say. I don't let her see the frown. Unconsciously, the pool I'd submitted looked like a scaled down version of the pool from the estate belonging to the Overlord in Branson, Missouri. I'd tried to get them to let me change it, but was too chickenshit to tell them it reminded me of Vicky. This would also be a real shitty time to bring that up as well.

"Do you like your pancakes crispy?" Stacy asks and I realize that I let the pancakes burn.

"Nah, just got distracted thinking about the structural requirements to make certain the pool never floods this place. Let's try this again with a new set of candidates."

Stacy accepts my lame excuse as I scrape away the first attempt and start over. Minutes later, we both had a short stack of tasty, buttermilk goodness.

"So, what happened next? You still didn't know Wendy was pregnant at this point, did you?"

In retrospect, Stacy is right; the chocolate chips seem like overkill. "All right, I'll tell you, but no laughing. Wendy was still on her personal leave of absence. Next, I guess would be me and a couple of José clones going to recover all the goodies from Tyranosorcerer Rex's lair. Looting sounds like such a bad word."

"Why José and not one of the others?"

"I figured if there were any traps, José could always grow new clones. Plus, he lost as much as I did when Patterson, or one of his flunkies, used that Robodestroyer suit to get rid of our robots in Florida. In fact, if you make some cosmetic adjustments to the Protector armor that Promethia put on the West Coast Guardian's to replace Patterson; it might match the profile of Robodestroyer."

"Strange coincidence," Stacy comments, and twirls final bits of pancake in the syrup on her plate.

"Yeah, I thought so, too. Is it my old pal, Joe Ducie, in the armor or is he pulling the strings behind the scenes?"

"I don't think so. The West Coasters have closed ranks lately. Athena thinks it might be Tape Delay inside the suit now."

"Who's that?"

"A Canadian named Amanda Rae Westfal, who can see seven seconds into the future. She's a very limited precog. Not an awesome ability by itself, but add a set of powered armor to it and it's a potent combination. Word is Promethia is using her to soften their image. They've also put First Aid into a set of armor as well."

"I'll keep that in mind," I say, and make a note to update the rest of the team. If that is the case, I could see Tape Delay could be a problem, even if the armor she is wearing is far outclassed by Mega. "Anyway, so I guess it starts with me figuring out where Rex's lair is, but I'm serious, no laughing."

"I promise," she says. I don't believe her because I know what's coming.

• • •

"I don't think there's anything you can do for him," one of Jose's clones said to me. We stood in front of the stone statue that used to be one of the most intricate pieces of technology in the world—Andydroid.

I scraped a sample off of the back of Andy's wrist and prepared it to go through a molecular analyzer to see if there were any signs that the process was reversing itself.

"I have to try," I said. Many people, and that used to include me, don't give José any credit. His power allows him to grow five copies of himself. At just shy of six foot and two hundred pounds, the Mexican kept himself in good shape and knew a decent amount when it comes to both martial arts and firearms, but he wasn't super strong or durable. It was more like having a small group of highly trained individuals who worked together so closely that they knew what the other one was thinking... except in Jose's case, they actually did. That's why I'd hoped to get him in my cheap sets of armor. Even those substandard suits, combined with his groupmind ability, would be a formidable combination.

"Why?" the clone asked. "His inventor said he'd just rebuild him and restore from the last time he was backed up. It's like me. If this body dies, I'll just make another one."

"It's not quite the same," I countered. "Yeah, I was there when the good doctor briefed us. His last complete backup of Andy was about ten weeks before the bugs showed up. That new Andydroid would be a stranger to me. This one is my friend."

In a sense, it was just like the situation with Aphrodite all over again. Maybe that's what bugged me the most about it, but I wasn't about to admit that to anyone if I could help it.

"Then good luck, Cal. I checked this week's supply shipment."

"Let me guess, just like last week. No synth-muscle. Effing Promethia!"

José nodded. "I used to admire Mr. Patterson, but now he is just a petty and spiteful man waging a war against someone who wants nothing to do with him."

His sentiments weren't exactly true. If an unarmored Lazarus Patterson walked through that door right now, I'd have no problem scooping up my pulse pistol and playing energy weapon piñata with his body. Then again, the Mexican member of our team had taken a hit in all this as well.

"Anything salvageable from our bots in Florida?" José was not very creative, but he was an excellent technician, with an eye for the details. Give him the instructions and he can do wonders. The six pack did the maintenance on the bots on the base, and after Patterson's ambush, the black haired man helped fix the armor I'd lost against the Dino magician, while I spent a few weeks hobbling around.

"All destroyed," he said, shaking his head. "The bastard took his time and turned them to slag. I'm in a bit of a jam with the monies I've committed to my family's new home. Are you sure there are no more of these bolt holes where we might locate new robots?"

Frowning, I'd hoped that I could scavenge the components out of the wrecked robots to make a new suit, but Patterson had blocked that option—not that a suit using recycled synth would last very long.

"I wish. Right now we're shit out of luck in that department. I'm on inactive status and only get half pay until then."

At that rate, it would take over a decade to rebuild my armor. I was weighing the offer Wendy sent to me about floating me a loan. It was an unexpectedly kind and surprising gesture from our absentee leader. She probably felt bad about Patterson's assassination attempt, or not being here for this latest debacle. Ultimately, I wasn't certain whether I'd want to be that indebted to her.

Plus, I'd probably have to behave if I took her money, and that was never going to happen.

"What about the dinosaur's body?" José asked.

"I already tried. Sheila let the government take it away." Not that I wasn't pissed about it, either. I killed it and should have had a say in its disposition.

José frowned and looked at the shards of that teleportation gate crystal spread out on an examination table. "Too bad these aren't diamonds or emeralds. We could have at least put them into necklaces and made something with them."

When he reached for them I shouted, "Stop! Don't touch those!"

My warning was too late and his fingers closed around one of the shards. His thumb broke the event horizon of the crystal; it just kept going through the material.

"*Madre Dios!*" He screamed, and jumped backward like he'd been burnt.

I'd been inspecting the pieces and trying to find a way to make them work for me. "Are all your fingers still on your hand?"

He flexed his palm and surveyed for any signs of missing digits "Thank the creator; they're all still where they are supposed to be."

I used a pair of tongs on the outside edges of the greenish material to move it back. Previously, I'd stuck a couple of things into them, but hadn't been brave enough to stick anything organic through them. Jose's blunder actually saved me a few hours of sticking carrots or celery through the gap before trying some kind of critter, like a mouse.

"I'd been worried, after seeing how much flesh Kimodo and the dinosaur had removed by these things. I'd have had to start calling you Frodo or something."

The clone got my reference and said, "So, this portal thing is still active?"

"Seems to be," I replied. "My guess is that the other side is just as wrecked as this side is. Cool stuff though, teleportation. That'd be a useful power to have."

"Then again," the clone replied, with a no-nonsense grin. "Just because the end of this portal is destroyed doesn't mean there's not anything valuable."

José was a man after my own heart. He worked pretty damned hard, and he liked to be paid. We quickly came to an understanding.

It took about two hours for me to cobble together a transmitter, power supply and GPS that I could slide through the largest piece, but we had a location shortly after that. The other end was deep in the middle of a swamp.

"Now for the big question," I asked both of the clones present. "Do we bring in the others, or do we just do this ourselves?"

"Sheila won't go for it," the José on my left said. "And if she did, we wouldn't see any money. Jin is already doubling up on patrols to make up for all the injuries."

I thought it over. "You and I are a little under gunned if there is anything guarding Rex's lair. I can scare up some of my pulse pistols. I'm on pretty good terms with Swamp Lord and it's his turf. He's going to want a cut, but I'd feel better if we had him backing us up."

The clones agreed and I started planning a trip out to the bayou. Old Hooch was still pretty ticked that someone beat him on his home field, and I figured it wouldn't take too much to get him interested—not so much payday as payback.

• • •

When people talk about going deep into the swamp, they invariably imagine scenarios where they are attacked by gators, snakes, and the like. Firing pulses of energy from the pair of pistols in my hand, I knew I'd never have to worry about those images again.

Those fantasies would be tame compared to this!

The thing might've been some kind of a constrictor at some point, but Rex's magic pushed it back a few notches on the old evolutionary belt, and turned what would have been a terrifying encounter into the stuff of nightmares. My pistols clicked empty as the monster thrashed on the ground. The long departed Maxine Velocity would have been impressed by my rate of fire.

My accuracy, on the other hand, left much to be desired.

"Don't rightly recall these things being here last time," Hooch said, in a barely corporeal form as he gestured at the muck next to a similarly transformed gator. Roots erupted from the mud and wrapped around the thrashing body of the creature, dragging it to the side and effectively demonstrating Swamp Lord's main power. This swamp seemed to obey him.

Sliding the spent pistols back into their holster, I yanked on the handles of the replacements. "A simple No Trespassing sign would've worked."

My feeble humor aside, this expedition seemed less Raiders of the Lost Ark and more Bungle In the Jungle—or more aptly put—Stumble around the Swamp. Even with a GPS telling us where the destination was, getting there was an ordeal.

A short distance away, a trio of José clones worked as a team to fry anything that wasn't human. Two carried military grade plasma rifles, and the third used my pulse pistols. Normally, I'd be bitching about someone using something other than my weapons, but in this case I was glad to make the exception. The rifles were crude, but had a certain effectiveness to them that I could appreciate.

Watching the roots and vines pull the hapless creature back into the brush, I sighed and said, "Hopefully, that's the end of the welcoming party."

"Could just be the warmup act," Hooch said, as pragmatic as ever. Enough of me agreed that I changed out the cells in the empty pistols for fresh ones, as one of the José clones consulted the scanner I'd put together to pinpoint our destination.

"Looks like it is a bit closer, maybe half a kilometer in that direction," he said while gesturing due west.

Turning to the semi-coherent mass of stench next to me, I asked, "Would you mind floating ahead while we finish cleaning up here?"

"Sure," the cloud said and drifted in the direction of the signal. Truth be told, I wasn't too keen on sending our heaviest hitter on ahead as a scout, but his physical invulnerability meant that I wouldn't have to risk myself or one of the clones.

It was less messy that way.

Giving Swamp Lord a two-minute head start, I finished changing my powercells and helped a clone adjust the backpack containing the energy source for his rifle. The connectors had come loose when he had to jump out of the way of certain death. His two other clones moved to the perimeter while I inspected his weapon for any damage.

"Nice shooting. Way better than mine," I offered him a compliment.

"All my practicing is starting to pay off," he answered.

The big chip on Jose's multiple shoulders was he knew that no one him seriously, except for me and the Bugler. If I was being honest, it was only a recent development on my part. Then again, Bo and I were the only people in this group of misfits who didn't have any super abilities. Given Jose's powers, I'd have my own engineering team and more completed projects than I could shake a stick at. In fact, I'd even have built a machine to shake a stick at all my completed projects.

Of course, that was the dream. The reality would probably be that I would watch five times the amount of porn. Hell, sometimes I'm such a slacker that I could even picture my clones arguing over who had to do something. So, I applauded Jose's efforts to turn himself into a group mind version of a SEAL team. That level of badassery could come in handy down the road—more power to him.

"All set?" the one I was working with asked.

"Yeah," I answered. "It should hold, but when we get back to base we need to swap out the lines. Let's find Swamp Lord."

When we arrived at the source of the signal, I scowled. It was on top of some marshy hillock infested with trees and scrub brush. Finding an entrance would be impossible without Hooch. His semi-tangible hand extended and he used his plant powers to probe the root systems.

"That group of trees over there," the man gestured to a thick cluster. "They ain't real."

"What do you mean?"

"I can't sense them. Must be some kind of an illusion or something like that."

To prove his point, he made a root from a nearby bush rip itself from the ground and snap at the fake trees like a whip. It passed through one side and out the other.

Impressed by the camouflage, I made a note to come back here and look at the illusion in the infrared and ultraviolet spectrums to see if it held up to that kind of inspection as well. Magic had always been something I'd relegated to a sideshow act. Sure, there were a few magic users out there who were heavy hitters, but the majority consisted of charlatans and fakes. My college roommate, Joey Hazelwood had dated one of those, a tattoo artist who could do some minor charms and the like. She used this one for mental clarity during her artwork that I let her try on me one time. In my classes there were some "normal" students who abused Adderall to try and get better grades. Her spell was sort of like that and lasted for about thirty minutes. I spent that time engrossed in the pixilation and details of her artwork as she created the souvenir demon fighting an angel tat on Joey's shoulder.

My OCD was basically tripping balls over that, and I vowed to avoid doing that again... ever.

Recent experiences hadn't exactly given me any reason to adjust my opinion of the mystic arts, either.

"Yeah, there's a tunnel behind them," Swamp Lord said, continuing his check of the area. "There's a whole building underneath this hill."

"Well, if anyone wants to back out," I commented. "Now's the last chance."

Greed overcame common sense and we started to walk through the illusionary cypress trees. It was strange, moving through a tree that both sight and smell screamed were real. The tunnel Hooch promised waited on the other side, with a reddish glow coming from inside.

"Trap?" José asked.

"Rex didn't seem like a trap kind of... guy... I guess we can call him that. It looks like it's just there to kill things."

"Well, then, lemme send something down thataway and see what happens," Swamp Lord said, and then concentrated.

In response, an old fern uprooted itself and came scuttling toward us using its roots like sets of insect legs. It was both impressive and creepy at the same time. The moment the animated vegetation crossed the threshold into the passageway, the red glow vanished. It was replaced with a low rumbling.

"Yup," I said. "That doesn't sound promising."

Swamp Lord took that moment to sublimate as the rest of us scrambled to stay upright. Suddenly, my decision not to bring a jet pack along became fodder for one of those self-assessments that begin with the words, "In hindsight, perhaps I should have..."

There was the briefest of pauses before the ground next to me erupted in a burst of mud and dirt, tossing me bodily aside.

Climbing out of the hole in the top of the hill was a dirt covered T-Rex. Shit just got real.

"What the..." I said, stopping short of saying the "F" word.

"Shoot it!" The pistol wielding clone shouted. My first thought was run, but his idea wasn't bad either. In fact, I could probably do both!

Backpedaling, I cut loose with my pulse pistols, hoping to hit something important, or at least slow it down. I didn't come all this way to end up as something's well-balanced breakfast. Plus, I was awfully high in fat content.

Bluish white needles of energy darted into the beastie. My attack pitted the thing's chest, and left me with a sudden and horrifying revelation. This wasn't a dinosaur in stasis that Old Rexxie left taking a dirt nap, this was some kind of stone construct that looked and moved like it belonged in Jurassic Park. It had red glowing eyes that might as well have been a targeting system—locked on me.

"Help," I said. The words didn't leave my throat with any real oomph behind them. Nor did they properly convey my sense of complete and utter panic. So, I returned to my original idea and started running, letting the foul swamp air fill my lungs for a second attempt.

"Help! Shoot it! Shoot it!" A frightened, young co-ed in a cheap slasher movie couldn't have done it any better.

On the plus side, it was made of stone and not terribly fast, but this chase wasn't exactly taking place over wide open spaces. I had to dodge around fallen trees, rocks, roots and everything else. All it had to do was follow the straightest path to me.

I ran past one of the clones carrying a plasma rifle who was trying to slow it down. All his high tech weapon did was leave some scorch marks on the surface.

Worse still, the T-Rex golem ignored him and kept following me. Secretly, I had hope that he'd draw the thing's attention and it would stop chasing me. For better or worse, the animated creation only had eyes for me.

"Try explosives!" I yelled, already finding my breath coming out in ragged gasps. Adrenaline and panic were compensating for my poor exercise habits, but the situation was degrading by the second.

"We didn't bring any!" The clone answered. "Remember? I said we should, but you said we wouldn't need any with Swamp Lord here."

I suppose I did actually say that, I thought. *Still, it's a dick move to remind me of it!*

Frantically, I looked around for Swamp Lord, however, unless you were within ten feet of him and looking for a distortion pattern in the air, it was like trying to spot the Semi-Transparent Man in a football stadium on game day.

"Hooch! Save me!" I screamed. This was his home turf. Inside a swamp the dude is damned near invincible.

A tree near me pulled itself out of the ground and ran toward the thing gaining on me. It fared about as well as a tree would against something that out-massed it by more than ten tons and was made of far denser material. Of course, better the tree than me.

"Cal," I heard Hooch say. "I have to go and..."

"No!" I shrieked. "Don't leave me." The words reminded me of the things my teenaged self might have said to any of the number of girls he'd tried to date.

"Just try not to get eaten," he said. "I'm going to round up enough swamp gas to do some damage!"

"Hurry!"

One of Swamp Lord's animated trees was excavating a trench—a low point where he could put the methane, I supposed.

Summing up my situation, I concluded that our weapons were useless and our most powerful member just ran out to get some gas. Things were so messed up right now that it seemed like a civil servant was in charge. Technically, I did work for Uncle Sam. Even if I had the time to rig my pistols to blow up like a grenade, it wouldn't do nearly enough damage.

So, I ran. I ran like never before. I ran like Tom Hanks in that one movie, but there was no girl to run to, only a series of desperate sprints and evasions to save my worthless life. I felt like one of the marbles on a life-sized game of *Hungry, Hungry, Hippos.*

My only advantage was my mind, I stayed just inside the underbrush and moved through as fast as I could; letting the dinosaur golem behind me clear the path that I'd use on my next lap. I did my best to keep it away from Swamplord's created monster, which was digging our own version of a tiger trap.

They sure look bigger on the screen; I muttered and dodged around a collection of trees and bushes. Of course, I was running out of juice fast and it could, and probably would, chase me to the ends of the Earth.

Time began to lose meaning, and my continued existence was reduced to that of a cornered rat. I'd considered trying to take it back down the hill to see if it would get stuck in the swamp, but that path back down wasn't for the faint of heart, and there was no guarantee that I wouldn't get stuck.

Twice, it had nearly gotten me and I'd scraped up enough adrenaline to skitter away from it, but now my body, less a well-oiled machine and more a sputtering clunker running on vapors, was giving out on me.

I fell and couldn't rise. On my hands and knees, I pushed forward another five feet and could only watch as the behemoth approached. There wasn't enough energy left in me even to scream. Something grabbed me from behind and I barely registered being tossed through the air. For a brief second, I though the T-Rex golem had snatched me from the ground and tossed me upwards to crush me in its jaws on the way down, but instead, I hit the ground and tried to figure out what just happened. It was Hooch's plant monster, interceding on my behalf and grappling with the behemoth to buy me another twenty seconds.

"Cal!" One of the clones called, shaking me out of a haze of lactic acid buildup and terror. "Get into the pit!"

Stumbling, with a new short-term lease on life, I made my way in the direction he wanted me to go. It was the best I was capable of. The pit was really some kind of sloped trench Hooch's destroyed tree soldier had dug. I could see the area of distortion that I associated with Swamp Lord, above me, and smelled the awful, rancid, methane pocket the Master of the Marsh held in place down here. The methane itself was odorless; however, all the contaminants were what generated the awful stench. At that moment, I didn't care. It was the best smell ever as far as I was concerned!

Another of Hooch's creations waited for me at the bottom in the hard to breath air, and a plasma-rifle-carrying-José was on the top of the slope I'd need to climb to get out. Hooch's monster was a long vine anchored into the side of the trench.

"Wait!" he commanded as I took a couple of steps in his direction. After all the motion I'd put my body through in the past however long it had been, standing still and panting felt strange. Every part of my body screamed that if I stood still much longer, I'd fall to the ground and never get up. Fighting against it, I held my ground, which shook with the approach of my executioner.

"Now," the clone commanded and my tired legs gave a half-hearted attempt to follow his directions. A second José appeared and dragged me the last few feet as the golem's leg stepped down into the trap. The vine snapped out and wrapped around the thing's ankle.

Seconds later, there was an eruption behind us. The clone who'd helped me up the slope, pushed me up those last few feet, and dived on top of me. A massive thud came seconds later and I dared to hope it was all over.

It wasn't.

The creature, with half his lower left leg removed by Swamp Lord's assault, still tried to move toward me. His arms and remaining leg flailed and propelled the creature slowly in my direction. The José who'd lit the fuse had died and the one who had pinned me to the ground wasn't in great shape either.

"Hooch!" I called.

There was a whisper in the air. "I'm still here. It's just... gonna take some time to pull myself back together. When I do, I'll have some plants make... it... so this thing can't get... out."

I thanked him profusely.

The two remaining clones and I pulled back and waited for Swamp Lord to collect his particles. Going on, at that moment, seemed more foolish than jumping back into that trench.

• • •

"I thought I said no laughing," I say, and jab an accusatory finger at the red-faced Love Goddess.

"I can't help it!" she replies, between gasps for breath, and mimics, "Hooch! Save me!"

I let her go on and have her laugh at my expense for much longer than I should have. If it were anyone else, I'm sure I'd find it more amusing. Lord knows, José Six-Pack used to give me all kinds of shit about it in private. Finally, I ask, "Are you about finished?"

She wipes away some of the tears that had built up in the corners of her eyes and nods, stifling a couple of more laughs in the process.

"Well," I explain. "Besides not wanting to give anyone reasons to think more about those pieces of crystal, you can probably see why that didn't make it into the abridged autobiography. It wasn't exactly one of my finest moments, which, given our history together, says quite a bit."

"What did you find?"

"Not a whole lot, or at least that's what I thought initially. Rex didn't have trap after trap lined up. He was probably too arrogant to believe that we mammals could be anything more than just a minor irritant. Inside his lair, we found the remains of the central mirror of movement; in larger pieces than the ones we'd already recovered, and a couple of spares that were intact. Later, I used the bigger chunks to run my stuff through after I cut matching pieces out of one of the spares."

"What about the treasure?"

Shaking my head from side to side, I reply, "Mostly a bust. Can't really say about his society, but Rex didn't care about gold. He liked silver though. His spellbooks were actually piles of silver slates. There were a few stones here and there, but almost all of them were of the semi-precious variety. Honestly, the plasma rifle we lost when the one José died cost more than what we pulled out of there. We also found the pieces of him and poor Kimodo that had come through to the other side."

"Didn't quite pan out the way you wanted?" Stacey says, seemingly not bothered by my casual mention of a bit of gore. I pick up our dishes and take them to the sink. Normally, I'd probably leave them for Andy, but since I'm trying to make a good impression with the gorgeous lady at my side, I start washing them off.

All I can do is shrug and reply, "It's like what Mick Jagger says about always getting what you want?"

"You can't," she finishes for me. "How'd you explain away the plasma rifle?"

"José lied and said it was destroyed when we fought Rex. It was pretty easy since he's the one in charge of keeping all the records. I was down in the dumps as well and was ready to chalk it up to another one of my misadventures. Of course, the real treasure was Rex's spellbooks, if you want to call them that, and the mirror fragments, but it took me a little while longer to put all that together."

"I'm sorry I laughed at you," she says, with sincerity.

"You get a pass on that since we're involved."

"Involved?" she asks. "Sounds like a complicated situation."

"I guess it's going to be as complicated as we make it," I respond. "Realistically, you're a member of the most powerful, sanctioned, superteam on the planet. I'm on the most powerful, unsanctioned team, with no real plans to get the UN's or Uncle Sam's rubber stamp of approval anytime soon. That's going to create some problems for us down the road, but only if we let it. The Olympians and the Reinforcements are bound to bump heads, but let's make a promise not to let that come between Stacy and Cal."

Pausing, I reflect on my sudden discovery of a new layer to my personality. The lady looks equally mystified. "It's been a long year apart, Stacy, and I've had a lot of time to do some serious soul searching. Why don't we go chill on the couch and wait for Gabby to wake up."

She agrees to my plan and takes my arm as we head back to Central Command. So far, things seem to be going great, which means that naturally I'm nervous as all get out. My new "depth of character" means that I will probably find some new and completely unexpected way of screwing this up. Paranoia and insecurity are threatening to pounce on me at any moment, but I want to put all my failed relationships to rest. If I can do that, maybe, just maybe, I can make this one work.

Chapter Four

It's a Magical Feeling, or Maybe Just Gas

"So, when last we left our intrepid hero, he was hauling away his ill-gotten dinosaur booty. What manner of adventure does he get into next?" Stacy inquires, following me into Central Command.

"Maybe we should take a break from story time," I reply. "You laughed at me."

She smirks. "Because it was hilarious and you know it. Too bad there's no video."

I plop down on the couch, grab the remote, and power on the monitor. "Maybe there's something good on."

It appears that Larry and Bobby had been playing their game before we got up.

"Ultimate Super Showdown?" Stacy asks, while lowering herself gracefully to the couch.

"Bobby and Larry spend hours playing USS; it's almost a religion to them."

"But not you?" she queries, with a hint of challenge in her voice.

"*Moi?*" I reply, feigning hurt. "I've been known to dabble. *Et vous?*"

"I thought you sucked at foreign languages, Cal."

"I did, but the necklace Larry is wearing definitely helped me out in that department. Really jump started things." Turning my attention to the game, I continue, "This one is a bit different. Andy modded the hell out of it, and Bobby and Larry keep getting new add-ons every time I turn around. Andy's coding has turned it into a poor man's battle simulator, where we can run simulations of two super powered people throwing down with each other. Just give me a minute and I'll shut it down. We can watch something else."

The Love Goddess smiles at my offer before a mischievous grin replaces it. "Or we could play and the winner picks what we do next. I'll have you know that I can crush you like a grape."

"Since when do you game?" High society is more her speed, or at least it used to be.

She scoops up the controllers and thrusts one at me. "You're not the only one who changed during our year apart. I cut back on public appearances and interviews. This is one of the things that helped me fill the free time. I'm sure my phenomenal reflexes make things a bit easier. So, are we going to play or are you going to admit my superiority?"

I guess I'm not the only one with a surprise or two. If I'm being honest, I didn't really keep tabs on her too much. As far as I know, she went on something like three or four dates. Considering she's the most desired woman in the world, that's practically joining a convent!

"Did I just hear a feeble attempt at smack talk?" I say, shaking my head from side to side and casting aside my inner thoughts. "Because that's what it sounded like. I'm pretty sure the person saying such things doesn't know what she's getting herself into. Just remember this was your idea when you're singing The Butthurt Blues at the end of the match. Best two out of three gets to pick our next activity."

Stacy began flipping through the characters on the selection screen before settling on the leader of the Olympians, Hera.

"You're not picking yourself?" I ask.

"No," she answers. "Robin's defense value is off the charts; plus her force field choke is a whole lot cooler than my finishing move."

She refers to Aphrodite's Kissy-Kissy final move where she grapples with the enemy and then plants a wet one on their face. The opponent falls to the ground and then starts worshipping Aphrodite. I could see why this would annoy her, which gives me inspiration.

"Well, I guess I know who I'm picking now," I say, and send a wink in her direction and select her as my character.

"You're such an asshole."

"Pucker up sweet cheeks! Either way, you lose, Stacy. But that's what you get for coming into my house and thinking you can take me."

As our two characters enter the battle arena she says, "I'm going to enjoy beating the snot out of you."

"You wish," I counter, and start working the controllers like a man possessed.

She isn't kidding about her reflexes! I barely take the first round and she gets the second, but I land a Cupid combo right at the end of the third that leaves the Hera wobbling with no energy to continue.

"Aw," I say, savoring my victory and punching in the five key sequence to activate Aphrodite's special move. "It's Kissy-Kissy time."

On screen, Aphrodite pulls Hera into a passionate lip lock and the other Olympian prostrates herself on the ground. I'm about to do my little victory dance when the synthesized voice, that really doesn't sound like Stacy at all says, "Come and let me show you what I do with my slaves."

The real Stacy looks at me and I shrug my shoulders as we both watch what's happening on the screen.

"Must be one of the new mods Bobby picked up," I say, and gulp as I see what the CGI characters are doing and shudder slightly, suddenly wishing I hadn't picked Aphrodite.

"Yeah," my recently reacquired girlfriend says. "Robin and I have definitely never done that before. We don't swing that way."

The cut scene lasts a full minute more and appears to have an accompanying horrible rendition of *Just a Friend* to go along with the moans and groans. As it finishes and returns to the main screen I stammer, "Sorry. I didn't know they had something like that loaded. We can shut it off and go back to story time."

"Oh, don't worry, I believe you. What were you going to pick since you won?"

"A nice backrub," I reply. "It's was a tough choice between that and something similar to what we just watched, but not when I'm supposed to be keeping tabs on my daughter."

Responsibility, it's a curse!

She considers my statement. "How about I give you a backrub in a little bit? Pick someone else and let me win this time, I want to see what Robin's altered move is, so I can give her crap about it."

"Okay, since I'm going to lose, I think I'll pick her," I click over to Athena. "What? I still don't like her. Don't think I ever will."

My gaming buddy laughs as our contest begins anew. "Why am I not surprised? Are you in this mod?"

"No," I confess. "I wonder what my finishing move would be."

"Biting sarcasm," she offers.

I make a half-hearted attempt to win, but Stacy crushes me after the force field choke sends Holly Crenshaw to the ground. Hera wheels out a rack, straps Athena to it and goes all dominatrix on her, whips and all!

"I may have to get a copy of this just to show her," Stacy says, in between fits of laughter. "I'm probably going to regret this, or need to sign up for therapy, but let's see the rest of the team."

As we rotate back and forth, beating each other with the various super powered characters in the game and watching the cringe worthy modified cut scenes, I start telling her the next part of the story.

• • •

After my little excursion in the swamp, I decided to build something, anything, to give me some more firepower. Even after swallowing my pride and accepting Wendy's offer of a loan. However, even with financing backing, I couldn't acquire many of the critical components to make a new set of armor. It was becoming the technological equivalent of cockblocking and was about as enjoyable as the real thing.

Lacking other options, I was in the process of dusting off something that should best be forgotten—my ManaCALes design. As sad as it sounded, I needed to get back on active status. As usual, it was about the money. If I was going to have to go to the Black Market to get the synth muscle and controllers to rebuild my suit, I couldn't really use Wendy's money.

The door to my workshop opened and Sheila entered followed by a pair of individuals. She-Dozer was in full tour guide mode with a pair in cloaks following. I stretched, sore from being hunched over my schematics for the new, and only marginally improved, ManaCALes, to see what had our temporary leader gushing like a schoolgirl.

"He's in here," she said.

I took a moment before replying, "Welcome to my humble abode. How can I be of service?"

Sheila gave me that same sour look you give the toilet bowl after you've taken a dump. "They're here for Andy, not you, dumbass."

Glancing over at the statue that used to be my friend, "In that case, anything you need. A few of the local bokers have been by, but the Voodoo they do, just no can do. Heck, one of them touched Andydroid and went running out of the room screaming."

"Comparing Voodoo to our branch of the magical arts is like saying Michelangelo was a house painter," the smaller one said, in a female voice.

I took a closer look at the guests and it was my turn to give Sheila the same look. "What are Patterson's bootlickers doing here?"

"I'd watch my tongue, if I were you," Mystigal threatened. "I could just as easily take away your ability to speak.

"Can it, Stringel! Before you get all pissy, Wendy asked Mystigal and the Grand Vizier to come here as a favor to her. You're welcome to leave if you don't want to be around them."

"Like I'd leave them alone in my workshop. No, thanks, I'll stay."

"I don't want any trouble from you then," she warned.

"Oh, yeah, I'm the guy with no powers in the room and they are buddies with the man who tried to kill me. Clearly, I'm the one who is going to cause the problems. How about we wheel Andy into the other room and they can examine him there?"

"Mr. Stringel," the Grand Vizier said, gently resting his hand on Mystigal's shoulder. "I understand your anxiety toward Lazarus. Rest assured we are no threat to you and we are only here to help, out of respect for all the good Andydroid has accomplished over the years."

I would have been more assured if it hadn't come out a few years before that the Grand Vizier wasn't Earth's Strongest Magical Protector. For almost two decades he'd perpetuated a fraud to hide that his protégé was the one with the real power. Still, he had the old grandpa crap down to a tee.

"My anxiety toward Lazarus? He tried to kill me and none of you even asked for an investigation?"

"It could have just as easily been the Overlord, as Lazarus said. Given his past and your past, I'm willing to give my teammate the benefit of the doubt," Mystigal said, in a callous tone.

My answer was, "Apparently, mastering magic doesn't require a lick of common sense."

"Stringel!" Sheila exclaimed. "Shut the hell up and let them do their job."

"All right," I said. "For Andy."

After all, these two were among the most powerful magic users around. If anyone could help him...

I did my best to relax and let Sheila smooth things over. Her efforts focused solely on telling the two of them what a moron I was. When all was calm, I turned to the still annoyed young woman, I said, "So, how are Spirit Staff and K-Otica?"

"My brother and sister-in-law are well and seem to be enjoying Mexico City. I didn't know that you knew them."

Making certain to look at Sheila I said, "Back when I was on the other side of the fence. They were the only two on this team who didn't annoy me."

In truth, I really only felt that way about K-Octica, but I was trying to be nice. Her brother was an arrogant shit with a magical bo staff. I kind of enjoyed the time I threw a dumpster at him. Shortly before the bugs showed up, Karina had convinced Spirit Staff to relocate South of the Border to be closer to her family.

"Let's just get this over with," the sorceress said, not really responding to my olive branch.

I couldn't have agreed more. Unwilling to go back to my work, I watched the magic happen... or not in this case. They lit candles in a pattern around my petrified amigo and walked around chanting and waving various objects at him. It was interesting to observe, and slowly I began to feel the hairs on the back of my neck begin to stand up. The room temperature fluctuated wildly and I felt chills. Grand Vizier had sweat glistening from his prominent forehead, and Mystigal wore a look that seemed to be one part concentration and the other constipation.

As my hopes for Andy's revival began to dim I thought, *Apparently, comparing what they could do to what the dinosaur could do, was like calling Da Vinci a handyman.*

Even my little mental jab did little to improve my mood. The dinosaur's words echoed in my mind; about how he called down the meteor that created the Gulf of Mexico to crush a rebellion and oddly enough, bring about the end of reptilian dominance. I wasn't sure if I believed it, but watching the two humans struggle against the curse, charm, or whatever the hell it was, made me doubly glad that I'd killed him.

Mystigal uses all sorts of protections on her costume. Maybe I could get her to put a layer of magic on my Kevlar vest? Hey wait! Did Andy's arm just move?

I got plenty excited, but it only lasted a few seconds. The Grand Vizier stopped chanting and breathed a deep sigh. He'd apparently tapped out of the match and it looked like Mystigal wasn't far behind. The old man in the crimson and purple robes pulled himself to his feet, looking far older than when he had entered.

"No dice, huh?" I stated.

"I'm afraid it cannot be undone," the man said, sounding like he'd just finished a five K. "The magics that permeate Andydroid's body are completely foreign to me. Asa is more stubborn than I am and will expend much more of her power before conceding defeat."

I pointed to some of my transformed armor chunks and asked, "I don't really know how magic works, but could you start on something smaller and work your way up?"

"Perhaps," he replied. "But I fear the results would still be the same. Undoing a spell requires some foundation in the discipline from which the spell was cast. We lack that grounding and the most we would be able to do would be to layer our own spells on top of what has already been done and animate him as a mindless living statue."

Pondering his words, I pictured the result and knew instinctively that Andy wouldn't want to end up like that. "No, I'm pretty sure Andy wouldn't want to be some kind of golem. Some of the things I recovered look like they might have this dinosaur's language scratched in to it. Would those help? They are these silver rectangular slates."

Vizier looked skeptical, but humored me and examined the silver platters José and I had brought back.

After a little over a minute, he rendered his judgment. "Even once this language is deciphered, and assuming they contain the spell he's using; it would likely take years to reach a point where the spell could be reversed."

I stopped short of asking him, "Well, what good are you?"

Instead, I went with an idea that just popped into my head, "What if I can get them translated?"

Chain Charmer's spare necklace! Maybe I can use it.

"Perhaps, but I still doubt it will provide the solution you are looking for. The person might very well have to start from scratch with this foreign system of magic."

"Maybe if we started with someone who didn't know anything mystical. Is it true that anyone can learn magic?" It was an age old question.

He nodded. "Everyone can, but most lack the potential to really do anything with it. Perhaps one in ten could ever cast even a simple spell without an augment. One in ten thousand has enough potential to cast one that does something substantial, and one in a million has the innate talent to become a sorcerer or sorceress."

"What's an augment?"

"A device, steeped in arcane power that increases magical energy. Why do you ask these questions?"

"Without a suit, I will probably need more protection. How much would it cost to get an enchanted cloak or vest?"

"I would not sell you such a thing," he responded.

That got under my skin really quick. "Why the hell not?"

"I mean no offense. Allow me to explain; an enchanted item can be powered by a totem like an augment, but if none is available, it then draws upon the host to power it. You would quickly find yourself incapacitated by the object's power demands."

I thanked him for clearing that up. So much for my enchanted armor idea, but maybe if I can learn this stuff, I could have an ace in the hole if Patterson ever does show up looking for revenge. Even if I could just turn his helmet to stone it'd lock his suit up completely.

Just as I started to ask a follow up question, Mystigal finally collapsed. I witnessed the look of frustration pass across the Vizier's face before he stepped toward his more gifted partner and helped the young Japanese American to her feet.

"There are some problems no amount of power can solve," he scolded the woman. "You should know this by now."

If the man appeared frustrated, she looked absolutely pissed. "Save the lectures," she hissed. "Can we just go now?"

The urge to say something petty was almost overpowering, but I've tasted defeat so many times in my life that I could describe the different flavors.

"Thanks for trying," was the best I could manage, under the circumstances.

She snapped a cold look in my direction before composing herself. "I can see the lies written all over your face. Don't bother denying it."

"Okay, I won't," I said. "I was just trying to be courteous. But if you want to know what I'm really thinking, I'll tell you; it's nice not to be the biggest failure in the room for a change."

"That's rich coming from you! I heard what you did to Mather. You're a cold blooded murderer."

"Asa," Vizier warned her.

"Don't worry," I said. "I'm not offended. I can assure you that killing him wasn't a cold blooded act. You weren't there, and you didn't see the little weasel taunting Wendy—the same Wendy who asked you to come here. He enjoyed making her do that and laughed about how he was going to use the system to get off with a slap on the wrist. I guess I slapped a little harder than he was expecting."

"Your justifications are as feeble as you are," she retorted.

"Tell me something, did your magic save you from the bugs? No, I'm pretty sure it was me. Now, can you get back to the part where you were leaving?"

"Yes, I think its best that we go," Grand Vizier said. "Good day to you, Mr. Stringel."

I nodded and watched them depart. The old coot seemed decent enough and told me straight up that it probably wouldn't work. Mystigal got all flustered and lashed out when her powers weren't enough to do the trick. I'd gotten as much help out of them as I was going to get. However, there was still a way forward.

He did say that anyone could do magic. Augments? They sound like a way to cheat the system. That sounded right up my alley!

I'd found a new hobby.

• • •

"I got it, but this is seriously one of your stupider ideas," the man said, and handed me the package.

Between the hours of making my new ManaCALes outfit, I'd spent my downtime watching video clips online about the wonderful world of beginner's magic. Most of the video-sharing sites kept the violent and dangerous stuff to a minimum. It was the greatest hits of "watch me pull a rabbit out of my hat" and "Little Rachel performs her first spell for the coven."

It was a unique combination of interesting and lame at the same time. I'd printed some of the pages from spellbooks uploaded to the Internet. Almost universally, the first step was to determine your magical potential. For that, there were official testing centers, but everyone who did it at the authorized locations ended up in a database. Even though I was currently on Uncle Sam's and Promethia's payroll, I didn't trust them one bit.

There was a home testing kit you could order, but that probably ended up flagging the same database. Good thing I am well acquainted with the wrong side of the law.

"Thanks, Bobby," I said, and looked around the Alabama base. He'd settled in again... and it showed. "I appreciate you snagging this for me. You didn't have any problems with the Wireless Wizard hooking you back up to VillainNet?"

"Nah, I'm good at lying. Everyone thinks you're down playing goody two shoes in New Orleans. So what's this about you and Aphrodite?"

"We've broken up," I said, flatly. "It's all, quite literally, downhill from there."

"But you still hit that right?"

I sighed under his questioning and the way he broke my relationship with Stacy down to that one sentence. On one hand, it was refreshing to have someone actually interested in my comings and goings. My team, with the exception of the Six Pack and the Bugler, couldn't really give a rat's ass what I was up to. Mom was still the same disgruntled woman when I called her, and Dad had to walk the fine line between being proud his son is finally "doing right by the name" and not pissing his wife off. José and his clones were cool, but usually tied up with his family or one of his get rich schemes, and Bo had only put in occasional appearances while using a wheelchair until his legs healed. I did offer to trick it out for him and maybe turn him into the sonic equivalent of General Devious and her hover throne—he declined.

"Yup," I admitted. "Twice."

Hillbilly Bobby seemed very pleased with my answer. "Well, all right, then! And that thing with you and the Tornado Girl?"

"Mind control. I killed the guy who made us do that."

"Shit, I woulda shook his hand," Bobby said, clearing away the trash on the table so I could start laying out the crystals in the kit.

"He was going to make her kill me at the end," I said, but at the same time, I think I still would have killed Mather, even if he hadn't mentioned it.

The man scratched his scruffy beard and considered what I'd said. "Well, when you put it like that I guess you did the right thing. I hope you brought something to eat. I'm about sick and tired of waffles and frozen dinners!"

"Groceries are in the van," I said. "Mind grabbing them?"

Part of keeping a low profile had my friend staying out of sight. It wasn't sitting well with him.

As I looked at the hand drawn diagrams depicting the order the crystals needed to be placed, Bobby got right to the heart of the matter.

"Cal, I need to start going out and doing some jobs. This place is almost worse than being in prison."

"What? You don't like my redecorations?" I asked, and gestured around the place.

"I'm serious, Cal. I'm bored shitless!"

Fighting back the urge to sigh again, I said, "Well, I can't really stop you, but I'd recommend you stick to low key jobs. Of course, Andydroid is out of commission, along with a good portion of my team, so you might want to take a big score. Just stay away from anything near us. Your cousin doesn't need a reason to be more suspicious of me than she already is."

"Fair enough," Bobby said, and shifted to scratching his ass. I tried my best not to cringe or look. "I reckon with Andydroid out of the way, that makes pickings in Atlanta easier."

Part of me wondered if I should really be giving Bobby advice on potential crimes. I was supposed to be working for The Man now. The other part wondered if I could get him to snatch enough synth muscle to get a new suit going. I'd already scrounged all that I could find here and it wasn't nearly enough.

With the ten crystals aligned on the table where the outlines of my hand was etched on the paper, I now had to prick the tips of each finger with a lancet that I'd picked up from a drug store. It was the kind diabetics used, and I hoped never to need it for that particular reason.

Bobby dimmed the lights as I touched the blood on each finger to the crystals. In a perfect world, each of the crystals would glow, lit by the nascent power of magic that flowed through my veins as I repeated the incantation on the page. Instead, there was a tiny, feeble light where my left index finger touched the piece of rose quartz... and nothing else.

Shaking my head, I consulted the accompanying paperwork. Light from that crystal indicates the presence of a passive form of magic, like, maybe, really good intuition. From the magnitude of the light, I reasoned that I shouldn't quit my day job any time soon. It was just a hunch or maybe my passive magic telling me that.

"Guess I'm going to need a lot of augmentation," I muttered.

"What did you say?" Bobby asked, from the other side of the room.

"I don't have hardly any latent magical talent," I said, and began sending out invites to my own private pity party.

My hulking brute of a friend started walking toward me. When he'd crossed half the distance, I noticed that all of the crystals were glowing now.

"Bobby?" I stammered. "Your powers must be magical in nature."

"Really?" he replied, sounding confused. "So, it was a bolt of magic lightning that made me and Sheila like this? Does that mean I can do spells and stuff?"

I wanted to shout at the unfairness of it all, and mutter how he can barely spell much less cast spells. Instead I said, "Maybe. I don't rightly know."

Pulling my hands off the table, I stood and saw the semi-precious gems continue to glow brighter, reacting to Bobby's presence. I felt suddenly exhausted, and all the things I'd read about how draining casting spells could be came to mind—just before I passed out.

• • •

"So, his power is magically based," Stacy asks, her fingers are doing a number on my muscles. She's being gentle, long accustomed to taking care with her augmented strength and what damage it could do to a mere mortal.

"Yeah, I guess it was magical lightning that hit the water they were swimming in. The regular kind probably would have killed them."

"So, has he ever tried to learn any magic?"

Recalling the few failed attempts on my friend's part, I say, "A couple of times, but it requires a certain level of obsession that he doesn't possess. Luckily, I do."

"Wonder it means Sheila could do magic?"

"Maybe, I didn't like her enough to tell her to give it a try. Right there, that's the spot!"

"You're tense," she states.

"More nervous than tense," I reply.

The backrub stops. "Why are you nervous?"

Turning to face her, I go with the only option available to me—the truth. "To be honest, I'm worried I'll screw this up again. My plans today included watching the Gab-O-Matic and working on all those projects that I'd been neglecting. Instead, you show up and it's better than I imagined. I thought I'd never again see the Stacy who'd spent weeks cooped up in this place with me."

The world had been ending and things had started out poorly between us, but we earned each other's respect along the way.

Stacy taps her head and says, "All the memories are back in here, Cal—the good, the great, and the not-so great. After I was wiped, I kept you around because I was curious what I could've seen in you, but I was looking at the wrong person. You're the same person you've always been, and I hope you never change, but I should've been looking for the changes in myself, instead."

"So, if we were a math equation, I'm a constant and you're the variable."

Tilting her head slightly she brushes her lips against mine. "I suppose, and I was trying to solve for you and make you seven when you were always an irrational number."

"Pi," I say. "If I'm an irrational number, I want to be Pi. Who doesn't like Pi?"

Laughing now, she shakes her head. "Whatever you want, Cal. I can do Pi."

She recognizes her mistake by the look on my face. "Oh, for crying out loud! What are you? Thirteen?"

"You already did Pi!" I exclaim, through my own chuckles.

"Grow up," she says, without any real malice behind the words.

I point an accusing finger at her and say, "Wait. You just said you hope I never change, and not five seconds later, you're telling me to change. If anyone's the irrational number here, I think it's you."

We kiss a few more times and my promise to not do anything with Stacy while I'm minding my daughter becomes more optional by each passing second. After all, the little maniac has probably another hour left on her nap. Just as things start to get serious, the buzzer goes off to inform me that someone's on the elevator. A glance at the monitor shows

Larry and Bobby coming back from fishing. Larry has a string of fish and Bobby has two, and looks perturbed. I can already tell that this is going to be one of those "he was using his mind powers on the fish again" arguments.

"Foiled again," I say, and push the Olympian back a few inches.

As the lift doors open, I heard Bobby complaining, "You might've caught one of those by yourself!"

Larry just shrugs and floats his string of fish toward the kitchen. "When are you going to admit, I'm just better at this than you? If I was using my powers, I could pull every fish from that pond."

"I still think you're a cheater!" Bobby proclaims. "Cal? Can you make something that'll tell me if Larry is using his mind stuff when we're fishing?"

"Don't drag me into this!" I protest. "I could probably rig up something, but that'd take me away from all the other things I'm supposed to be doing. Andy is still on my case about building him a better body."

Extraordinary Larry shakes his head and says, "Go ahead and build one when you get the chance, Cal. I'd really like to see the look on his face when he realizes I'm that much better with a rod and reel than he is."

Sighing, I tell them I'll put it on my list of shit I'll probably never get to, and we all laugh as I pop the top on a can of cola.

"Anybody hungry?" Larry asks. "I figured I'd go ahead and fry up a few before I inflict more damage on Bobby's ego when I spank him at Superhero Showdown."

"Maybe later," Stacy answers. "We ate just a little while ago. Although I wish I could get my hands on some pie right about now."

I about choke on the pop I am swallowing. *The wench just got me good!*

Sputtering, I try desperately to reclaim my coolness, or look less like an idiot. The carbonation burns my nostrils like the fires of Hell.

When I can speak again, I point at her and change the subject. "You should see Stacy play. How about we grab two more controllers, and me and her wipe the floor with you two losers."

Both men immediately forget the dispute about fishing, because that was trivial. I'd just thrown down the gauntlet and shit was about to get real!

Chapter Five

Obligatory Superhero Teamup

"Robert, my good man?"

Oh boy! Here comes the gloating.

"Yes, Lawrence?"

"If I recall correctly, one of our recent victims said, and I quote, 'Between my tactical genius and her phenomenal reflexes, we are going to take you losers to school!' Or, at least, something to that effect. Is that what you recall?"

"Sure as shit, I do!" Bobby said, abandoning his fake accent. "I'm pretty sure we kicked their little asses!"

"Indeed, we did," Larry drawled, now sounding like a professional wrestler doing his act. "A quick check at the final score, and it looks like the school bell is going to toll for them!"

I might not like to use the F word, but my middle finger is fully functional. Clearly, I am taking the loss harder than the Love Goddess. Then again, she doesn't live with these two buttmunchers.

"Watch the language," I admonish and point at the squirming child in my lap. Gabby's imitation of a howler monkey proclaimed to the world that she had finished her nap. It either spoiled our magnificent comeback, or put us out of our misery, depending on your perspective.

"Like her mother watches her mouth?" Bobby retorts, with a sly grin. He has a valid point. When Wendy stopped trying to be "Little Miss Perfect," she decided to go all the way. Most young women her age rebel and get tattoos and piercings, start sleeping with the wrong guys, and get knocked... never mind, the last two sort of fit. Our little wild child took the job of leading a rogue team of the most powerful individuals on the planet. It's laughable that I'm even part of this, but I've come a long way from the guy who first laid eyes on this cave and considered going back to prison as a better option.

I answer Hillbilly Bobby by defending my daughter's mother, "Well, running an unsanctioned super team, and flaunting it in front of her politically ambitious father as well as her hero mentor, carries a certain amount of stress. I say give her some leeway."

Stacy agrees, "There's a big rift between her and Bolt Action right now. I've never seen him that angry. Her father is probably the only one more pissed right now."

"Honestly," I say, and look at the woman beside me. "In every sim I've run, Wendy takes Bolt Action and I'm pretty sure the head of the East Coast Guardians already knows he wouldn't win. As for the not-so good Senator, he's used my book as an excuse to justify his little personal power grab. If it were up to me, I wouldn't mind finding out what his Manglermal form would be. My guess is a weasel."

The law of unintended consequences can be a foul tempered bitch.

"He would have found another way," Stacy says and leans forward to make faces at Gabby, providing a stark contrast to her words. "Senator Laguardia wants to be in control as much as the Overlord. He's just going to try and do it from inside the system rather than conquer it."

"I'm guessing that's part of the reason why Athena and Hera want to recruit us. Get us to toe Uncle Sam's line?"

She gives me a look with those beautiful eyes of hers. "I already know your answer, Cal. You're not going back."

"It'll be a cold day in hell before I let them watch over me!" Larry says, interrupting whatever I was about to say.

"Damned straight, that ain't gonna happen!" I say to reassure him. My problems aren't really with Uncle Sam, but rather the superheroes who jacked me over. Larry, on the other hand, has an ax to grind. The government gave up on trying to help him and focused on containment and getting what they could out of him. Somewhere out there were five children by the four volunteers or actresses who had played his high school sweethearts during each of his "resets." It's a safe bet that some three letter agency out there is running their own little improved human program.

As his memories of all his lost time returned, I found him out in the nearby woods, yanking pine trees out of the ground with his mind, with no more effort than I'd expend pulling a weed, and grinding them into pulp.

I don't ever plan on getting on his bad side. If he ever decides to go on a rampage, I'll either get out of his way or, more likely, join in.

"Hey, Stacy," I say, figuring the conversation is headed in a darker direction. "I guess I'm up to the point in the story where I tell you about convincing Chain Charmer to loan me the necklace. My only question is can you handle the excitement of an obligatory super powered team up?"

"You didn't have to sleep with him?" Bobby interjects.

"No!" I shoot back, and use my head to gesture at Ms. Mitchell. "Hello? I go that way."

"I guess," the big man replies. "But suppose the only way he would give you that necklace was if you would sleep with him. Would you do it?"

"Why are you even asking me this?"

Larry jumps in. "Now I'm curious as well."

Glancing at Stacy for some help, I see she is fighting pretty hard not to laugh. Annoyed, I say, "To be perfectly honest, Jin never showed any interest in me. Let's just leave it at that."

"Not a chance, Strings! You're all the time saying how Andy is your best friend in the whole wide world. So I just want to know how far you'd be willing to go!"

"I am so not answering that question," I declare the matter finished.

Naturally, Bobby has other ideas. He nudges Larry with his elbow and says, "He would've done it!"

Larry concurs, as I consider going to get my suit and killing the two of them.

"Based on all available facts," a new voice says, and we all turn to see Andydroid reaching the top of the stairs. "There is an eighty-seven point three six percent likelihood that Calvin would have complied with such a request."

"*Et tu, Brutus?*" I ask

Andy does the mechanical equivalent of shrugging his shoulders and replies, "There is no malice in my assessment of the given scenario. Given your circumstances at that point in time, and that you hoped that accessing the reptilian magic would provide you with a weapon to use against your nemesis, it is the most likely outcome to that hypothetical situation."

"It's bad enough when I have to take this crap from these two butt nuggets, but you don't have to help them."

With no hint of emotion in his delivery, my mechanical *compadre* dismisses my comment. "Engaging in rampant speculation is one of the traits that separate the human race from the rest of the creatures who inhabit this planet. Of course, one of the principles my creator endowed me with was to seek out a greater understanding of humanity. By interjecting my analysis and participating in this conjecture, I have come one step closer to reaching that goal."

Knowing Andydroid as I do, I am pretty sure that he is screwing with me. Sometimes he has a childlike curiosity to his actions. Last year, during the holidays, we watched *National Lampoon's Christmas Vacation* several times. Shortly afterward, Andy pushed Bobby down the stairs. The strongman was plenty angry, but Andy said that he knew the fall would not be sufficient to injure Bobby and that he wished to gather real-world data on the humorous effects of physical comedy.

I can't say I was pleased six hours later when he dumped a bucket of ice water on my head, so I could see where Bobby was coming from.

"I think your calculations are off, Andy," I say.

"Doubtful," he answers. "You entered into a business relationship with a known criminal organization in order to build your next powersuit. A singular same-sex encounter carries a significantly lower level of risk than your actual actions. Therefore, my margin of error is less than five percent. Now, considering we have identified each other as being best friends, I will offer you a suggestion that you proceed with the retelling of the events that transpired, rather than invite further speculation on this matter."

"I think he just told you to quit while you are ahead," a red-faced Larry says, and pounds the armrest of the couch with his fist.

Bobby, the instigator of all this, is obviously amused. "Who says Cal was ahead?"

Stacy gives up on trying not to laugh, and I realize all is lost.

For my parting shot, I say, "You guys suck!" Then I start into the story before this gets any worse.

• • •

Flying a hoversled wasn't my specialty. I was a little shaky at it and wouldn't be doing any riding stunts anytime soon. I liked my jetpacks and my armor better, but after being shot in the arm, I shelved the jetpack in favor of using the weight for a stronger force field. It reminded me of that two week period in my life, just after I got my first paycheck from Promethia, when I was determined to master riding a motorcycle—or how I ended up with road rash, a cast on my leg, and selling my bike for less than I paid for it.

Chain Charmer was a natural at it, and made operating one look easy. He gave me a disgusted look and said, "Try to keep up."

Sheila hadn't been impressed by my injury while stopping some bank robbers, or that I'd killed one of them. Unlike the rest, I wasn't impervious to small arms fire, didn't have unbreakable magic chains that I could use as a shield, or the ability to fire streams of paralyzing goop that extrudes from my skin. So what if I killed one of the robbers in the process? They were the ones who brought automatic weapons to a force blaster fight.

Resisting my urge to be a smartass was difficult, but I was trying to keep my eyes on the prize. I needed to be... nice. For me, that was probably going to be more difficult than flying this piece of crap. Maybe it was because my first encounter with this technology was when I intentionally killed for the first time. I also saw how easily these things exploded and dropped from the sky.

It wasn't very comforting.

Our hoversleds hadn't been upgraded to the newer models, so the best they could manage was still one hundred and twenty miles per hour. It was funny how the other three Guardian teams got the better gear first—the trickle-down theory, as it applied to super heroics if you ask me. We were headed for Waco where there were reports of some villains running around causing problems.

To make matters worse, I'd had dealings with both of them in the past. Blazing She-Clops used to buy weapons from my catalog. Jeannie Richey De Gruccio shot explosive bolts from her remaining eye. The lost eye came from trying to escape Graham Adzima and his discs. They were struggling, and she tried to blow his head off. The Dynamic Discus' energy absorbing and reflective abilities saved his life and made a terrible mess.

Her lackey was an old block mate during my stint in prison. The Passive-Aggressive Menace was decent to be around at select times. Dave Evans was twice as strong as Hillbilly Bobby and only about a tenth as sane. He was one of my more interesting students in the engineering course they let me teach. Every few minutes he'd switch from a shy introverted big man into a borderline lunatic—not too much middle ground there.

My thoughts went back to that lecture where I'd discussed how hard the Menace had to hit the Biloxi Bugler to splatter his brains everywhere. Even my increased shielding seemed dubious against his strength, but I wasn't certain whether I should try to take him on, or pick a fight with a woman who could look at me the wrong way and blow me to pieces.

I was under no illusions. I was backing up Chain Charmer and not the other way around. Given a choice between having Stacy back or my suit at that moment, I was pretty sure that I'd take the hardware.

A backrub, I thought two hours later to relieve my boredom. *I'd trade my suit and Stacy for a good backrub.* Toting around all that extra weight was murder on my neck and lower back. Maybe the Bugler was right all those times I'd told him to get some armor. Without synthmuscle this was more irritating than ever, and I realized that I should have packed the gear into a bag and put it on when we got to Texas.

Unlike a regular patrol where we circled around a general area and listen for emergencies that we could assist with, this requires us to go and meet up with the local police and coordinate our actions with them. It wasn't anything like my villain days where I could just show up, blow open a wall or a safe, grab the goods and make a getaway.

Sure, I'd been through this song and dance before when I had my suit, but this time it was much more tedious. I couldn't simply switch over and watch funny videos on the internet while one of the others hashed out the details. Instead, I kept my eyes on the scooter's autopilot and watched Jin using his chain link appendages as arms while the rest of him was in an animated conference call with the state, local, and federal agencies.

Look at me! I can multitask! Oh wait, he's pointing at me. Better see what he wants.

Switching over to the conference call frequency, I hear Jin introduce me. "I thought Stringel was already online, but he's joined us now. Do you have any insight as to why She-clops and the Menace would be in Waco?"

What do you know? I'm the resident expert on the criminal mind.

"Well, bank jobs are always high on the list. It is college football season, so which major school is there... Texas Tech? No, that's not right."

"Baylor," someone supplies, sounding annoyed. I was annoyed too. If I'd had my suit, I could have easily pulled it up. The LCD screen in the middle of the panel wasn't situated where I wanted it and the controls were awkward to use.

"Right. Are they playing someone at home this weekend and is that someone ranked?"

"Florida State and they're number three."

"What's the spread?"

"Eleven," the man sounded even more irritated. Must be upset that his team isn't getting any respect. *I don't get any respect either, so suck it!*

"Well, that's a possibility. As much money as there is in a bank, there's way more money tied up in the bookies and making certain they don't cover the spread. You may want to step up security around the visiting team's hotel. If that isn't the target, I'd look for them to use the game for cover to pull whatever job they are trying to do."

It's what I'd do in their place. Snatch someone important to the FSU game plan, like, their Offensive Coordinator, but not so important that they'd cancel the game. Kind of a dick move, but they are villains and that's how they roll.

"Reasonable theories," a second voice on the call said, this one female. I decided I liked that one. "I'll have our racketeering unit check out the major books in Vegas to see if there is a surge in bets going to Baylor, and monitor it."

Must be a fed, I decided, and liked her a little less on principle.

"Next," I continued, deciding that I'm on a roll. "How did you become aware of these two? Did they let themselves be seen or did you get a tip?"

"Why's that important?" the man asked.

"Simple. If they let themselves be seen, they want the attention and there might be more running around and this might be bigger. If you got a tip, then you got lucky."

"It was a tip from a reliable informant."

"Fair enough," I said. The Menace wasn't sane enough to orchestrate a bake sale, but She-clops—I wouldn't trust Jeannie further than I could throw her unaugmented. She might be smart enough to leak her presence to stir up some trouble.

• • •

Even when I was at UCLA, I didn't care for college sports. Yes, we had a great sports program there. My scholarship there didn't rely on whether I could throw a baseball or run a deep in route. For me, game days were a nice day to get around the campus without the constant mass of people. My roommate, the unfortunately named Joey Hazelwood, was really into everything Bruins-related. His side of the dorm sometimes made me a little nauseous. Heck, I even pretended to be really into Nebraska for a little while in freshman year, just to annoy him. *Go, Cornhuskers! Yeah, whatever.*

With that in mind, I found it odd to be parked on the roof area of Floyd Casey stadium, above the boxes, watching the Baylor Bears doing their best not to get blown out by the team from Florida State. Since the fact that I was still breathing was a testament to the life of an underdog, I was kind of pulling for the home team, aside from the fact it was fourteen to three with the final seconds winding down in the first half.

"Charmer, you think you can get a couple of hotdogs and a drink sent up? The view up here is lousy." I inquired into the communicator built into my ManaCALes helmet.

"You know what your problem is, Stringel?" My partner was in the oversized FSU windbreaker, trying to blend in with their visitor's training staff and keep his chains concealed. "You never think before you open that stupid mouth of yours. Always with the smartass remarks. Never knowing when to just be quiet!"

"Well, since you're in such a pleasant mood, I was wondering if you would let me borrow the spare necklace for an extended period of time."

There was a long pause before he replied, "Why? You already know what it does for you."

"Yeah, but I was thinking I could use it to translate all that lizard scratch and see if there's anything that will save Andydroid from spending the rest of his days as a statue. The Grand Vizier thought a translation would be helpful."

Technically he never used those words, but I wasn't above name dropping to help my cause.

"I don't know," he said. "She-Dozer has requested that I let others try it on so that we can recruit the person it grants the most useful power to."

The whistle blew as Baylor's long field goal attempt dropped short of the goalpost and rolled through the end zone. I waited until the whistles and announcements subsided before speaking again.

"I'm just asking for a loaner, Jin. If you're uncomfortable with Sheila's idea, tell her you're letting me borrow it while you think it over. I'm just trying to help Andy."

"I will consider your request," he spoke, after another few seconds of silence.

"Thanks," I said, and pondered whether or not to try my luck with another hot dog request when the vacated Florida State bench erupted in some kind of fire and began to burn. "Charmer! The bench is on fire!"

It looked like a metal bench, maybe aluminum and my mind started generating a list of things hot enough to burn metal.

Jin's reply was drowned out by the screams of people below, but I could see his chains shred the windbreaker he wore seconds ago and he moved like a giant daddy long legs toward the burning metal. Players from both teams began sprinting for the tunnel, followed by the frantic disarray of the marching band that had been trying to take the field, along with the cheerleaders, and any other unfortunate soul down there.

Switching over to the circuit law enforcement was using, I said, "Whatever is going on, She-clops and the Menace are making their move. I'm going airborne."

Activating the hoversled, I eased it off the top of the stands and got over the field while the announcer called for everyone to remain calm. Charmer's longest chains, the forty footers, wrapped around the burning bench that was already beginning to sag to the ground and melt, and flipped it over.

I jumped back onto our "Guardians Only" channel. "What's the word?"

"Some kind of enhanced thermite. I'm going to put it all in one pile to contain it all and not let it spread."

Surveying the scene below, I concluded, "Hurry up. I've got a hunch that they're nowhere near this stadium."

"Why do you say that?"

"Because, if they were looking for hostages, injuries, or anything else they'd have done it while the players were sitting there. Instead they wait for halftime and cause havoc without the injuries. It's a diversion. The real stuff is going down somewhere else. Neither of them flies and there's no way in hell they'd get themselves caught up in this mess. Come on, we have to go!"

"I will contain the situation first and then follow," he said.

"It's a crowd control issue, leave it to the stadium security," I protested.

"People come first," he said in an adamant tone.

I began accelerating on the sled and muttered, "Jin, do me a favor. If I ever start acting like you, shoot me."

Pulling up the map of the city with the locations of every bank and credit union in Waco with the current traffic patterns shown, I narrowed it to three suspect sites and informed the locals and the feds. They replied that they were directing a helicopter to one of the locations.

"I'll take the one that's near the on ramp to the interstate. Be careful on the approach. She-clops can shoot you out of the sky," I stated. It's the one I would pick in the situation. I wanted to kick myself as soon as I said it. I could've just as easily picked the other and let the cops show up where the robbery was in progress. No! I had no intention of turning into a clone of Jin. In this case, being right was more important. There was that TV head doctor who always asks people if they want to be right or happy, well I'm happiest when people realize I'm right!

Traveling as the crow flies; I cut across the city with ease. I also took my own advice and dropped to the rooftop levels. There was less of a chance of me ending up as a splatter on the pavement. Without my armor, I felt practically naked up here.

Approaching the credit union, I saw a non-descript black van backed up to the rear entrance and it brought back memories of the "good old days." I banked away and set down on a nearby warehouse while calling it in. Toggling the vision enhancement built into my helmet, I took a gander to see if I was dealing with a Saturday cleaning crew or Jeannie and Dave.

"Unless cleaning crews carry shotguns, I think I've found the spot," I said and chuckled. "Then again, this is Texas!"

Blazing She-clops must've hired some local muscle to help with the heist. There were five altogether. Thermals told me one was in the driver's seat and that he was the getaway driver. Two were loading and the other two carried what looked like your typical off-the-shelf Remington pump action shotguns. Provided I didn't try to go toe to toe with them, my heavier shield should be able to take it. For a change, I felt I had the edge.

That should've been all there was to it. Instead, I cringed as I heard the sirens rolling up the street; I knew that it was going to be a long afternoon.

Ah yes, the stealth approach, I thought.

Climbing back onto my sled, I flew the opposite direction from the one that the six squad cars and SWAT van were coming from and hoped their noise would help cover my landing on the credit union's roof. With any luck, the hired muscle would be so distracted by their immediate problems that they wouldn't notice that I'm right above them with the high ground.

Using the crude voice commands built into the helmet, I dialed up a level three pulse from my force blasters and fired at the right front side of the van. The tire exploded, and I probably bent the axle. The van wasn't going anywhere in the near future. Instinctively, I ducked as one of the men swung the business end of the shotgun in my direction and fired. Yeah, my vest would've protected me, even if it had gotten through my force field, but I possess an aversion to being shot at. Reaching into my belt, I fumbled with a tear gas grenade and lobbed it down into the mix. My helmet worked like a filter, and I could still see these yahoos with my thermal scan.

Switching over to taser pulses to save energy, I popped over the low wall and snapped off a couple of shots. One hit, but the other missed, badly. Six SWAT team members take advantage of the men reeling from the tear gas and charged in to overwhelm them. I was just about to do a mini-victory celebration dance when someone roared and the van was pushed aside like it was a Radio Flyer wagon.

Dave Evans, The Passive-Aggressive Menace waded into the fray, tossing friend and foe aside. He stood about six foot six inches tall and had short curly black hair. Clearly the aggressive side was in charge. Gunfire simply bounced off his skin and there was a crazed look beyond anything I'd ever seen on his face. Sure, I'd seen him lose it, but on some level he still knew that he was in prison and held back.

We weren't in prison at the moment, and he didn't seem interested in going back. He hadn't seen me at the moment, and the chickenshit part of me wanted to keep it that way, but I decided to suck it up and pretend to be the hero no one actually thought I was.

"Level four," I said, and pushed my right hand at him. The burst of energy slammed into Aggressive and knocked him sideways. It was a good sucker punch and he definitely felt it, but it wasn't going to be nearly that easy.

Cutting over to my private circuit with Jin, I said, "Move your ass, Charmer! The people you claim to care about are getting their asses handed to them!"

"I'm on the way!" His response wasn't nearly as good as, "Turn around, I'm here already." However, it was a damn sight better than, "I haven't left the stadium yet."

I'll take what I could get.

Though it had been tempting to dial it up to level five and hit him with a full alpha strike, I knew two things: my luck isn't all that great and he has a partner. My limited charging capacity meant that if I wanted a decent rate of fire, and to actually have enough juice to last more than a minute, I had to cycle one blaster at a time and I couldn't go higher than a four without the risk of losing my force field.

Dave didn't seem to recognize me, but it wasn't like we were buddies or anything. The only thing that mattered to him was that he hurt me.

His weapon of choice, the getaway van! *Holy shit! Holy shit!*

Since prayer wasn't going to help me, I dived to the left and released my chambered force blast at the mangled wreck, with the screaming driver still stuck inside. My bolt created enough of a nudge that I didn't get the opportunity to see whether my single shield generator was actually Ford Tough.

The van impacted on the roof behind me only a few feet from my hoversled and that caused me to breathe a sigh of relief. I'd have flown back commercial rather than ride behind Jin all the way back! Seconds later, the vehicle dropped into the building.

That's going to make a mess! I thought and wondered if there was a chance She-clops was now pinned underneath it.

There was a chime inside the helmet that let me know the recharge cycle on my right blaster had finished and I was armed again.

"Come down here and let me kill you!" Dave yelled and ripped through the steel weighted net one of the SWAT members had tried to subdue him with.

"Can't we just talk this one out, Dave! It'll be just like old times." *He's bound to revert to Passive any time now, just keep him talking.*

"Who? Oh, that's you, Stringel! Where's your fancy suit? I was hoping to rip you out of it through your arm socket.

"It's at the dry cleaners," I quipped, and fired just after my left blaster finished charging. He easily dodged my energy pulse this time.

"Well, since you ain't coming down..." Aggressive said, and leapt.

My suit had a really nice tracking suite which would have really helped my targeting right then. As it stood, the Mark I eyeballs were all I had to work with, and my blast clipped his legs and sent him pinwheeling into his less than graceful landing.

"That hurt," he growled.

Of course, I'd been trying to catch him center mass and knock him back to the pavement. Instead he was up here, on the roof, with me, and I was already backing up. The indicators for my force blasters seemed to crawl in comparison to how fast Aggressive was recovering.

I ran toward the hoversled as fast as the heavy equipment would let me. Dave reached me first and his fist hammered into my right side sending me flying through the air and down the hole made by the van. My body hit the roof and made a Stringel sized dent in it. I struggled to my knees and rolled down the hood and onto the debris covered carpet, probably looking as bad as I now felt.

Ow! Ow! Ow! Dammit to hell!

The force field and protective vest I wore absorbed most of the impact, but I knew I'd have the mother of all bruises on me—assuming I lived through this. My shield was almost completely down from his single punch and now everything was charging even more slowly than before. It took both hands to pull me up and help me stand, using a nearby desk as a crutch.

"Hello, Cal," a female voice said, snapping me out of my *AmIStillAlive* mode. The icon indicating my right force blaster disappeared, going offline. That actually helped me since I no longer had to distribute my limited power supply three ways.

"Jeannie," I said. "You look nice. How are things?" She wore a red headed wig as part of the whole "Blazing" theme she was going for. Also, wigs can get dropped when fleeing and make it easy to blend into a crowd.

"Well, let me see. I was trying to score a decent payday when this loser asshole dropped in and ruined everything, but now I get to kill him!"

Since the right blaster wasn't working, I grabbed the World's Number One Mom mug from the desk with that hand and chucked it at her.

A ruby lance of energy from her eye destroyed it.

"Pathetic, Cal," she said. "See what happens when you go over to the other side? Consider this a mercy killing."

I dropped the force blaster to a level two and fired, our energy met and cancelled each other out, but I was already moving. I jumped behind a couch, not that it would do me a world of good against her. Still, it gave me enough cover to yank one of the two remaining tear gas grenades out and pull the pin.

"Catch this!"

As expected, she destroyed it, but that merely dispersed the gas faster. Sure, my shield was about as good as a thin bed sheet at the moment and half my weapons were offline, but my helmet sure had a nice filter on it!

Who's the sucker now?

Blazing She-clops realized what was going on pretty quickly and began coughing and screaming. Her eye bolt lashed out and destroyed the couch in front of me. The explosion sent me on a short trip through the air where the nice hard wall was waiting to arrest my momentum.

• • •

"He's coming around," a voice intruded through the throbbing mental fog I drifted on. I started to mumble for my armor to start a diagnostic sequence and initiate repairs. Seconds later, I recalled why that was a stupid idea.

I'm really beginning to hate the sight of paramedics, I thought. Jin was standing next to the man, with his chains flexing back and forth, almost like they were nervous.

"What happened?"

"She-clops nailed you, but the gas made her easy to subdue. The Menace was more difficult to capture, until he reverted to his more docile persona. You should have waited for me."

I coughed as the EMT told me that it was bruised ribs and maybe a concussion. As ManaCALes, I'd been beaten soundly by the Bugler, but this time was more of draw with an advantage to me. My track record was improving, but it still hurt.

Rasping, I answered Chain Charmer, "If I had, there'd be a whole bunch of dead police officers."

Jin smiled, which he rarely did in my presence. "So, people do come first? Does this mean that I get to shoot you, now?"

"No!" I hacked out a protest. "If too many of them had died, I'd have had to fight The Menace and She-clops at the same time, because my partner thought a damned aluminum fire was more interesting to look at!"

Charmer actually laughed. "You sound like you almost believe that. They're taking you for precautionary X-rays and we will leave in the morning, if you're able. When we get back, remind me and I will lend you the necklace."

Something had changed his mind and I wasn't about to ask him what, because I probably wouldn't like the answer.

I'd gotten my ass kicked many, many, in fact too many, times. This was the first time anyone ever offered me jewelry afterward.

Yeah, I've got a head injury. I decided as they finished loading me onto the gurney. With my helmet off, I could see Jeannie surrounded by the Feds. Her wig was off and one arm was in a sling. They'd forced this ridiculous piece of headgear onto her that looked like a bad mix of *Phantom of the Opera* meets a fishbowl. I found it more amusing than she obviously did.

"Hey, Jeannie!" I called out.

"Go to Hell, Stringel!"

I waited a second, and then said, "Hey, Jeannie!"

"What?" she demanded.

"So how are things?" I repeated my earlier question as if nothing had happened.

Her profanity laced rant wouldn't heal my wounds, but it soothed my aching spirit. Since I wasn't going to risk pissing off Jin, I had to get my jollies somewhere else.

• • •

"You're a lot more heroic than you give yourself credit for," Stacy says, and runs her fingers through my hair.

"No need to go insulting me," I say, and act hurt while making faces at Gabzilla.

"I think Clops had a thing for you, Strings," Bobby comments. "I ran into her on a... job... recently and she was asking me a bunch of questions about you. Maybe that's why she was so angry about you working the other side?"

I laugh and say, "I never really thought about her that way, but if you say so. Music. Play *Don't know what you got till it's gone*."

Naturally, this starts an argument about whether or not Cinderella counts as Classic Rock.

Chapter Six

I Can Haz Magic, but Does I Wantz Magic

"You don't really believe that?" Stacy asks, while admiring the rail gun. I'm down in what used to be the prisoner area, checking on Andy's suit maintenance while he watches my daughter. After getting Bobby all riled up, I thought it best to bring my newly reunited girlfriend down to this level and continue the story.

Laughing, I respond, "Nah, I just like to yank Bobby's chain. It's fun to see him get all spun up from putting Arena rock bands in with his beloved Lynyrd Skynyrd. Honestly, he'd be less likely to hit someone who says a bad thing about his mother then if they insult his favorite band."

"That's low, Cal."

"Well, I am a petty man. Hell, I already immortalized my pettiness in a novel for the whole world to see! Anyway, that's like saying the Semi-Transparent Man passes for a real superhero. I have to admit, when I was in prison with him, I had no idea he was really a mole for Unky Sam. What's with the look?"

Stacy banishes the "I just swallowed a glass of sour milk" expression from her face. "I had dealings with him before and let's just say he's about as pure as the driven snow."

I'm tempted to ask if STM belongs in the same group as Mather, but reminding her of the other guy I killed, pretty much in front of her, could be a downer. It doesn't seem like a good time to mention that.

"This is cute," she says pointing at the graffiti decorating the barrel of the rail gun, where it says *Knock, Knock Mother Fu*.

"Bobby's contribution. If you get close enough to Megasuit to see the end of the pistol, you'll see the C, K, E, and R. The movie poster from A Christmas Story is my idea. Except my Red Ryder uses three inch diameter BBs that travel at supersonic speeds. They'll do more than just put an eye out."

Holding up a pair of the rounds for her inspection, I gallantly offer to let her hold my balls.

"Really," she says and crosses her lovely arms. "You're going there?"

"It seems appropriate."

"And that's why you are you," she concludes. "Maybe later, I'll try holding your balls, but you seem to be enjoying holding them right now."

"That's not nice," I protest.

"Whoever gave you the impression that I was nice?"

Even I have to admit that's a good comeback.

With a grin on her face and a wink, she continues, "One thing is certain; your balls hit harder than Bolt Action."

"I may have to use that line down the road. Actually not much harder," I confess and explain. "The force is concentrated over a smaller surface area. Your typical shield generator is going to try and cover as much area as possible. Nothing Promethia puts out commercially would stop it."

"So, how do you defend against it?" Stacy inquires.

"Well, duh, your best bet is to not get hit," I quip.

"Seriously, Cal," she says. "I have a good idea how you think. You already know how to stop it, don't you? Admit it?"

"I could tell you, but why should I tell one of Unky Sam's sanctioned superheroes how to stop my boomstick?"

She sighs, which is somewhat distracting. "I guess it is time to set some boundaries. Outside, we can be Aphrodite and, is it Megasuit you've settled on? Okay, good. When we're here, it's your girlfriend Stacy asking. I disabled the GPS in the hoversled before I came here because I fully plan to protect your secrets. Does that sound acceptable to you?"

I can feel some heat in my cheeks and realize I must be embarrassed. *Odd feeling doesn't happen often.* "Yeah, I can work with that. To beat it with a shield generator, you'd need a narrow beam focused shield and a computer to calculate where to put it. If it were me, I'd tie Andy into my suit and let him run my shielding, like I did against Lazarus. Your buddy, Hera, or someone like General Devious could probably do it instinctively with a cylindrical shield or an angular one that would deflect it away. Even then, it still might not work. I didn't build this to screw around, and if you ever see me pointing it at something or someone, it's because I am fully prepared to obliterate my target."

"I'll keep that in mind," she says. "Frankie was joking that we need to find out what your weapon was and upgrade the defenses at Mount Olympus."

"How is Ares anyway?" I ask. Patterson's pet atomic robot had curbstomped the God of War in San Francisco. I consider him to be one of the least annoying of my girlfriend's teammates.

"He should be back on the active roster in four weeks," she said.

"That soon?" I reply. "He looked pretty rough. I thought for certain he only had a fifty-fifty shot of making it to the hospital."

"It was touch and go for the first two days. First Aid showed up to do what he could."

"And to show that he wasn't on Patterson's side..."

She nods. "Probably, but as soon as Frankie made it through the first forty-eight hours, I knew he'd make a full recovery. We heal fast. The powers that be almost decertified the West Coast Guardians after you faked your death."

It's my turn to nod. "Wendy didn't think it would amount to anything, even with her pappy leading the charge."

"No, there's some fallout from all that. We used to have a total of two government liaisons. Now we have six and they are considerably more intrusive."

"They had one assigned to the Gulf Coasters. He was hardly ever sober enough to meet with us. I think he was somebody's son and he had a bunch of juicy dirt on someone."

She doesn't bother trying to deny this. "I heard he was replaced by three bureaucrats. And if they are anything like ours, they're annoying and a hindrance."

"That's why you should come over to the unsanctioned side of the tracks. We throw better parties!"

She looks skeptical and I can't blame her. Cracking under the weight of the stare, I stammer, "Truth be told, our parties are lame. Larry turns off the porn whenever Wendy is here, because he gets embarrassed. Bobby, as you can well imagine, has no problem with having it on all day. Hell, he wants me to invent LCD contacts that would allow him to watch porn whenever and wherever he wants."

"Sadly, I could see it," my girlfriend admits. "So, did you?"

"No," I say. "The logistics proved to be too much of a problem, but I'm sure someone will do it in the next fifteen years. It'll be a big seller."

I am also sure that when that happens, they'll discover a patent I filed in Bobby's name concerning flexible LCD screens inserted over each eye that allow for a full package of entertainment features. Bobby wants to call it Pornovision, but I'm still holding out for a better name. My fingers are crossed, concerning its approval.

Being an Intellectual Property Slimeball might make a good backup plan if all this super powered business doesn't pan out. Three cheers for being a Patent Troll! Where're my licensing fees and my goat?

"So, do you remember where you put them, or have you forgotten why you brought me down here?"

Of course I had, but I'm not about to admit that! I roll my eyes and lean under a workbench and fish around. Pulling out a storage tub marked Cal's socks and underwear. "Here it is."

She points at the labelling and I answer, "If you were stealing stuff from this base, would you bother with a bin that says this?"

"Probably not. You win."

Those last two words mean a lot to me, and I begin pulling out the silver plates containing the ancient dinosaur magic spells. Spreading them out on the workbench, I call her over. Each of them is about seven and a half inches wide and fourteen inches long."

She leans closer and I hand one to her.

"So you can really understand all this without the necklace?"

"I had to make up some hand translation guides, but yeah. The one you have in your hands is a simple one for controlling other reptiles. It's the first one I managed to cast."

• • •

"Thanks for dropping in," Bo said and pushed his wheelchair around the kitchen. It was a nice place, a French Colonial style from the Civil War era. Technically, it didn't belong to his family. The city of Biloxi owned the property and let him and his family live there rent free. The more jaded side of my personality applauded his scam, while the other side knew that the man was far too gracious to take advantage like I would.

The first time he had dragged me kicking and screaming for dinner at his house, I'd finally made the acquaintance of his lovely wife. Melinda was a kind-hearted soul with long blonde hair and eyes that had probably seen more than their fair share of sorrow. She greeted me with a big hug and said her man had told her that I saved the world. I shrugged my shoulders and replied that he was giving me too much credit.

"Bo isn't one to exaggerate. So, if he said it, I believe it. Besides, the way I see it, that pretty much squares the books on that time you almost killed him."

From that moment on I had a good idea that Melinda can always be counted on to say exactly what is on her mind. It was a refreshing quality to find in someone, when the majority of my days were spent with people capable of speaking out of both sides of their face at the same time.

Today, she was picking their youngest son up from the airport and might have mentioned to me that her other half was in a bit of a funk. I'd been in a rut since my armor was destroyed, so I figured misery loves company, and told her that I'd be happy to come over and hang with him.

"So, are you making any progress with the magical stuff?"

Shrugging, I looked at him, and responded, "It's tough. I can read the words, but sometimes it's hard to understand the context. I was hoping it would be a little less complex and more along the lines of eye of Newt and so on.

"So, it's kind of like speaking a Cajun dialect of French, and then going over to Europe and being misunderstood."

"Pretty much," I reply. "But it's more like speaking English and then going back in time to the Ancient Rome and trying to hold a conversation, if you know what I mean. Now how about you? When are you going to be back on the active roster? I could use a patrol partner who doesn't drive me up the wall."

"Sadly," he said. "This old body just doesn't heal as quickly as it used to. But you can bet that I'll be serving up the stanzas of justice before too long."

"Sometimes Bo, it actually makes me physically ill to hear you speak like that! I'm still pissed that they wouldn't send First Aid out here to help you."

"Now, Cal," he began, and took on a lecturing tone. "I know you want to see a conspiracy behind every corner, but he does have other responsibilities, and he has a tremendous gift, and a terrible burden."

"Sure, he'd have to sit around with broken legs for a day. Tremendous burden? I heard about his deal. If you're lucky enough to see him for a serious disease, and he heals you, you have to sign a contract donating ten percent of your income to his foundation for the rest of your life."

Bo scratched his neatly trimmed beard and said, "I'm not talking about that, besides his foundation helps people all over the world. Frankly, it's a way to have the rich donate ridiculous sums of money. First Aid's healing powers make him live under constant threat. If it's not some desperate parent taking hostages to try and cure their child, it's cultists who either want to sacrifice him or worship him as the next prophet of the Almighty. He's been abducted by his own bodyguards twice in the past decade."

"Want me to get you a drink from the fridge?" I offer, changing the subject. I was supposed to come over here and cheer him up; not let him rain on my parade. Someone like First Aid—everybody wants something from him. I'm kind of on the other end of the spectrum.

"Sure, I'll take a can of diet soda. There's no beer, if that's what you're looking for. Melinda's worried that I'll put on weight during rehab and that it would bring back my Type Two diabetes."

"Yeah, you don't want to play around with that crap," I answered, and pulled a couple of aluminum cans from the refrigerator. "So, did you ever give any thought to my improved helmet design? Since I can't scrounge up enough synth to create a suit, I need to improve my ManaCALes equipment and a cut down version of your design would work decently. Heck, we could even go into business and make tactical helmets for the military and the police when you decide to hang it up for good."

Mentally, I patted myself on the back for my own personal development. A few months ago, I'd have just taken the design and run with it. Unfortunately, that meant that I was growing fond of this man. The thorax piece of my destroyed armor was a bigger, badder version of the design I'd sent him.

"I think it will work, but you'll be operating at less than peak output because of the space constraints. As for your other idea, I don't think I'd like to see my invention mass produced and put in just anyone's hands."

There was a point to be had in his argument. "Still, sonics, as a weapon, are tamer than plasma and is better for something like crowd control than Tasers. You have to admit that. Some governments are using cheap versions already; maybe it's time to cash in on your design?"

Bo shook his head while taking a drink. "Cal, it's not about the money. Look at your nemesis, Lazarus Patterson. He has more money than some countries. It doesn't seem to make him any happier or a better person."

"I'm beginning to miss the days when you were my nemesis," I replied. "Things seemed simpler back then."

"Ah, the good old days... was your getaway driver really a blow up sex doll, or am I thinking of someone else?"

"Yeah, that was me. I had trust issues, back in the day. Not too long ago I also had a suit. Now, I'm looking forward to a sonic upgrade to my helmet."

"Well, you were pretty good with your floater and roller," Bugler offered. "If you can't get the materials to build a new suit, why not build more drones? You don't need synthmuscle for them. I was impressed by your floater."

"Cal Stringel—The DroneMaster? Nah, how about TechnoDrone? Has a decent ring to it. Naturally, I'd have to figure out how to work a name with Cal in it, for old time's sake. Meh, maybe I could make it work. Wait a sec! Does that mean you really didn't like Roller?"

"Oh, that one was a brute to be sure, but the hover drone, now that was a piece of art and precision engineering. Your Roller was good enough in a scrap, but remember when you used Floater to track down E.M. Pulsive? Once you knew where he was, you called in Zeus and took him into custody without a fight. Sheer strength alone doesn't always win the day."

"Damn, Bugler! Are you sure there's nothing in these sodas? You're making too much sense."

We spent the rest of the day going over potential drone designs. I especially liked the one that took Roller and made three times bigger, adding a control chair inside of it for me to command my platoon of drones.

It wasn't going to compare to having a real suit, and I certainly wouldn't be able to fly, but it would definitely increase my prospects of living until I could build a replacement suit.

• • •

"C'mon!" I muttered in frustration. The little caged gecko wasn't going over to the twig like I wanted it to. Instead, it sat there, mocking me and basking in the light of the warming lamp. I'd been losing this particular exercise for the better part of eight days, with nothing to show for it.

This was my feeble attempt to cast one of the first spells I'd managed to translate from the collection of plates that I loosely termed Rex's spell books. There were sixty-three of those, but some covered more than one of the plates. The rest of them consisted of his long winded biography and manifesto—at least I was pretty sure that's what it was.

I didn't find the "pull an asteroid out of orbit and smash it into the Earth" spell, which meant he was either a braggart with a keen sense of astronomy, or perhaps he didn't want to leave something that destructive lying around for any potential enemies. It was difficult to say. Me? I was having enough trouble convincing a tiny lizard to go check out a twig.

Asserting your dominance over the lesser species is a necessary skill. Superiority opens the pathways to much greater manipulation.

"It sounds less like a magical system and more like installing a rootkit in a network," I muttered and stared at the uncooperative animal. Reaching into the leather sack, I pull out the petrified carcass of a bat. This thing cost me four large from a bokor that Swamplord considered mostly trustworthy—or at least the voodoo priestess was too afraid of Hooch to screw over one of his friends.

As augments go, this was supposed to produce a threefold improvement over whatever innate magic I had in me. In other words, three times almost nothing might equal something.

I attempted the incantation again. Wait is it moving? No. It just reacted to the sound of my voice.

Then again, maybe it doesn't' mean crap.

"What am I doing?" I shouted in defeat. Futility was an old familiar friend I'd grappled with on many occasions. This time it looked as if it had the better of me. I looked at the rough drawings of the drones I'd put together with Bo. Instead of wasting my time with this I should be working on my squad of drones—the little tracked guy with the forty millimeter grenade launcher and eighteen round capacity, would pack a decent punch and wouldn't set me back an arm and a leg. I had a spare grenade launcher back with Bobby in Alabama and could use the targeting system from a Type A robot. There would still have enough space to mount a forward facing shield generator.

Yeah, I guess I should be doing that instead. My awesome magical talents don't seem to be getting me anywhere.

Glancing over at the statue of Andydroid, I tried to tell myself that if I started the whole drone project, I'd never come back to this. Lying to myself was easy. Hell! I could be a prodigy when it came to that.

Frustrated, I walked over to Andy and put my hand on his shoulder.

"If I give up now, I'm pretty much writing you off, pal. You know how stupid I can be; despite not having any real magical abilities, I wouldn't let that stop me! But maybe it's time I face the facts—I'm just not cut out for this. I've taken pictures of each plate and added my translation to them and put it into a database. Maybe down the road I can hire someone with more magic to try and tackle this."

The expression on Andy's face didn't change and I tried to determine what he would say and knew, deep down, that he wouldn't be angry with me, just slightly disappointed. Even turned to stone, Andydroid was probably ten times the hero that I could ever be.

"Sorry, Andy. Bo was telling me the other day that strength alone can't solve everything, but you have to have something to start with."

Like the idiot I was, I looked for reassurance from Andydroid. Finding none, I wanted to be angry. He was the last witness to the one great thing I did in my life. Even if Stacy got her memories back at that very moment, I doubted that we'd ever be the same again.

"This sucks giant donkey balls," I told the statue. "But I can't help you. That sonnuvabitch had more magic in his little toe than I'll ever have."

When the words came out of my mouth, it was like the light had been shined in my eyes after weeks of blundering around in the dark. I looked at Andy, and said, "Are you thinking what I'm thinking? I might not have his little toe, but I do have one of his clawed fingers!" I stared down at the shriveled up bat I'd still been holding and chucked it on the workbench. Digging through the items in the small dorm room fridge next to my bench, it took me a solid five minutes to find where I'd put that thing. José had laughed when I took it, and joked about making it into a necklace or something to commemorate my victory, and to be honest I'd forgotten I'd even had it.

In an ironic twist, the engineer pushed aside the plans for a group of drones. They became the back burner project as new life was breathed into this extremely dodgy venture.

Now, all I had to do was figure out how to turn Rex's claw into my own little magic totem. Addressing the digit, I said, "Let's go see what Mr. Google says I should do with you."

• • •

"Yes," the woman said, fondling my finger, well technically Rex's claw. "This has some serious potential. I can feel the power that can be tapped with this."

Was it my imagination or did the voodoo lady just lick her lips.

Her name was Patrice and she'd originally set out to be a pharmacist. Along the way, she'd discovered a similar, but vastly different, calling. She'd been one of the few Voodoo types who'd made a determined effort to break the spell on Andy. I'd been skeptical of the blonde haired woman, but Hooch said she was legit and that was enough for me. Even so, she looked the part of a PTA mother and not a person who deals in questionable magic.

The outside of her house looked like almost any misbegotten structure you'd find in the backwoods of bayou country. Inside, it looked completely modern and like something out of Better Homes and Gardens.

It was also my first time standing in the room with an, "I shit you not", zombie. I'd seen one or two in the occasional traveling carnival freakshow, and figured out that on most of those occasions they were just actors in makeup.

This one, however, was no actor; right down to the leathery, desiccated flesh, and the sunken eyes that didn't blink. Doesn't smell nearly as bad as I thought it would.

Patrice noted my curiosity and chuckled in amusement. "My boyfriend in college. He swore he'd love me forever, and then broke my heart. In return, I did something else to his. Does that bother you, Guardian?"

"Not nearly as much as it bothered him," I replied, and shrugged my shoulders. "What exactly do you use him for?"

"Round the clock housekeeping service mostly. He also helps with the vermin problem. You didn't answer my question."

"Oh, that?" I said, looking indifferent. "I'm still trying to adjust to being on this side of the fence, Ma'am. The 'don't kill unless absolutely necessary' rule is still a work in progress for me, so I can sympathize. Back to business, there's no way to get the rest of Rex's body back from where my team leader donated him. Instead, I've got a dead American crocodile, fresh from southern Florida instead."

"A pity," she commented. "The substitution will no doubt dampen the power of the augment."

"Yeah, but without any other dinosaurs really available for this, I had to go with a second cousin or what have you." I mentally added the one count of poaching to the things I'd need to be covered in my pardon, assuming I ever get it. "I'm still new to all this occult stuff, but I'm well versed in the manufacturing of powerful devices. So, after trade in credit for the petrified bat, how much is this going to run me?"

"Something with this much potential needs to be done right. The bat, and throw in another seventy-five hundred dollars."

I let out a low whistle. This was getting more expensive by the minute, but it was still not out of the realm of what was financially possible for me.

"However, when the augment is completed, I can try to free your robot friend again. If I can do that, you won't need this anymore, and we'll call it a fair swap."

I sense much greed in this one.

"Maybe. I do have some other things on my list to try with it, so we will have to see. For now, I will put together the money."

"Very well, Mr. Stringel," she said. "It will be ready in two weeks."

Hooch was waiting for me on the boat at the dock. Instead of a motor, he used four gators as locomotion. I wouldn't have had to go to Florida if he hadn't objected to me offing one of his subjects. People get so sensitive about things like that.

"How'd it go?"

"She said it would be ready in two weeks," I replied as we shoved off at a leisurely pace. I waited a couple of minutes before saying, "Patrice seemed pretty enthusiastic about how powerful of an augment she could make from Rex's claw. How likely is she to double-cross me?"

Swamp Lord reaches over the side and swirls some of the water before turning back to me. "How much is she charging?"

"The bat plus another seven and a half. She offered to try and fix Andydroid again with it and implied that she wanted the claw if she did."

"Well, shit," he said. "I guess I'd better come back with you to pick it up. If she's offering to do something at cost, I don't think she's planning on parting with it. Better come ready for a fight."

"Yeah, I didn't like the gleam in her eye. Well there's a first, a woman who won't give me the finger!"

He laughed while letting me know what his part in all of this was going to cost me – more pulse pistols. It was cool; I had things to do in my workshop anyway.

• • •

"Thanks for calling me. I really appreciate it," I yelled over the sound of my force blaster discharging. The nearest group of zombified nutria exploded into a gooey mess. "I'm having Rodentia flashbacks."

"After our little talk, I decided to keep an eye on her. Yeah, I was hoping it wouldn't come to this," the semi-vaporous man next to me said, as a tree limb scooped me up out of the way of the horde of rodents. "You should have brought the rest of your team."

Patrice really does have a vermin problem! She also seems to have done something about it. "And have them blame me for this, I don't think so!"

Imagining the shrill voice of She-Dozer blaming me for unleashing a zombie outbreak, I figured this was best left on the sly, unless I die, in which case, I'd probably be regretting it for the rest of my shambling existence.

The animated tree cut a swath through the army of dead animals.

Patrice's cackling laughter rang out. "You realize that with this, I can even challenge you, Mighty Swamp Lord." A second tree uprooted itself, but this one wasn't under Hooch's control. "Let us see if you're really the force you claim to be."

"This is still my swamp, Patty!"

"But, unlike you, fool, I can leave and still be just as powerful!"

While they exchanged pleasantries, I was trying to avoid a terminal case of splinters. The newly installed sonics in my helmet were pretty useless against zombies and, from this distance, only mildly annoying to the voodoo priestess.

My force blasters, on the other hand, could still affect things. One of my two beams went wide right and the other plowed into the ground a few feet in front of her, sending mud flying everywhere. "This wasn't part of the deal, Patrice!"

Yet, people always look at me funny when I say I have trust issues.

She scampered back behind some cover, which was a pleasant change. I'd been half expecting her to conjure some kind of shield like Rex did and mock me. So, I actually took a bit of reassurance in the fact that the traitor didn't want be shot at.

Another salvo was impossible because the two animated constructs began wrestling. I concluded that I was better off trying my luck with the zombie rats in the muck than getting crushed up here.

"Leave now, Stringel, and I won't kill you! This is between me and Hooch."

I tried to come up with something witty, but I was having enough problems dodging massive root balls that could cripple me.

Not having enough juice to hit the rock Patrice was hiding behind with a full broadside, I settled for sending a level four pulse her way, which I suspected would get her attention.

Hooch screamed in pain. Whatever she was doing hurt him directly, even in his gaseous state. His tree stumbled and splashed into the bog. I got the feeling things were beginning to shift in her favor.

"Shoot again, Stringel, and I will kill him!" the woman warned.

Swamp Lord had been a decent enough friend, and besides, I needed some time to recharge my blasters.

"That's better," she said, emerging from her hiding spot after a few seconds of nonviolence, and grasping the necklace with her hand. "Now drop your gauntlets."

"Into this muck, not happening," I replied. "Do you have any idea how much these things cost. Let me walk over to that dry spot, over there, and I'll do it."

The remaining zombie critters followed my steps closely.

"I really must thank you, Mr. Stringel. This object is amazing. It's at least a twelve fold augment. It's everything I've ever wanted."

"Except for the fact that it belongs to me," I said, reaching the small spot of raised land. "I guess that means you have no intention of honoring our deal?"

Her zombies, including the boyfriend, formed a protective wall in front of her. "Well, I suppose I could reanimate you and let your corpse hold it now and then. Would that be acceptable?"

"Well, I'm sorry it has to be this way, then," I said. "Don't say I didn't warn you."

"What?" she demanded.

The drone floating high above shot an arrow-like missile down at her and she dove to the side.

"You missed!" she declared, pointing at the floating weapon.

"I didn't have to hit and I'm no longer standing in the water," I said and trigger the heavy electrical charge from the drone.

The feedback blew the drone up and I added several more thousand dollars to this lesson in dealing with the occult. The zombies around her collapsed, save for one, and the giant animated tree joined Hooch's animated tree beastie. I was just happy I was still around to hear it and get the joke.

Sloshing through the muck, and looking at the floating carcasses surrounding her, I made my way to where a haggard looking Swamp Lord was pulling himself together.

"Is she dead?" he asked.

"I'll tell you in a minute," I replied, and kept my blaster trained on the sole remaining zombie. He made no move to attack. Slipping one of the gauntlets into the holster on my hip, I felt for a pulse and found none. I slipped the necklace off her neck. It felt warm, and even my pathetic level of magic reacted to its presence.

"She's either really good at faking it, or she's a goner." Standing up, I step away from her and her reanimated boyfriend. "I guess she's all yours."

The zombie moved forward and cradled the deceased voodoo priestess. He lifted her limp form and began a slow march into the depths of the marsh. It was a surreal scene, to say the least.

"I'm beginning to hate magic," Hooch growled, and joined me.

Regarding the necklace, I saw Rex's claw suspended inside a crystal, surrounded by crocodile blood, and who knows what else. The necklace was croc skin and decorated with teeth. It had a very savage style to it. "I can't blame you. Do you think this thing possessed her, or was she power mad to begin with?"

"She was always a little too eager, if you get my meaning," Hooch said. "Maybe you ought to be careful with that thing?"

"Sadly, I don't think it will make me powerful enough to ever reach that level."

• • •

"So, it works that well?" Stacy asks.

"Yeah," I say. "Instead of levitating a water bottle, I can pick up about fifty pounds and chuck it. I even managed a mage bolt with it... almost fainted afterward."

"And it didn't corrupt you?"

"Stacy," I say, and allow a big yawn to escape. Not that I'm complaining or anything, but I didn't sleep very much last night. "I'm about as corrupted as I usually am. Besides, I haven't broken it out in a few weeks. I'm doing a bunch of meditation and exercises to build up the amount of magic I can do on my own."

"I'm already sufficiently impressed. Do you think you'll ever need it?"

"You never know. Nobody who knows me would ever expect me to bust out some magic. It might save my hide somewhere down the line."

When I yawn for a second time, she smiles and asks, "Stamina problems?"

"Not everyone has your Olympic endurance, sweetheart. When Gabosaurus Rex goes down for her next nap, I might join her."

"In that case, I'm going to get going. I'd better check in and make sure my team knows I'm okay. I'm due for a week off after the members of the team who were hurt in the battle for San Francisco are back on the active roster, but I can definitely slip away this weekend and come back down here for the night. Is that all right with you?"

I feign a lack of interest and say, "So, I'm a booty call, now?"

"Does that bother you, Cal?" she asks, approaching me. We kiss for a few seconds while I compose a suitable answer.

"Not in the least. I'll be the star sixty-nine to your booty call. What?"

"That line? Seriously?"

"Oh, come on! That was a great line, and it's funny on multiple levels."

She doesn't seem convinced. "Anytime you have to start explaining how a joke is funny, it's already over. Give it up."

With no other options, I kiss her before she can come up with more reasons why that perfectly good line didn't resonate with her.

After a minute or so, things are getting rather heated. Pulling away, I stare into eyes so enticing that they almost have a hypnotic quality. "I thought you were leaving?"

Stacy winks. "You said you would take a nap when your daughter goes down for one. You seem a little more awake now. I'm guessing that's another thirty minutes to a full hour. The question is what can we do with that time? Got any ideas?"

"Now that you mention it, I do."

Chapter Seven

Go West Young Anti-Hero

I will never say that I spent more time than usual in central command monitoring the movements of a certain Olympian. Bobby, however, has no problem telling me his thoughts on the matter.

"She's got you good, Strings," he says.

"Oh, will you please shut up!"

That only manages to generate a round of knee slapping laughter from the big man. "See? That's what I mean. Normally, I'd expect you to ask if I was jealous in reply, or find some other way to try and use it to get under my skin. Instead, you get all onery and indignant! Like I said, she's got you good!"

There is nothing that I can really say in response to that. Even giving him the finger is the same kind of inadequate.

"I'm just worried that when she gets back to her friends she'll realize what a colossal mistake she's making and then rat us out to Athena and her ilk."

"Nah," he says, dismissing my concerns. "I saw the way she smiles around you. When she's up on the monitor looking pretty and all that, she'll smile and wave to the crowd. But when she's down here and hanging around you, well, that smile gets a whole lot bigger. I reckon if there's one piece of advice a surly bastard like myself can offer you, it's to not screw that up."

Bobby Walton, love guru and all-around thug. Also, now show-casing his skills as a spy.

"Thanks, I guess. Just try not to worry about my love life too much, and keep your eyes open. The Apostle is a tricky son of a bitch, and he's tied to almost everyone who is anyone. Watch your ass, Bobby."

"I'd look kind of foolish staring at my butt all day. Don't worry about me, I'll be fine."

I start to say something, but the intruder alarm goes off and I see a hoversled landing.

Bobby draws himself up and takes a long breath. "Well, looks like your lady friend is here. I'll send her down when she's done with a real man!"

"Stay classy, Bobby."

• • •

The Love Goddess enters, wearing jeans and a leather jacket. She has a bag over her shoulder and is carrying her flight helmet in her left hand. *Damn she's hot!*

"Bobby was trying to flirt with me up there... I think. Do you know why he would do that?"

"Because he's scrotum lint," I answer, and give her a kiss. "Actually, I think it was his idea of a joke. Part of why no one likes his jokes except for him. How's the superhero business?"

"It's a booming industry," she says, not missing a beat. "Did you see the fight?"

"Only the highlights and the press conference afterward. You know what would have ended the fight sooner?"

"Me wearing my armor? Don't start. I would have, but I had the upper torso open and was installing the fake power cell with the crystal shard you gave me when the call came in. I didn't want delay our response, or put it back together too quickly and have something fail on me because I was sloppy."

Her conservative approach made sense, and unlike me, she has her own powers to fall back on, and a large team. I just wanted to see her in her armor—call me selfish, but she can make a set of armor look sexy. Frankly, I can't pull that off.

"Well, at least it's installed now, and your suit can pull power from my grid."

I also have an alarm on that feed to let me know when the flow starts. I have to keep an eye on my girlfriend, don't I?

"I'd bring the suit down here, but I don't think I can get away with it."

"Well, I can always meet you in the field with Megasuit and slip through the poop chute."

"The poop chute?"

"It's the largest crystal shard. I use it to get into the suit when I want to and if I need to do any repairs. Right now, I'm working on a casing to hot swap one of your front arc shield generators."

With Stacy's armor, I have to make things cosmetically appear to be normal armor components, hence the fake powercell, as I'd done with the suit destroyed in California. It's a shit I don't have to give, with Megasuit.

I follow her into my bedroom where she drops her bag. "Your place looks cleaner."

"Well, I figured I could make an effort to make my bedroom a place where two people could actually spend time together, and moved most of my clutter downstairs. I'm told it's the little things."

"Who told you that?"

"Andy," I answer. "He's already working on the relationships between Flora and her husband. He's going for authenticity. Just yesterday he was grilling me on my problems with my parents."

She scowls slightly. "Do they know you're still alive?"

"No," I say, and let her look at me in disbelief for a few seconds. "I think they took a lot of heat from the book and I couldn't trust them to keep the secret. More of my unintended consequences, I guess."

"You should tell them," she insists.

"Probably, but now isn't really the time. Before you say anything else; I know they care in their own way, but sometimes there's too much ill will. Let's just say that water under the bridge doesn't really count if the bridge is already burnt. I don't have the kind of relationship you do with your parents. I wish I did, but I don't."

The Olympian crinkles her brow in thought and takes a moment to compose her response. "I'm not going to meddle. Every instinct is telling me to, but I'm going to pass on this one."

Clearly, we're a work in progress, but I can see that she's willing to put in the effort. "I appreciate it, and if anyone can convince me down the road that I should reach out to my folks, it's you. By the way, how are your folks?"

"Good. Dad's in Europe lecturing and consulting on a project at the CERN supercollider. Mom is doing her lobbyist thing."

"I don't suppose she would take me being alive very well?"

"It's been over a year now and people still make off color jokes about the ink blot test, so I'm thinking no. Of course when we did gag gifts for the holidays, it didn't help when my brother gave me a set of ink blot cards."

"That's... wow!" It takes quite a bit to shock me, but that's pretty hardcore.

"Yes, he's got an unusual sense of humor. You'd probably get along with him. Where're Larry and Andy?"

"Andy is up topside, surveying the house before it comes down next week, and Larry went to Charlotte to catch a Panthers game. Something wrong?"

She continues to rub the back of her neck with one of her hands, and replies, "Long flight on the hoversled. Mind giving me a backrub? What's with the shit eating grin?"

"Sorry, I'm just trying to picture how this would sound in an adult magazine—I never thought it could happen to me, but there she was, the Love Goddess herself, sitting on my bed and asking me to rub her back."

"Well, if you play it right, you might get lucky," she offers, and discards her jacket. The top follows and I'm already agreeing to whatever she wants, which also includes continuing my story.

Just for the record, I never did think this could happen to me.

• • •

"So, how does this work again?" Bobby asked. "You're really into this magic shit these days."

"I'm working both sides of the fence. Believe it or not, the two can actually work together – like so," I answered. "I run this cable from the powercell bank through the piece of the magic mirror and hook it into my force blasters. The array of 3 C-class power cells would provide more than enough power to run an entire battlesuit. I just need for it to handle the load from my wrist mount and shield vest."

Manacles 3.0 was suddenly a whole lot more viable with the addition of these bits and pieces of old Rexy's teleportation mirror.

Demonstrating how it worked for my escaped felon *compadre*, I proceeded to fire several level three pulses in rapid succession at the target. "When I get my hands on some synthmuscle and can build a new suit, I will pound Lazarus Patterson into a pile of goo. This little trick is going to let me build the most powerful set of armor ever imagined."

"You should just let me steal some for you," he offered, not quite grasping the situation.

"Believe me, I would," I said, and connected the shield vest into my new power distribution system. The whole thing fits nicely into the empty chassis of another C-class power cell. Hopefully, no one will notice how much juice I seem to be getting from that lone device. "But you can bet that any theft would be traced back to me by Promethia."

"What about the black market?"

I threw my hands helplessly in the air, and said, "The two big suppliers were the Overlord and General Devious. The Overlord is presumed dead, his distribution channels are all silent. Even if he is still alive, most of his production capability was wiped out when he lost his last base. The general isn't offering any for sale, and what little is out there has been marked up over 400 percent. What a bunch of damn criminals!"

Bobby laughed, and asked, "Well, what the hell did you expect?"

Even though he was right, I didn't want to admit it. If I still had all that synthmuscle that was blown up along with my junkyard base, I'd be using a portion of it to take advantage of the dramatic increase in price myself.

"Now that I'm back on VillainNet, I've got a smash and grab lined up at some research facility near Cape Canaveral. Somebody wants to get their hands on NASA tech. If you don't object, I'm going to take that one."

The big man sounded a bit antsy, so I tried to lay out the situation for him. "I can't really object. Just keep your eyes open and keep track of who is doing what and where they are."

"You ain't trying to make me into a two-bit turncoat?"

Jesus Bobby! It's not like we have membership cards and union dues!

"C'mon Bobby," I said and used my best disgusted face. "Do you think those goody two shoes will be happy with me when I finally whack Patterson? I'm pretty sure I'll be back on the other side of the fence when that happens, unless I can make it look like an accident. All in all, I'm a pretty lousy hero; just ask anyone! Your cousin has already tried to get me fired at least once that I know of, but WhirlWendy shot that idea down. That could easily change when she gets back next week. The only reason I even went along with this stupid idea can be summed up in one word—Aphrodite. Well, now that's over and I'll be honest with you, the grass is only greener on the other side because the heroes use a better quality bullshit to make all their scams look legit! Most of 'em have fan clubs and foundations they milk for money. Until Wendy took a leave of absence, Sheila was spending most of her time doing appearances and cashing in."

"You're talking a good game," Bobby said, and scratched at his beard. "And I understand what I'm hearing, even if I don't completely believe it."

"Oh, for the love of..." I muttered, and went to the table where I'd left my bag. Fishing around inside of it, I retrieved a thumb drive and inserted it into a port on the computer. "Check this out!"

"What is it?" he asked.

"After I got shot, Sheila put me on monitor duty and Patterson dropped by to rub salt in my wounds."

• • •

In my mind, I still heard She-Dozer saying, "With Andy gone, everyone has to take turns on monitor duty. It's your turn tonight."

My old sparring partner, Graham Adzima was speaking. The Dynamic Discus had gone to the East Coast Guardian team to be the deputy team leader under Bolt Action. Obviously that job was better than being top dog at this dung heap.

"East Coast reporting situation normal. Preditaz was finally apprehended downtown six hours ago and is in the secure holding facility under guard and awaiting transport. We had a handful of sightings of CyberThor in the Boston area. Nobody knows what that nut job is planning. Bolt Action and Sea Raider are headed down there tomorrow and will coordinate their actions with Freedom's Militia."

More like, tell those idiots what they're supposed to be doing, I thought. According to rumors, the Militia was so dysfunctional it made my team look like a well-oiled machine.

Sitting in the big chair, I stared at the screen split four ways. The three other Guardian teams occupied their spots and the last was reserved for the Olympians, who almost always had one of their regular human employees there, and tonight was no exception. Bolt Action still had that Marine mentality and always had one of the East Coast heroes here for the nightly rundown. The folks in Montreal were hit or miss, with tonight being a hit. I recognized the speedster called the Ivory Comet, waiting for his turn.

Naturally, the West Coast team usually followed the Olympians' lead and had one of their employees handle this and brief them in the morning, but not tonight. A quick check of the attendance database showed that it had been over three years since the last time Lazarus Patterson sat in on one of the sessions; yet, here he was, radiating that condescending smugness that surrounded him like an aura!

Coincidence? I think not.

Graham finished his report by noting that there were no team members on inactive reserve status. The same could not be said for the Gulf Coast Guardians. I typed in a couple of quick notes that summarized the East Coast for the others to read in the morning. It wouldn't be nearly as detailed as the virtual transcripts Andy was able to provide, but it would do.

While the northern frontier team member delivered his report in rapid fire fashion, I could feel Ultraweapon's gaze fixed on me, or maybe it was just the rampant paranoia that seemed to rule my life.

"Thank you for that report, Comet," Patterson said. "Why don't we hear from our friends along the Gulf Coast, next? How are you this evening, Mr. Stringel? I heard you took a bullet in the arm yesterday. I hope it's nothing more serious than that."

"It's just a flesh wound," I replied, in a really bad British accent, and noticed Graham cracked a smile, obviously getting the Monty Python reference. Despite the bad blood between the two of us, he seemed to treat me professionally enough so far.

"That's good to hear," Lazarus said, oozing false sincerity. "Just remember to keep your head in the fight when you're not in your armor. Keep a cool head and temper your reactions, unless of course you intended to kill that man."

He was goading me, and it was working. "Well, he did try to kill me. I don't take kindly to that. The old karma boomerang caught up with that fella a few seconds later. For some others out there, I suspect it's going to take a little longer, but since you seem to have a firm grasp of what's going on down here, would you care to give the report for me?"

"No. No. I was merely wishing you a swift recovery. I seem to be doing that a lot these days. I hope it doesn't become a trend."

"Don't worry about me, Mr. Patterson, I'll be fine. But your concern is duly noted. Other than the foiled bank robbery that we just discussed, things are relatively quiet along the Gulf Coast. We have reports from several pest-control companies in Baton Rouge about an increase in rat activity, which usually means Rodentia is in the area. Louisiana authorities have issued an advisory. She-Dozer, Anemone, and several members of the Six Pack, all left for South Florida to assist The Pelican in a counter narcotic operation that may involve supers. When they return, Chain Charmer and I are headed to Texas to investigate sightings of Blazing She-clops and the Passive Aggressive Menace in the Waco area. Our inactive roster includes Andydroid and the Biloxi Bugler. WhirlWendy sent word that she would be back in ten days."

"You seem short on good people down there, Mechanical. I'm sorry, Stringel; did you still want to be called that?"

"Frankly, I don't give a rat's ass what you call me."

Patterson smiled and seemed amused. "You seem awfully angry, Mr. Stringel. Perhaps you should rethink the superhero business. It doesn't seem to be agreeing with you. If it were anyone else, I would try to locate the components you require to create a new set of armor. However, after further consideration, and coupled with the knowledge that the blood of several of my employees is on your hands, I could not, in good conscience, provide you with any assistance... ever. It is my deepest hope the gears of history will grind you up and spit you out like the irrelevant little maggot you are."

The look on my face probably betrayed how deeply his barb struck, but I wasn't the kind of person to take something like that lying down.

"Tell me something, Lazarus; did you incorporate a mindwiper into your suit—for when your dates discover what a limp dick you are? Now, if we're done, do you mind giving us the West Coast report or have you got something else you'd like to talk about?"

There was the slightest change in his smug disposition, and I hoped that I scored at least one point in retribution.

• • •

"Yeah," Bobby agreed as the video ended. "I can see why you think he needs killing."

"Like usual, I thought of a dozen things I could have brought up. From him blowing up Maxine's bombs and killing those hostages to the fact that Maxine might have been his half-sister."

"Really?" Bobby said, sounding surprised. "Max V?"

"Yeah, thought I told you that. I don't know if it was true, but she sure as hell thought so. Every time since then, when I'm on monitor duty, he's there like clockwork. I should feel special. He's spending time screwing around with me when he could be porking some model."

"Too bad you can't use all this against him."

Nodding I said, "He's as shady as they come, but he pays his public relations department well. No one in their right mind would go up against... wait just a damn minute! There is someone I could go to."

• • •

Megan Bostic was waiting for me in the hotel's virtually deserted restaurant. Most anyone staying here was out enjoying the nightlife New Orleans had to offer. Her dark wavy hair had lightened through the years, and I concluded that she was still out of my league. She'd graduated from a woman obsessed with bringing down Lazarus Patterson, to being the face of the Anti-Hero movement. After all, taking down the one who scorned her appeared too petty. Taking them all down, now that was the sign of a crusader. Even so, the ease with which she'd agreed to meet me told me that Ultraweapon still had a place in her heart, or at least destroying Lazarus still did.

It's important to have a goal. I've learned that over the years. "Good evening, Ms. Bostic."

"I must say, I'm astonished that you actually showed up," she said, and tilted her wine glass to me as I sat. "People in the superhero community rarely call me unless it is to deliver the threat of another lawsuit. For one to actually want to meet with me borders on the astonishing."

"Well, I wouldn't exactly call me a member of the community, but if you're going with that analogy, I'm the guy who just moved in and is driving down everyone else's property values."

She let out an amused laugh before saying, "I'd put you more at the registered sex offender status, given your little romp with WhirlWendy."

"Oh, you know that wasn't me," I replied, and sipped my water.

"Of course it wasn't, and strangely enough, no one has seen Michael Mather since then, and dear Wendy has been on a personal hiatus since that night. Could we just skip over the part where you pretend I'm that stupid?"

"Oh, no offense intended, Ms. Bostic. I just promised Wendy that I would deny it publicly, so I'm going to keep doing that. Ask again, and you'll get the same answer. Read into that what you will."

"Fair enough, Calvin. May I call you that?"

"Actually, call me Cal."

"So, do you seriously want me to help you write and publish your memoir?"

"Confessions of a D-List Supervillain, and yes, I do."

"I like the title," she declared. "Sounds catchy. However, what makes you think it will sell. Granted you spent a few weeks as Stacy Mitchell's bed warmer, and that will garner some interest, but my time is worth more than an all too brief 'boy lands the dream girl and proceeds to lose her'."

"My suit. Before it was recently destroyed," I began. "It recorded almost everything, and I archived it offline fairly religiously. The book would practically write itself."

Pulling my tablet out, I handed it to her. "Here's a little slice of the dirty underside of the superhero world that everyone works so hard to stop the public from seeing. I think you'll find it interesting."

She practically snatched the device from me. I'd chosen the part where I was arguing with Athena about the public story giving Ultraweapon credit for stopping the bug invasion, and culminating with Patterson zapping Aphrodite with a mindwiper.

"This footage could be faked," she said, but the unhealthy gleam in her eye told me she'd already taken the bait.

"Sure, it could be, but it isn't. I've got lots and lots of juicy stuff and no qualms about letting it all hang out. I just need someone to be an editor and agent for my manuscript. Since you're an award winning journalist who already has several excellent novels out concerning the problems presented to society by super powered human beings, I could think of no other person on this planet who is better positioned to help me make this dream a reality."

"How long did you practice that bit of sucking up?" she inquired.

"Long enough to memorize it," I replied. "I'd like for us to be able to do business, but there are a couple of conditions."

"There always are," she commented. "All right, let's hear them."

"First, we can't release anything until I get that pardon they keep dangling in front of me like a carrot. It's one thing to give a massive middle finger to everyone in a cape and tights, but it will be hard to enjoy the victory from several hundred feet below the North Dakota countryside, if you know what I mean?"

Megan nodded, and said, "I can see why you want that. Anything else?"

"Actually, now that I think about it, that's the only one that will really hold things up. Obviously, you'd be signing an ironclad nondisclosure agreement, but that's just a technicality."

She appeared surprised by my sudden reversal. "Why is that Cal?"

Leaning forward, I tried to seem nonchalant while answering, "For a moment there, I almost started acting like one of them. I'd better watch myself. The truth is that if you screw me over I won't be in a position to bring a lawsuit against you, because I'll be either in prison or on the run again. For your sake, you'd better hope it is prison. Otherwise, you, and probably anyone you care about, won't have much longer to live. After all, there's a reason the title has the word supervillain in it. I have what I like to call extremely flexible morals. So, stab me in the back and you'll get the answer to where Mather is."

"I've had my share of death threats, Cal. It'd take a lot more than what you bring to the table to rattle me, but I'll take you at your word, and will go ahead and do a nondisclosure agreement. One thing about the 'tell all' industry is that the real money is made when you're on the talkshow circuit. That won't happen if you're on the run or in prison, so it's in my best interests to ensure that you are able to sit on a couch with a camera in front of you and talk about your book. So, do we have the beginnings of a partnership?"

I took her offered hand and said, "I do believe we do, Megan."

Of course, in reality, I was waiting for the pardon before releasing the book so that when I killed good old Lazarus I already had a built-in alibi, and perhaps the sympathy of the general public. As far as I was concerned, it was never too early to consider something like that. We spent the next thirty minutes hashing out the rest of the details before agreeing to meet again in my home state of Alabama.

In truth, this little get together had gone much better than I had hoped, and I was already close to becoming a best-selling author.

Now, the only trick was making sure I would be in a position to enjoy the accolades.

• • •

My most optimistic plan called for a patient year-long wait while I located all the components for my new armor. You can only imagine my surprise when none other than Paul West showed up and asked what I needed to make the next version of Mechani-CAL a reality. Now, instead of years, I could begin thinking in terms of months."

Given the fact that I could barely stand that no-good sleazy bastard, it was a remarkable reversal of fortune. Even though I'm not one to believe in signs, on the surface, this was about as fortuitous as I could imagine.

Driving a rented U-Haul through the gates of the Branson Missouri mansion owned by The Evil Overlord, or one of his shell companies, brought back memories of Vicky, which felt like so long ago. My time with her had been a slow build of something incredible; cut short way before its time. Now, I couldn't help but compare it to the fast-moving train wreck with Stacy. With the Olympian, our interactions were volatile and desperate on both our parts. Vicky allowed me to be happy with the person I was and not feel like I needed to change. Conversely, those few weeks with Stacy before she was mindwiped, had challenged me and made me actually want to become a better man. Despite the fact that it was pointless to debate the merits of my two failed relationships, I couldn't help but wonder which of the two was closer to being the *real* thing.

In all likelihood, I'd take that question to the grave with me.

Taking in the surroundings, I felt a sense of nostalgia. With the exception of a different paint color on the shutters, the main house looked exactly as I remembered. Part of me wished that I could walk around back to the hot tub, and find Vicky enjoying one of her trashy romance novels.

Instead, Paul West and two of his goons stepped out the front door and began walking to me. Sliding my right hand into a waiting force blaster gauntlet, I wasn't going to simply accept Mr. West and his employer's gracious offer like some doe eyed newbie.

"Good morning, Mr. Stringel. I trust you had a pleasant drive."

"It had its moments," I said. The trip had been a good way to blow off some steam after another late night session of Patterson and the nightly report.

"Very good," Paul answered. "If you would back up to the garage, we can get the items you requested loaded."

I was still waiting for the other shoe to fall, but did as he directed while my mind ran through any and all scenarios of how The Overlord could be screwing me over. *His men could easily slip a bomb into one of the crates, but what does that get him? It's not like I, or the Gulf Coasters are a threat to his organization. Bugs and listening devices? That's probably a given, but I can sweep for those easily enough at the storage unit where I'm going to take this, so I can inspect it before transporting it to our headquarters. So far, nothing I can come up with is better than The Overlord wanting me to keep Ultradouche occupied.*

Deciding that I'd have the next several hours to overthink this whole thing, I shut off the engine and climbed out of the front seat. Walking around to the rear, the men already had the back open and were lowering the ramp. Inside the garage, I saw six spools of synthmuscle, which would get the new suit up and running with at least a spool to spare. It clearly wasn't the high grade Promethia brand, but beggars couldn't be choosers. I popped the top on one of the crates and saw several sheets of armor plating—the material definitely looked dated, but serviceable. When I set up the power feed from my Alabama base, my shields would, hopefully, be almost impenetrable and these substandard components would work quite nicely.

Paul West made his way over to me as I was inspecting the crates. "All the items you requested are here. My employer would like to remind you that you are to be an irritant to Lazarus, but he reserves the right to be the one who delivers the final blow."

He bothered to spell that out? That's micromanagement at its finest.

"Paul," I said. "I am supposed to be one of the good guys, now. That's frowned on nowadays."

"Of course it is, Mr. Stringel. But given the fact that less than 100 feet from where we stand I recall you threatening my own life... You've also killed a bank robber, and should I even mention the rumors swirling about the death of that one hero at Mount Olympus?"

"Accidents do happen, Mr. West." There was no use denying anything he said.

"Granted. And though no one believes you could best Patterson in armored combat, murdering him outside of his suit might be something you would consider. I'm just making sure you understand the ramifications of such actions."

"Well, either he or your boss lured me into an ambush filled with robotic assassins. Considering the Overlord's generosity at the moment, I find it difficult to believe he would go to such lengths to engineer this scenario. This also means that Ultraweapon will probably try to kill me again. I will defend myself, naturally. I hope your employer understands that. But for the sake of moving forward, I will also say that I won't attack him if he isn't in his armor."

Of course, he has no idea what I'm planning!

After a minute or so of awkward silence, I asked. "Any word on General Devious?"

Paul scowled at me. "Even if I were privy to any information, Guardian, what makes you think I would share that knowledge with you?"

"Point taken," I responded. "Didn't want to step on her toes as well."

Not that she could feel it with her paralyzed limbs!

The good general had managed to survive the Bug Invasion by virtue of her telekinetic powers. However, her organization, which had mounted several rescue attempts, had been decimated by losses. True, she did fair better than the roughly five hundred million who were too sick, or otherwise unable, to work in the New World Order. Ultraweapon and the Overlord probably slept just fine by blaming each other for the unimaginable loss of life.

There was the temptation to ask Paul to let me walk around, but I figured I'd watch his steroid abusers load the rental.

It was also tempting to remind Paul of the time he said I was going to get my ass handed to me by Patterson's little band of suit hunters. *Pompous Jerk!*

Thinking back to the actual encounter with Promethia's employees and the previous roster from the Gulf Coast, I recalled the notion that I should have faked my death and high-tailed it out of there. Were I to actually off Patterson, I'd then have to be ready for Devious or the Overlord to try and kill me.

That's no way to live a life!

Bolt Action had implied that his "best case scenario" was we finished each other off. Already, the wheels were beginning to churn out the beginnings of plan that killed him and allowed me to walk away unscathed.

Yeah, that could work! I thought. *Poor Mechani-CAL, you're almost ready to be recreated and someone had to go and plan for your impending doom.*

"Sounds like you were considerably more premeditated than what was in your book."

"Branding and imaging, I suppose. If you must blame someone, blame Ms. Bostic."

The beautiful Olympian looks like she wants to say something. Whatever it is, she takes a breath and swallows the words back. I appreciate that she doesn't want to go there. "So, that's when you decided to fake your death?"

"Pretty much. My first instinct was to build something similar to Megasuit, but instead, I just used a couple of the mirror fragments for the suit to run the extra power and ammo feed for the grenade launcher along with the remote operating setup. All the rest was going to be a bomb to take out Ultraweapon and make it appear that I died trying."

"Why did you wait to go after him, then?"

"I was all set to do it, but then Wendy had a bombshell of her own to drop... that she was pregnant."

Chapter Eight

The Idiot's Guide to Victory

Stacy and I were enjoying a picnic on the grounds when Wendy arrived, toting my daughter. I knew my leader's moods well enough to recognize the waves of anger radiating from the young woman.

"What's wrong?" I ask.

"I caught one of Dad's cronies trying to slip a tracking device into Gabrielle's stuffed bear. Long story short, he tried to have me taken into custody."

Standing up, I held my arms out to take my slightly wind burnt bundle of joy from Wendy. The Gabster immediately grabs my nose to show how much she missed me.

To the pissed off superheroine I say, "Simmer down, Wendy. Just dial it back a couple of notches."

"Don't tell me how to feel!"

"I'm not trying to tell you anything, except that if you start making more than a localized barometric change, the feds can track your position using weather data. So, either get it together right now, or go hover out in the Gulf and see if you can create a tropical depression."

For the next three seconds I get her death stare, before she mutters in frustration, "Shit! I hate it when you're right."

"It's usually a surprise to me as well," I reply, and continue. "What happened this time; did your father's push polls say it was the right time to put his foot down?"

"I don't know!" she snaps.

"Wendy," Stacy says and points at the picnic basket. "When was the last time you ate? We've got plenty."

With an incredulous look, Wendy stammers, "Who gives a shit about... Actually, I am starving."

"Eat first," the Love Goddess says. "The other problem won't solve itself that easily. One of the things you two may be overlooking is that just because the senator is leading the charge for more legislation and control in our world, doesn't mean that he's the only one out there. Trust me, I'm certainly not trying to defend him, but others in his movement may be leaning on him to go after you, since they can spin it as a father trying to correct his daughter's behavior problem, instead of a government official trying to harass a rogue superhero."

I'm ready to admit that I hadn't thought of that, but the other party in the conversation wasn't so easily swayed. While making the world's most haphazard looking sandwich, Wendy counters with, "It sure sounds like you're defending him! Has your position on this changed any, Olympian?"

"I'm just the pretty one, Wendy," Stacy answers, with the slightest hint of disgust in her voice. "My opinions are rarely sought on these things, but since you asked, I've been playing by the Government's rules for years now and I can deal with it, but I can see where you three are coming from."

"Five if you count Andy and Bobby," I interject. Andy can't really express bitterness, but he does show gratitude and knows that everyone but me wrote him off as replaceable. Suffice it to say, it has altered his worldview. Bobby? As far as he's concerned, he's tired of being considered a lightweight and likes the idea of running with the big dogs who answer to no one.

"You five, then," she corrects. "So, here's my deal; as long as you're not engaging in wholesale murder and the like, I'm going to feign ignorance."

"Did you find what Cal did to Ultraweapon objectionable... or Mather for that matter?"

Wendy isn't the kind to take ultimatums sitting down and isn't afraid to challenge someone. I didn't want to muddy the waters by stating that both those situation weren't that cut and dried, but I can deal in oversimplifications. I've spent a lifetime doing exactly that.

"At the time I did, but that was the heat of the moment. In retrospect, both were justifiable. I'll give you guys the benefit of the doubt as long as I'm not questioning your actions on a daily basis. It is for your benefit as well."

"How so?" Wendy inquires.

"Right now, you're the most popular one of us out there. You've got the public on your side, which is why you're getting the kid gloves treatment. I'd be prepared for a PR offensive from the government that will try and chip away at your reputation, if I were in your position."

"Just remember," Wendy says. "If it ever comes out that Cal is still alive, you're bound to get swept up in all this as well."

"I'll cross that bridge when we get to it," Stacy answers. In truth, I hadn't considered that angle either, but apparently both of these ladies had.

Noticing the weight on my shoulder had shifted, I see that the drool machine has passed out. "I think all that fresh air during your trip wore her out. I'll take her back down and get her into her pac-and-play."

Wendy shakes her head. "No, I'll do it. It probably won't happen, but I'll lay down with her and try to get some rest. Maybe things won't seem so bad after some sleep. It's a nice day out and you two should enjoy it."

I hand my daughter back over to her mother and watch the duo depart. I wait a few seconds for Wendy to get clear before I say, "I told her going in that this was a possibility. She's as stubborn as she is powerful and is determined to change the world. I didn't have anywhere near her ambition at that age. Unfortunately, I think she's about to find out just how resistant to change the world can be."

"She's your public face. Part of the reason Robin and Holly are always so intense is the constant sea of bullshit they have to wade through from everyone pointing fingers. What about you?" she asks with a sly smile on her face. "Did you sign on to change the world? Or to show off in the Megasuit?"

"I'm hurt," I protest, with a false frown on my face, and resist the urge to comment on the root cause of Athena's intensity. We all know it's the stick up her ass anyway. "I thought you knew better. I really, really, really wanted to show off in the Megasuit."

"You're the most honest quasi-criminal I've ever met, Cal."

"I try. So, how did you figure out she was hungry?"

"It's a subset of my empathic powers. Concentrate enough and I can sense what the person's most immediate desire is. For Wendy, it was a combination of anger and hunger radiating off of her."

No, that's an interesting nugget of information. Thinking really hard, I offer, "So what's my most immediate desire?"

Stacy rolls her eyes and says, "I just ate. So that's definitely not going to happen, but maybe if you bribe me with some more of your story we can arrange something suitable in trade."

"If I were to embellish this section, does it improve my chances?"

"Just stick to the facts, Calvin."

"But we're getting to the good part. Oh, okay. If I have to..."

• • •

Fatherhood! Well, smack my ass and call me Sally! Somehow, I managed to successfully mate with another human being. My first thought was that I should call at least five people I grew up with and rub that fact in their face, but I was still standing there in my workshop, where I'd been stuffing some of the innards into my new armor, with a stupid expression on my face.

Naturally, reality slapped me across the face like a wet fish.

I'm going to be a shitty dad! I'm a card carrying self-centered narcissist; an ex-felon with so few morals that, like a vampire, I shouldn't be able to stand on holy ground.

Okay, maybe I'm not that bad, but I need my own semi to carry around my emotional baggage.

More importantly, and back to the narcissism, how is this going to change my plan to kill Patterson and fake my demise? Could I still do it?

Yes.

Should I do it?

Tougher question.

Should I just stand here debating this or wait for this armor to finish itself?

Hmmm, self-assembly feature? Probably ten or fifteen years from that. It'd be cool though. Damn it all! Get to work, Cal!

I tried to push the random thoughts aside, but they kept intruding. Considering what a one-track mind I possessed, this was doubly annoying. Picturing junior or juniorette on the playground and hearing the other kids' taunts.

"I hate you! Your dad killed Ultraweapon!"

"You're a loser. Your dad was killed by Ultraweapon!" That one was noticeably worse.

I grunted in frustration and began unwinding the synthmuscle I'd just knotted. I was using a pair of mirror shards to run the power through, along with a third, larger shard that had the tip of an M-19 belt-fed 40mm grenade launcher sticking out of it. Instead of a twelve round capacity, I could link up dozens on the belt, and just keep firing until the ammo boxes ran dry. It would be a sight to behold! Now, I just had to make it cosmetically look like the regular grenade launcher I mounted to my suit. In the casing where I normally kept the grenades, I could slip in an extra shield generator for some win-win action.

Even so, I needed a big stick. The mini-gun was nice and I had already made a replacement for the one turned to stone, this one mounted to my left arm and was fed by suit power. But, it didn't have the kind of oomph that would make someone like Ultraweapon think twice—something more was required. My exploration of the magical world wouldn't give me anything useful for at least three years.

A quick review of my recent catalog was depressing, and showed a distinct lack of inspiration. The maul and the hammer both had potential, but fell dreadfully short of realizing it. Maybe I should stick to pumping electricity into my punches and have a pair of high voltage brass knuckles. In reality, I should avoid punching and stick to ranged combat. The pulse rifle I'd made, for the fight with the bug controlled Olympians, was better when I overloaded it and chucked it at Ares and Apollo. Floater and Roller both had their uses, and I was still loving the whole Dronemaster idea, but I'd need a genuine horde of drones to make Patterson take notice.

Roller was another addition to things that do damage when they blow up.

Wait just a damn minute! I should make something that goes boom! That's how I made my name in the first place. The self-destruct that I'd used escaping New Orleans put Ares out of commission for a while. I could weaponize another powercell. That's an expensive proposition, but I do have one or two to spare. If I make it the payload of a missile...

Yes! That would wreak havoc on his shields, and if I could focus it enough, I could drop a whole quadrant on his armor. It would probably be the most expensive shoulder launched missile ever built, but it would be glorious! The lovechild of Nicky Tesla and Robby Oppenheimer, or at least someone in the Oppenheimer family.

In my best Yoda voice I said, "Powerful, this will be. Build this, you must!"

• • •

"You think up some wild shit, sometimes," Bobby said. "But I gotta tip my hat to you on this one. If I didn't know any different, I'd never suspect that you're not in your suit."

"Thanks," I said, and took a swig from my beer. He was in a chipper mood after successfully pulling another job. Technically, I was supposed to be on the lookout for him, but I was horrible at following orders. Also, I probably shouldn't drink and operate my suit at the same time... sure enough; the arm emulated my motion because I forgot to disengage the puppeteer interface. It was something I needed to get used to doing and why I was here for a long weekend. After all, it would look odd if my suit is hanging around the base and suddenly walks into a wall because I'm not thinking, or simulates taking a dump.

I had one of those outfits on that was similar to what the green screen movie makers' use. My Direct Neural Interface picks up my actions and transmits them to the armor. So far, it's been easy as pie. Mixing science and magic has never been so simple! Sadly, I hadn't been able to get back to my lizard magic translations yet, the drones I'd like to make, or any one of a dozen things I should be making.

With so much to do, I was spread thin. At least here, I'd have Bobby's help with some of the heavy lifting; he wouldn't ask questions, and I wouldn't have to lie about the answers.

"I still need to make the powercell bazooka, but I'm glad I have the suit finished. It means there is a good chance I will never have to step foot in the Gulf Coast Guardian headquarters—ever again."

"You seem happy about that," Bobby remarked and gulped down the beer he was drinking and reaches for another.

"You wouldn't believe me if I told you, but before you crack open another cold one, Cochise, do you mind going topside and letting me put the suit through its paces? I want to do a little combat practice."

"So, you're wantin' me to mess up the paint job on your fancy new tin can? I can do that."

His grin troubled me, but I figured it was better to have my shakedown run against a somewhat friendly foe.

One week, and a couple of alterations, later, I had the opportunity to try it against a considerably less accommodating opponent.

• • •

"Major Garner," Wendy keyed the intercom. "What's our ETA?"

The female Marine pilot, who was part of a flight team Uncle Sam assigned to us as Andy's replacement, replied. "We're thirty minutes from the airspace around St. Louis, but word is coming in that the fighting is getting close to the airport and they may have to evacuate the tower. If that happens, they're leaving a runway empty for us, but we'll have to go in with no assistance."

I tried to dislike the brunette woman on principle, but Janine had one of those "difficult to hate" personalities. On the other hand, I had an easy to dislike personality and though she was polite and professional to me, I could tell that I was being tolerated as part of her assignment.

Our leader replied, "I have every confidence in your ability to get us down safely, Major, but Mechani-CAL and I will deploy over the combat area and carry our teammates."

"Understood," our pilot acknowledged. "I'll contact the FAA and get priority clearance to drop to a lower ceiling. Good luck to you all."

"Okay, people," Wendy said. "The major will get us as close as she can to where the Silicon Sisterhood is getting their ass handed to them by Earth Quaker."

"They must be in a bad way if they're calling us for help," Anemone said.

Wendy bounced Sanford Acojo a reality check. "The Olympians are in Europe, and the other teams won't get there before we do," Wendy answered. "Earth Quaker isn't going to wait for anyone else. It's time we hero up and show the world what we can do!"

Earth Quaker was a heavy hitter. A coal miner from the western part of Pennsylvania who'd left his religious order to go and make "real money"; he was buried in a cave in before he got his first paycheck. It was weeks before the recovery team made it down there to find what they thought would be his body. He should have died down there, and maybe he did. The rumor mill said he made some kind of unsavory bargain with some power that shouldn't be dealt with.

The recovery team didn't make it out alive.

"Charmer, you catch a ride on Mechani-CAL and use your chains to carry the rest of the team. When we get to the ground, we take the fight to him. He's some kind of earth elemental, so keep moving and don't stay still for too long. Cal and I will pound him from above. He's tough, but not invincible. We just need to lead him away from the civilians so there is less collateral damage. Try to get him close to a place with enough water, and I'll drench him in a waterspout. Water jacks up his powers and makes him weaker, but he is aware of that, so it won't be easy."

An oversimplification of the problem, but she certainly has the enthusiasm.

"Cal, do you want a beer?"

I click off my external speaker so I can answer Bobby. "No, we're about to take on Earth Quaker. I shouldn't be drinking!"

Flipping up the flat screened helmet that allows me to see what the suit does, I shot Bobby an annoyed look.

What used to be the prison area was now just open space. The place could use a paint job, but it was an improvement over what used to be here. Coming from the viewpoint of an ex-convict, I never liked the idea of having cells of my own. My skills as a warden were somewhat lacking, and I'd rather not do that again... ever.

"Try not to interrupt me when I'm about to fight a supervillain."

"Well, shit!" He exclaimed in a drawl. "*Excuse* me for trying to be helpful!"

In my earpiece, Wendy was asking me if I'm ready. Flipping down the faceplate, I replied. "Sorry, I was just running a quick diagnostic on the armor before it goes into combat."

"You'll be fine, Stringel. Let's get moving."

We all followed Wendy into the rear of the jet and I checked my instrumentation. We were descending to a reasonable level. Even so, Chain Charmer and the others grabbed oxygen masks. On the external display, I saw two of his shorter chains wrapping around me and seeking anchor points. Our Amazon wrapped him in a hug while the Manglermal on our team grabbed on to another set of chains. We'd left all six of the José clones back in New Orleans. Not a whole lot the Six Pack could do in this situation.

In my base in Alabama, I pulled up the local news channel footage on one of the external monitors. The Sisterhood was already out of action. Andy's sisters would probably have to be rebuilt again. The only thing left fighting the thirty-foot tall man inside a golem was Sherman, The Haunted Tank.

Haunted Tank was one of those odd heroes that was tough to figure out. It had a mystical element. Hell! It's been blown to scrap metal hundreds of times, but the next day it is back on a concrete slab outside of a nearby VFW that brought it back from one of the Pacific islands looking just fine. The details were kind of sketchy, but there was a battle at some ancient and abandoned shrine between the Japanese, the tank crew, and something that they disturbed. Best anyone could tell, all three parties lost. Fifty years later, some explorers found the site of the battle and a pristine M-4 Sherman tank that was sort of alive. They identified it by the serial numbers, which brought the son of the tank's commander to the island. The tank followed him like a giant steel puppy back to St. Louis, and has been protecting the city ever since.

It doesn't need fuel, or ammo, but it's only as effective as a World War 2 tank. Non-supervillain crime rates in St. Louis were at record lows. However, most supers could handle an old tank; it was one of the reasons Eddy used to operate out of this area.

HT's 76 mm main cannon and two animated machine guns chipped away against the golem's body, but the cracks sealed themselves too quickly for the damage to accumulate, while an attached loudspeaker boomed static-ridden patriotic music.

The blocky humanoid made of earth, asphalt and concrete advanced against the much smaller tank, and hefted an abandoned pickup truck. The Chevy S10 smashed into the ground next to the evading tank.

To HT's credit, he/it was trying to lead it toward a park, where it's slightly better maneuverability would help it, but Earth Quaker must've recognized the tactic, because the next vehicle landed behind the retreating tank and the elemental began blocking the escape path. The tank slowly pushed the truck aside, but by that time, Earth Quaker added a city bus that completely blocked the way.

Haunted Tank must have realized the jig was up and stood its ground, firing as fast and furiously as it could until the monster was on top of it and began hammering away like a battering ram.

As the siren blared and our jet's cargo ramp began to lower, I wondered if a possessed relic of a long ago war could feel pain.

"He's taken out Haunted Tank," I announced and activated my jets with most of the team clinging to me.

There was still an oddness attached to the suit flying while I'm not in it—almost a phantom feeling that I should be moving, but wasn't. It would take some getting used to as the Mark III Build II suit descended onto the battlefield.

Delivering my cargo a block away from Earth Quaker, I left the other Guardians and accelerated toward our opponent. He kind of resembled a walking Easter Island statue. A mental command spun up the mini-gun and I raked the elemental with pulses of blue-white energy as I strafed him.

The M-19 responded to my next set of commands and I pumped out a trio of 40 mm High Explosive Armor Piercing grenades into the head to get his attention.

Detonations, like tiny pops, didn't generate what I hoped for, but I'd expected that. Haunted Tank was throwing bigger shells his way and it hadn't been effective, but it did grab Quaker's attention.

Too bad I hadn't finished the powercell bazooka. It was twenty feet away from me in Alabama, half assembled. Earth Quaker would have been the perfect test subject.

The city street and the stores surrounding it were a war zone. The concrete and the asphalt were being sucked into the golem's body, repairing the cracks I'd just created. My base would run out of power before he ran out of St. Louis. That's where Wendy came in. I glanced at where she hovered over the retention pond, pulling the water up into a waterspout. Water and earth were opposites. Once Quaker gets wet, it becomes harder for him to repair himself.

The Sisterhood tried using a fire truck against him. It didn't work out so well for them. We had someone with a little more going for her.

Concentrating my weapon fire against the left leg of the villain, I hit him with the minigun, the helmet mounted blaster and the grenade launcher, and immediately began wishing that I'd added twice the amount of weaponry to the suit.

"Here I come," Wendy's voice yelled though the static coming across the communication channel. Her approach reminded me of when I helped her against Imaginary Larry in Charlotte. Her twister was tightly focused and a credit to her ability to concentrate. She was trying to deliver her payload and do as little damage as possible to the city, at the same time.

Even with my jaded morals and questionable ethics, I had to give her props for that. I can't say I would be nearly as careful if our positions were reversed.

The man inside the golem figured out what was coming, because he attempted to reverse his direction. Unfortunately for him, Chain Charmer had used all our distractions to get into position. His two forty-foot chains snaked around one of Earth Quaker's ankles while the other four chains anchored the hero to the ground. I added a pair of grenades and more pulse bolts. The combination caused Earth Quaker to tumble to the pavement.

Wendy released her portable monsoon. Thousands of gallons of water flooded the area and I kept an eye out for Jin, to make certain he wouldn't be washed away.

She-Dozer appeared from nowhere with a pair of makeshift rebar spears and performed an ad-hoc acupuncture session on the construct's left shoulder.

Sheila should get her own personal weapons, I thought. *Even Bobby has those stupid clubs! She relies too much on her MMA training.*

Of course, if I had my way, everyone would have their own suit of powered armor—Chain Charmer's would look especially cool. Then again, that would require me doing all kinds of free or pro bono work, and I've got enough going on without adding more to my plate.

While the golem tried to rise, we descended on him like a pack of wild dogs. Charmer's longest unbreakable chains kept the legs wrapped up and the others smashed into the muddy creation time and time again, breaking away chunks.

Not actually being there left me detached enough to really analyze my team, as I used my weapons to smash the arm Sheila wasn't mangling. Sheila was a liability. She was nowhere near as good as she thought she was and had pretty much peaked.

Wendy, even with her foul mouth, was the only real redeeming thing about this team. She had the intangible quality of greatness about her. Being around her made other heroes better by association. Watching her drench Quaker without mercy made me slightly proud to be her baby daddy.

Anemone, who was currently using one of those infrared cameras and calling out the humans location so we villain, didn't accidentally kill them was a jackass. I just didn't click with him. Other than his suit, he didn't give a shit about technology. He liked soccer, rum, jazz, and flaunting his abilities.

Me? I didn't really care for any sports. Rum was my second least favorite drink behind scotch. From my perspective Jazz is where drummers who couldn't make it in a real band ended up.

Chain Charmer? He's a loner, ill-suited for being on a team for an extended period of time. He didn't like taking orders any more than I did. The death of his husband left him searching for a direction in life, and anyone with two eyes could see that it was only a matter of time before he walked.

Lastly, outside of a couple of magic spells, I had no abilities to flaunt except my mind. My creativity was an asset, but my decision making was a definite liability.

Earth Quaker was beaten, but even with our victory, it still took ten minutes for us to finally dig out the drowned rat of a man and let Sanford give him the paralyzing venom treatment. Most of the world, and me especially, short-changed the squad. It was a rare occasion when we were hitting on all cylinders, but when we did, we were actually an elite superteam.

Anemone asked, "Where do you think they'll send him?"

"Probably Guam," I replied. "They kept Amydillo there until she died fighting that sea monster, a few years back."

In the aftermath, Wendy landed beside me as I was trying to figure out the best way to flip Haunted Tank over. "Nice work today, Cal. Are you happy with the way the armor is performing?"

"It works good. But, you know a guy like me is never satisfied with just good. Hey Haunted Tank, can you rotate your turret and use your barrel like a jack?"

The small machine gun mounted at the front of the chassis nodded. I was talking to a possessed piece of military equipment after fighting a golem. I no longer questioned how strange my life had become.

"Boss when he starts to get unbalanced, do you think you can give him a push?"

"Sure, why not. But let's get Jin and his chains over here along with Sheila, and make this a team building exercise."

"Guardians together?" I offered our lame battlecry in a half-hearted question.

She shook her head. "It just doesn't sound right when you say it, Cal. Although, I think that's the first time you've ever even attempted to say it."

Ultimately, it took me and Sheila using Charmer's chains while Wendy conjured an updraft to get the tank back on his treads. I noticed Wendy looking a little pale and unsteady afterward.

Watching the damaged tank roll away, I said, "The police just took custody of Earth Quaker from Sanford. That means the press will be here soon. Sheila, why don't you warm the crowd up for the boss while she gets her second wind?"

Wendy glared at me. I wasn't certain if it was for the pun or for calling her out. "I'm fine."

"You just lifted a tank after draining a retention pond. Take a moment. You've earned it."

Wendy motioned for Sheila and the others to go ahead and get moving, and put her hands on her hips. "I don't need another mother, Stringel."

"Special cargo, bosslady," I said and tilted the armor's head down at her. "Taking good care of it means taking care of yourself. I'm just looking out for the both of you."

Her expression softened, and she said, "Just don't get overbearing. Mom is already talking about hiring a bodyguard. My luck, it will be an asshole."

"In that case, I'll be happy to forward her my rates. That's my specialty," I replied and laughed.

"That'll never happen. Besides, I'm going to need you to help Sheila with the team."

"You want me to be Sheila's second in command?" I didn't have a method of determining the temperature in hell, but I had a guess of what was happening down there.

"I'm considering it, Cal. You told me that you want to be a part of the future, so I'm thinking you might want to demonstrate that you're ready for more responsibility."

"Well, I've always thought She-Dozer is a bit childish. It should be good preparation, but I'm not going to change her nappy."

"Please, never say that to her," Wendy said.

"Hey, I just thought of something!"

"What now?" she said, sounding exasperated.

"It's my turn to give the nightly report. Wonder if my good buddy Lazarus will be there."

Just don't say anything that's going to start a fight," she warned.

I didn't have the heart to tell her that the fight had already started.

• • •

"Congratulations on taking out the elemental," Patterson said. "He's a tough opponent."

If you listened closely, you could hear the false sincerity in his words and I made a mental note to send off the most recent updates to my memoir to Megan Bostic. She was chomping at the bit to release it, but I had to keep reminding her that if it screwed with my pardon, there would be consequences.

"I see you're enjoying your new armor there, Stringel. So much that you're still in it. Doesn't look like you made any improvements."

"Well, gotta test the prolonged comfort features. You know how it is. Did you ever get that access plate installed so you could get a hummer without getting out, or did you decide to put it on the back end for some quality fudge packing?"

I figured I'd get the insults started early tonight, but I needed to pace myself—it's a marathon, not a sprint.

"Crude as always, Stringel. You must be feeling great, having rebuilt that third-rate clunker, but I wouldn't get too cocky, because all those substandard components won't last long. I'm worried about you, Stringel... Those ancient designs are destined to fail."

The other screens watched on in interest. Psycho Mountie from the Northern Frontier team even had a bucket of popcorn, but the Canadian was slightly off—hence the psycho part of her name.

"You say ancient, I say well tested. Besides, I'm sure you have more things to worry about than just me... But, you know what I worry about, that RoboDestroyer suit. It hasn't shown up in a while, and if you want my opinion, it looks like whoever was in that suit had access to more of your tech than I do. I'm guessing your security isn't nearly as tight as you think it is."

"Thank you for your concern, Stringel. We are still investigating the matter."

"I'm sure your people will be able to track him down. I'm just glad we aren't enemies anymore and don't have to fight. Maybe, if your people do catch up to him, you could pass on that info to me, since I have a score to settle with that poser. I'd fight him any day of the week!"

Patterson looked thoughtful for a few seconds before replying, "I'll see what they turn up, but even someone in the equivalent of my suit from five years ago would hand you your ass."

"I wouldn't be so certain, but we'll never know until we find out. Anyway, that's the report from New Orleans. Since it is way past Bolt Action's bedtime, I'll hand it over to you, because you all know how cranky he gets."

Ultraweapon delivered his report and we broke for the evening. Bolt Action stayed on screen after the others signed off.

"So, you're calling him out, Stringel? I didn't think you were so eager to die."

"If he wants to come after me in an old suit, David... I figured I'd give him an out. I've got a better chance against that suit."

"My friends can call me David. You're not one of them, dickhead. And I wouldn't be so certain, if I were you. Patterson probably has some of his next generation tech on that suit."

"Probably, but the bottom line is that if that suit was better than the one he uses, he'd be wearing it. Besides, I'm full of surprises, so don't count me out just yet."

The founder of the Guardians laughed and replied, "You're full of something, Stringel, and surprises ain't it! But hey, it's your life. How you choose to die is completely up to you."

"I'll definitely keep that in mind. You should try more fiber in your diet and see if it mellows you," I said. With my tele-operated armor, I could probably contradict the head of the East Coast team, but I had no intention of going there.

"Keep up those cracks and you won't have to wait for Patterson. I'll kick your scrawny ass myself," he said and cut the connection.

I killed my external microphone and kicked back in my chair, back in 'Bama. "Yanking Bolt Action's chain is even more fun than spinning Wendy up."

Bobby laughed and used his teeth to maul one of the grilled cheese sandwiches piled on his plate. "Pretty smooth move, trying to talk that rich fellow into using his other set of armor."

"Maybe it will work," I said, and decided that I could probably go for something to eat as well. "If I were to take him out in that armor, there'd be enough questions about why he was in it for me to weasel my way out of the legal side of things. I'd still have to worry about General Devious, and the Overlord, but I'd be legit, and could call on all of those goody two shoes to protect little old me."

"Have you thought about making a second set of armor yourself? Seems to me that you could go after him and still have the perfect alibi 'cuz your suit'd be in Louisiana while you put that fucker down like a wild animal. This thing could work both ways, or am I just not thinking it through? C'mon, Cal, tell me why it won't work."

I was stunned. Bobby, Hillbilly Bobby, my buffoon of a buddy, had once more provided the most obvious answer that had been sitting in front of me all along!

"I... I... How did...? No, you're absolutely right! It would work! There's no reason why it wouldn't!"

In truth, I'd like to think that I would have reached that conclusion at some point. Bobby had just hooked me up with a way out of this that didn't involve blowing up a perfectly good set of armor, and disappearing to Costa Rica.

"Where are you going?"

"I have to start designing the suit that will kill Lazarus Patterson and let me get away with it!"

Having spent the majority of my life on the losing side of most situations, I was well-versed in the art of defeat. This excruciatingly long partnership, kind of like karma's version of having genital warts, had left me all too familiar with how things could go wrong. That's why I planned to cover as many of the angles as possible.

With any luck, Lazarus Patterson's days were numbered, and if I'd built up some good mojo, maybe the universe would let me do the final subtraction.

• • •

"So you were always planning on attacking him?" Stacy says. I could see the glimmer of disappointment in her eyes. We'd avoided the eight hundred pound gorilla in the room for as long as possible, with laughter, fun, and make up sex, but I guess it is time to address it.

Probably not getting any tonight. Shouldn't have gotten wrapped up in telling the story.

"You wanted the unvarnished truth. When I was a nobody, he let his people ruin my life. Sure, I made my own decisions, but he made his as well. Later, he sent people to kill me so they could field test technology he wanted to use against the Overlord. I barely survived the one time I fought him in person during HORDES. Back then, I was still just a minor irritation to him. Later, you came along and called me out with my obsession over him and I was ready to let it go, because you made me want to try and be a better person."

"Cal," she starts, but I ask her to let me finish.

"Then, he took you away from me just because he was a sore loser. Even that wasn't enough for him, so he sent robot assassins after me!

Each and every day, I do something stupid that I should apologize for, but killing Lazarus Patterson won't ever be one of them."

"Are you finished?" she asks, and pulls me close to her. Damn, she's strong.

"Yes," I answer.

"Good. It's my turn then. Until I got my memories back, I didn't know what I saw in you. You're brilliant, but I've dated others who had your level of IQ. You did pretty good in your suit, but there are plenty of other heroes out there."

She puts her index finger on my lips to silence the smart ass comment that was on the tip of my tongue. "But you did something the others never did, you challenged me to become something better than I already am. The rest? They were content with me being Aphrodite and I was content just being her. You put me in a set of armor and pushed me to go a step beyond what I was capable of. Most guys will say that I make them want to be better, but you were the first guy who made me want to better myself, and challenged me to save the world. That's what makes you special. That's what I didn't have with Lazarus. And that's why I came back to you. Do I wish you hadn't killed him? Yes, I do. But if I can't accept you for the person you are, then Lazarus did win, and I'm not about to let that happen. So, here's my deal—you challenge me to be a better hero and person, and I'll keep challenging you at the same time, because together is a lot better than apart. Deal?"

That pesky knot in my throat takes a second to swallow, but I reply, "Deal."

"Good. Now that we've gotten that off our chests, let's get something else off as well."

Her one hand starts pulling my shirt up and the other sweeps the picnic basket off the blanket, making room. The look in her eye no longer reflects disappointment, as she pushes me back and slides on top of me. My mind flashes back to right before we broke up at Mardi Gras, when she'd been this aggressive and I'd felt like I'd auditioned and failed for a part in her life.

This time, we both know what we want and why we want it. That makes all the difference in the world.

Guess I need to apologize to myself tomorrow, for thinking I wasn't going to get any. They say confession is good for the soul, but so is this, and trust me, I'm no priest!

Chapter Nine

Reports of My Death have been Greatly Exaggerated

"That was rather vigorous," I say, or rather pant. "I am going to have to start a serious workout regimen to stay up with you."

Stacy, propped up on one elbow, chuckles and slowly drags her right index finger in a swirling motion across my chest. "If you want my opinion, I think that was much better than the hot fudge sundae fiasco. And there's less mess to clean up afterward."

"Yeah, definitely going to need to hit the cardio. Consider my booty called and then redialed."

She's about to say something when a third voice interrupts, "Calvin, if you and Stacy have concluded your session of intercourse, perhaps I can interrupt? Otherwise, can you give me a time to return?"

Turning my head, I see Andydroid standing about twenty feet from us, in the shade of a pair of trees.

Stacy shrieks like a schoolgirl, and uses the nearest object to cover her chest. It happens to be my hand, so I'm not too terribly broken up about it. I roll to block Andy's view of the Love Goddess in her natural state.

"How long have you been standing there, Andy?"

The robot answers, "I've been in my present position for seven minutes and thirty-seven seconds. The two of you were otherwise engaged, and did not detect my approach. Thus, I encountered what you humans refer to as an awkward situation. I did not wish to interrupt, and based on the material you, Bobby, and Larry watch, it is customary for the third person in this position to watch. If I had been female, it would also be customary for me to begin touching myself."

Stacy gasps with something between a choke and laughter, before saying, "How much porn are you letting Andy watch?"

There's no good answer to her question, so I ignore it. "What's going on?"

"It appears that an arrest warrant has been issued for Wendy LaGuardia on the grounds of failure to comply with the instructions of a federal marshal, resisting arrest, evasion, and child endangerment. Several

US military helicopters began monitoring the position of the Megasuit as it conducts firefighting operations. When I detected an increase in the volume of radio traffic and several other approaching aircraft, I opted not to engage and sent the suit into the fire zone."

"Well, that didn't take long!" I say. "Andy, go back downstairs. Stacy and I will be along in a moment."

My companion frowns. "The military isn't going to attack. They are waiting for the superheroes. I would be willing to bet that if I went back to my hoversled, I'd find an emergency recall message waiting for me."

"Probably," I answer. "But then again, your team is still a few people down. I do know one team who didn't lift a damned finger in San Francisco. Let's go see what the West Coast Guardians are up to."

• • •

Andy relinquishes control as soon as I jack in to the command circuit. My senses expand and I connect to the suit. The external temperature reads one hundred and thirty-five degrees. It's probably messing with my paint scheme, but I'd been thinking of redoing it anyway. The sky above shows seven helicopters circling like angry moths over a campfire.

"How many helicopters were here initially?"

The robot answers, "Two Apaches escorting the lone Blackhawk. I will go alert Wendy to the situation."

The slightly protective side of me thinks we should let her get some sleep, but the side that doesn't like being yelled at by our fearless, and foul-mouthed leader says, "Go ahead and get her."

Turning to Stacy, I ask, "What do you think? Talk to them or just walk away?"

She shakes her head and replies, "With the warrant out on Wendy, I don't think you should talk right now. They will try to force your hand and use it as an excuse to try and round up your group."

"Sounds sensible enough," I admit. "Now, all I have to do is avoid their little dragnet. They'll have satellites blanketing the area, trying to find me."

Andy's hidden area turns out to be a cluster of burning pines. The armor is built to withstand much greater heat levels. This is child's play. As we wait for Wendy to come down from her bedroom, I show Stacy more about how the connection to Megasuit works, and point out the single power connection I have running to her suit.

"That is, if you're ever going to wear your suit."

"If I beat you up, would your suit experience my attack?"

Unable to resist needling here, I say, "Cute, but seriously, you rarely ever wear it."

"I already told you, I would have worn it during our last fight, but it was in several pieces and I didn't want to try and throw it together while everyone was waiting on me. Sheesh!"

"Did you just 'sheesh me'?"

"Get on my case about my armor again, and I'll do more than sheesh," she says sticking her tongue out at me.

Further banter is cut short by the arrival of a bleary looking Wendy and Andydroid. "What's the situation, Cal?"

"I'm still hiding in the burning forest. Figured I'd let you make the call on how to handle this one. You want me to go talk to them, or do you want to go through the poop chute and do it with me backing you up?"

The petite young woman stifles a yawn. "Talking to the government in a remote area isn't going to get us shit. See if you can get out of there undetected and find a decent sized television market. I'll slip out the poop chute and go give an impromptu interview to get my side out there. Aphrodite's right that the people love me. But if we don't get out in front of this, my father and his cronies will tell the story the way they want the public to hear it. I'm going to go get a shower and change. Aphrodite, would you mind helping me look my best when I do the interview?"

"Sure thing, Wendy."

As Wendy heads back upstairs, I look at the Love Goddess and say, "I must have been hanging around Bobby too much. I was ready to kick a little ass."

She points at the poop chute. "I still can't believe you slide through that and come out the business end of the Megasuit."

"It makes moving the team around very easy. Uncle Sam's little thugs are going to be surprised as hell when she turns up at a news station in... looks like my best choices are San Diego, Albuquerque, or Phoenix. I've always wanted to take a wrong turn at Albuquerque."

She groans at my Looney Tunes reference and asks, "Why not Vegas? Not much farther and it'd be easy to get out of the city afterward."

"Yeah, I suppose I could go there as well. I've been banned from going there for so long that I don't even think about it. Guess I need to start thinking differently."

"That's right!" she says. "Didn't you go on some kind of drunken rampage through the city?"

"My armor did, but I wasn't in it."

"Sounds like a good story," she says. "Want to tell it?"

"Not particularly, but it involves way too much scotch, a clone's bucket list, and an obscenely bad hangover. How about I just keep with the current story and you can add that to the list of what you want to hear next?"

She scrunches her nose in the most attractive way and says, "Well, okay. Is there anything major before the battle in Los Angeles?"

"Not unless you want to hear about my epic rematch with Seawall, the living douchebag, or the gripping story of me trying to talk a jumper out of committing suicide."

"I think I'll pass. I've heard Seawall's powers only work when he's concentrating."

"Yeah, you could probably flash him and that'd be enough to make him drop his guard. With me, it takes a bit longer, and usually involves a great deal of pain—on his part, not mine."

"What about the jumper?"

"He did. I caught him, but broke his leg while doing it. It ended with him screaming that I'd ruined his life which was the only thing remotely amusing about the story."

Laughing, Stacy tells me to move on to the exciting stuff and I'm happy to comply.

• • •

"Bobby! Get up!" I said and banged on his door like a kid on his first day of a Disney vacation. "C'mon big guy! The shit's about to hit the fan!"

"What're you going on about?" The man grumbled.

"The Olympians are flying everyone to Los Angeles. Patterson's gone loco and tried to kill Jade Lyoness because she found out he's been building banned tech. We're taking him down, and I need you to feed the ammo to my grenade launcher."

"All right. All right. Get me when you're almost there."

"We are!" I shouted. "Apollo's Chariot hauls some serious ass."

"What about your new suit?"

"It's not ready, but I don't need it! Patterson made an atomic powered robot! That's forbidden by more treaties and laws than I have fingers! Even if I don't kill him, he's going to prison."

It's a good day to be me! Best day ever!

There was more grumbling. "Have I got time to take a dump?"

And, back to reality. Yeah, those are the kind of things I have to put up with.

"Just be downstairs in ten!"

I damned near fell on the steps going back down the stairs. That would have been pathetic! Hopping on the ankle that I had just turned, I jacked back into the control system and became immersed in all the input Mechani-CAL offered. While I was upstairs, I could still see and hear everything going on in the chariot, but now I could move again.

Flipping the visor down, I looked around. The chariot was an interesting construct, tied to the mind of Apollo. It could get from one side of the country to the other in thirty minutes. When damaged, it would fix itself just like Haunted Tank. Through magic or psionics, it possessed an atmosphere and was capable of reaching escape velocity. The Olympians had fought in space and been to the moon. It even adjusted size to accommodate the number of passengers.

My disposition toward magic had softened since I was dabbling; in what little spare time I had. Aphrodite stood off to one side in hushed conversation with Athena. She wasn't wearing her armor and that annoyed me. Part of me wanted to go over there, she looked miserable, but there was precious little I could add to the situation. Somehow, I doubted Stacy would want to hear me say, "I told you so."

Instead, I stuck to the side of my team who, outside of Wendy, didn't care whether I lived or died. Most any person on the planet would be a gibbering idiot, going for a ride in this company. Instead, I was still wondering what in the hell I was doing there.

Bolt Action came up beside me and was staring at my powercell bazooka. After giving it a critical once over, he grunted and said, "It will only work if you hit, Stringel. Two words—don't miss."

"I don't intend to."

"Got a special assignment for you, you might even like it."

I replied, "Okay, you've got my interest."

The older black man said, "He's got a weak spot when it comes to you. Lure his ass out. Call him names. Say whatever the hell you think will get him out of his private bunker. I'm just asking you to be an asshole. I suspect it's the one thing you excel at."

"Seems you've had some practice in the art as well, David. Are you going to be sad if Patterson doesn't walk away from this?"

I knew he didn't like me using his first name, which is exactly why I did it.

"We want him alive. Lazarus didn't used to be like this," the old Marine stated. "He's changed over the years. Everyone changes, but not always for the better. You'd do well to remember that, boy!"

"I got your boy right here! I couldn't give two shits about what you think. Just don't get caught in the crossfire, because I won't be holding back!"

Our discussion attracted the attention of several others and I could see Aphrodite looking at me.

"David," Wendy interrupted. "Mechani-CAL is a member of my team. Why don't you see to your own people and leave him to me?"

"Listen Wendy..."

"No! You listen! You don't run my damned team, and you don't run me! Back the hell off!"

Now everyone was focused on our little conference.

Discus jumped in, "Listen, everyone just calm down. We've got enough problems without turning on each other."

I took morbid amusement in watching both Wendy and Bolt Action tell Graham to shut the hell up. This was an instance of putting the "fun" in dysfunctional. This would be another interesting section to add to the memoirs. Ms. Bostic would be salivating over this. Then again, I don't know if the general public would rest easy seeing all of this.

Strange time for a moral dilemma.

Bolt Action left, and Wendy didn't seem pleased.

"Save the anger for Ultraweapon," I offer. "No sense in picking fights until the one that matters is taken care of. Make sure you stay safe out there, Wendy. Don't take any unnecessary risks."

She created a swirl of air around us to "Do I need to give you the same speech about butting out that I gave him?"

Looking down, I commented, "You've changed your costume to prevent people from noticing that you're developing a bump. I'm not trying to run your life, but I am telling you not to be stupid. You're one of the most powerful people in the world and you're the best team leader I've ever had."

"I'm the only team leader you've ever had."

"Nah, I've worked for villains, too. You're loads better than they were. All I'm saying is focus on being a great hero and don't worry about what kind of leader others think you are."

"Thanks," she said. "It goes without saying that I'd like to bring him in alive."

"Then you'd better get to him before I do. Just saying. I'm pretty sure whacking his ass or not whacking his ass won't change anyone's opinion of me, so I'd just as soon do it, even if it costs me the pardon."

"I could ask you not to do it, but won't. You didn't hesitate to back me when it came to Mather, and I won't ask you to forsake your revenge on Patterson. Maybe that's not the hero way, but my view of the world is a lot different from the eight year old girl who first discovered her powers."

Her eyes held a weariness that seemed out of place in someone just barely over the age of twenty-one. She was a bona fide force of nature, but that power, that life, had exacted a price from her by taking her innocence.

"When are you going to find out the sex?" I asked, searching for a way to change the subject.

"Ultrasound in three weeks. You want to come?"

"I will have to check my calendar, because I'm such a busy person, but yeah, if I can. Are you going to go with one of those weird names that celebrities give to their kids? With your last name, you could call the kid On Time and make the middle name To."

"On Time To La Guardia?" she asked and laughed.

"Well, how about Clear Skies Over?"

"No way in fucking hell!"

"Watch your language, Wendy. Little Delay At La Guardia might hear you."

"Stop, Cal. Just stop."

"You know that's not likely."

She sighed. "Watch yourself out there, Mechani-CAL."

"Thanks for being one of the few people who actually try to say my name right."

• • •

"I'm still trying to figure out why you don't just try and shack up with her," Bobby commented, knocking back a beer.

My mouth waters slightly, but I resist the urge, and grab a sip from a water bottle. "Dude, she's not my type. It's just not there. Part of me wishes it was! When she told me she was pregnant I offered to marry her, and she turned me down faster than Hermes can circle the block."

"Sounds harsh."

"Yeah, but she's one of the only ones who actually respect me. I get the feeling that if we had tried that would've been the first thing to go."

As strange as it sounded, I'd rather have Wendy's respect, than have her as a girlfriend. Just goes to show how badly my priorities have been screwed up.

"Maybe you're still too hung up on the one that got away."

I don't bother trying to refute his statement. Stacys and Vickys don't come along that often and I'm already looking closer to forty than thirty.

Instead of dwelling on the sad state of my personal life, I focus on the important task at hand, killing Ultraweapon. On the side monitors, I pull up available imagery and layout of Promethia's sprawling industrial complex. Sure, I'd worked there, but that was more than a decade ago.

There was a perimeter set up by the police and the military. The inside looked like a robot convention taken to the nth degree. There were robots everywhere and they were armed to the teeth, and I noted a distinct lack of non-lethal ordinance. Patterson wasn't going to give up without a fight. There was no sign of his new nuclear tinker toy, and I hoped it wasn't ready to make its debut, because there were plenty of Type D Warbots to go around.

There were very few humans to be found. Thermal analysis showed less than a dozen living people. Fanatics or loyalists, did it really matter? I wondered if the people I used to work with were in the sublevels below the main compound. Was Joe down there or had he gotten out when Patterson went over the edge?

No one on the chariot seemed interested in speaking with me, though I did catch Stacy looking over in my direction, twice. At the moment, it seemed like there was only the burnt remnants of a bridge for all that water to run under. The realization of just how much I didn't belong with this crowd hit me. Screw them! They don't belong with me.

"Bobby, can you link those belts of grenades into the launcher. Might as well get ready for the action."

My available grenades went from twenty-four up to sixty-four in a few quick seconds as the chariot drew closer to the Promethia complex. My radar lit up with a barrage of surface to air missiles fired from launchers. Hera stepped forward to erect a shield, while several of the others flew off the back of the chariot. I waited for the first wave to be intercepted before joining them. I didn't unlock the launcher yet. Ultraweapon needed to show up first.

Instead, I concentrated on attacking the warbots before opening up the broadcast channel and letting the insults fly. To be honest, I might have done this without any prompting from Bolt Action. My spleen needed to be vented, and I hadn't realized how much anger I'd been toting around. Lazarus had this coming, and I was more than willing to let him know what I thought of his predicament.

It might have been my mocking, or maybe Patterson decided he was losing too many of his toys. He finally came out to play and I was ready to make the most of it.

My minigun, now tied into the suit's power system, sent a steady stream of energy at him. His force blasters bludgeoned my forward shields. If I hadn't had the additional two generators in the upper torso, my armor would have been in trouble. Raising my suit's left hand, I grabbed the handle of the powercell launcher and slid it off the back. The HUD updated and added the targeting grid for the bazooka and I continued to spray energy in his direction.

Cursing the heroes who kept interfering, I'd inched closer and closer to bracketing him, when Wendy insisted on my presence. I resisted until she conveyed threats of physical violence. I can freely admit that I was being a complete tool over wanting to finish Lazarus first, but I caved, rather than let the young lady with my bun in her oven do all the heavy lifting against this thing.

At least, I got to see how much damage my launcher could do, even if it wasn't against Ultraweapon. Bobby let out a whoop when the hip assembly detonated.

• • •

"Shit! I'm so stupid!"

"So that thing's engine is gonna blow anyway?"

"Probably," I said, and looked for anyone who could take care of the situation... anyone other than Wendy. Finding none, I knew I'd have to sacrifice this suit. "It's up to me."

Switching over to my external speaker, I tell Wendy that the fusion reactor is my problem and that I'll get it to the ocean and then cut it off, as I lift off with my deadly payload.

"Bobby! Pull the grenade launcher out of the crystal and take it upstairs. Then, come back and grab everything you can and get it upstairs, too."

"What are you doing?"

"I'm transferring control up to the computer upstairs. There's going to be a nuclear explosion on the other side of the suit and those three little entry points are going to let a little of it get through to here. I'd rather not be down here, if it is all the same to you."

"Can't you just shut those things off?"

"No. I can use the crystals, but I'm still a long way from figuring it out what makes them work. We'll need to block the stairwell. I can spin them so they aren't pointing toward us. That should keep the radiation risk low."

"You're nuking my damned base!"

His priorities seemed out of order. "Yell at me later, Bobby. Move now!"

Taking my own advice, I unhooked the suit umbilical after putting the automatic pilot on the suit. Next, I spin the C-clamps holding the crystal shards toward the wall, and grab as much of the stuff on the workbench was I could carry. All those heroes, who barely acknowledged my existence at best, or acted like I was the walking equivalent of herpes, were now trying to say something to me. At the moment, I was a little too busy ensuring that my fake death was really going to be a fake death, to answer. Heroes get off on this whole self-sacrificing bullshit. Mechani-CAL was going to die today, but there was no reason in Hell that Cal Stringel had to buy the farm.

Up in central command, I made certain the suit was still on course and told Bobby which things to toss into the stairwell.

"You could help," Bobby said, tossing a locker down.

"I'm a little busy with the reactor right now and I'd just be in your way."

"You're speaking words, Cal, but all I hear is stupid."

"Whatever," I declared. "In the main storeroom, there's a box labeled Radiation Kit. Grab it and meet me in the elevator. We have about 2 minutes."

Bringing up a blank message, I quickly type.

Megan,

Looks like we don't have to wait for the pardon after all. I'm programming the transfer of the last group of video footage from my servers. It may cut off when I blow up or it may continue until it finishes. My proceeds go to Wendy's kid, for obvious reasons. Gotta go nuke myself, now. You will have to enjoy Patterson's downfall without me.

Cal

I'd be able to scrub anything that I needed to, and Megan will just believe that it is the lag behind it. I trigger my transmitter and then give my final speech. Ever since I'd first considered faking my death, I'd made up a few versions of this speech, and I steal what I need from two of them, winging the rest of it...

I'd like to think that it was a pretty damned good speech. I didn't have time for anything else. Meeting Bobby in the elevator, we rode it upstairs when the suit hit the water and the reactor detonated. The lights in the elevator dimmed, but we continued our ascent. Once safely at the top, I broke out the gamma radiation meter and began a quick survey. After a minute, I breathed a sigh of relief; rad levels were at background levels. Sixty feet below us might be a different story.

"I outta kill you," Bobby muttered.

"Didn't you hear," I said with a laugh. "Cal Stringel just died. You're too late!"

"I hate you sometimes, Strings. You know that. What do we do now?"

"Let's wait a day or two before going back down and seeing if there is any contamination to clean up. Want to go get something to eat? We'll have to do a drive thru. I can't risk showing my face."

Bobby had a look on his face, a cross between angry and constipated, so I asked him what was wrong.

"My damned keys and my wallet are still downstairs. We ain't goin' anywhere."

"Well, that stinks."

• • •

Stacy's laughter makes recounting the story worth it. "How bad was it?"

"Actually, not too bad," I say. "I overreacted. Some nasty crap got through, but the shards exploded a few seconds into it. The C-clamps, or what was left of them, went into a lead lined box and we had to get rid of some other stuff. Don't tell Bobby, but I used it as an excuse to get rid of the prison cells. He was really paranoid about the radiation levels and I might have used it to my advantage."

"You?" she asks in mocking accusation. "Use a situation to your advantage? I can't possibly imagine that."

"Easy on the sarcasm there, Stacy. But yeah, I didn't really go into that day planning my death. It just sort of played out that way. Good thing I already had a plan in place."

"Good thing," she agrees, but I don't hear the sincerity.

"Well, I did need to protect myself from Devious and the Overlord. There's been a large amount of chatter on VillainNet about how they are already after Megasuit. Straight up, I can take both of them, but she's Devious for a reason and the Overlord won't come alone. Fortunately, I have Larry and Wendy on my side. They're a big step up from the folks I used to team up with, and less likely to stab me when my back is turned."

"Are you talking about the villains or my team?"

"I was talking about the villains, but I guess it could apply to Holly and the rest. Though Holly didn't really stab me in the back so much as spit on my face and rub my nose in it."

"Not going to let that go, are you?"

"Not anytime soon. I wouldn't hold my breath, if I were you."

We laugh a bit, and I check the GPS on the suit. "Better call upstairs and tell Wendy to get ready for her close up. I'm about thirty minutes from Phoenix."

"Actually," she answers and starts toward the staircase. "I promised to help her with her makeup, so I'll go. She might be in for a disappointment. My powers give me a natural beauty and, as a result, I don't have to use very much of it at all."

"I won't hate you because you're beautiful," I offer to her retreating form, and get a single finger in reply. "Now that's a rude gesture, Stacy! What would your fans say?"

Chapter Ten

Make Way for Captain Unintended Consequences

"I can see why you call it the poop chute," Stacy says, as I replay the video of Wendy sliding out the backside of Megasuit, behind the CBS Phoenix affiliate's dumpster. "It looks like you just crapped out a superhero."

Mega remained behind the dumpster as Wendy walked with purpose into the building, intent on getting an interview. I didn't have the heart to make fun of her, as someone who has also had warrants for their arrest out on them.

"Andy? Can you help me hack directly into their cameras and their interior security system?"

The robot processed my highly questionable request and said, "I can do that to ensure Wendy's safety. I also have no known location on the West Coast Guardians. The other Guardian teams are accounted for, and the majority of the Olympians remain in Europe, are listed as inactive, or are seated next to you. There are no reports of local superhuman activity in the Phoenix area at this time."

"Good, continue to monitor. My guess is the West Coasters were on the way to back the government up with me, so they'll be in the area."

"What's going on?" Larry asks coming down the stairs.

"Wendy and Mega are in Phoenix so she can do an interview. Uncle Sam is trying to crack down on us. Mind suiting up and being on stand-by? We might get a visit from the West Coast Guardians. How was the game?"

"Panthers won. I always thought Sundays were supposed to be a day of rest."

"No rest for the weary or the wicked, take your pick as to which one applies to us," I reply and wink at Stacy.

"All right," Larry says and turns toward the staircase. "I'll get into my costume and be ready in ten."

I begin monitoring the security cameras inside the station. Naturally, the fools inside are hesitant to believe that one of the most famous supers in the world just walked in off the street and requested an interview. The main lobby experiences a sudden windstorm before someone runs to fetch the general manager.

There's a brief wait, until a woman in business attire rushes down the corridor to greet Wendy and escort her to one of the smaller studios, while one of the junior reporters appears to be teetering between eagerness and panic as she rushes into the makeup chair.

"Well, it looks like we have some more time while she does her interview," I say. "Are you ready for more story?"

"Sure," Stacy replies. "What happened after you died? Did you go into the light?"

"If you mean the light in the bathroom, I went in there all the time."

• • •

"...In conclusion, Calvin Matthew Stringel was a flawed man. His story is a lesson in perseverance and rising to the challenge when it matters the most. It often is said that one way to judge a man is to see how he behaves when he thinks no one is watching, but I submit to you that the opposite is also true. You can also judge a man by what he is willing to do when everyone is watching. Heroes step forward when needed and something you can take away from Cal's life is that whatever your past, even if you aren't a well-liked person, or an especially nice one, you can still make the choice to be the hero you were meant to be. I don't know if Cal considered me a friend, but I shall always consider him one."

Not everyone gets to watch their own funeral, and I'll confess I was a little choked up by Bo's words. I'd been hard on the Biloxi Bugler, mocked him mercilessly at times, but it was because he was the genuine article. What he lacked in power, he more than made up for in conviction. I was on the fence about considering him a friend, but he'd more than earned my respect.

Bobby pointed to the monitor and proceeded to kill the moment, "You sure you weren't seeing the Bugler on the side?"

I gave Bobby an incredulous look and said, "No."

"He sure seemed to like you. Just saying."

My empty casket memorial was in Biloxi, Mississippi of all places—also Bo's doing. In attendance was a who's who in the superhero world and even a smattering of political folks, including Wendy's father. My guess was that the PR folks had worked overtime to convince most of them that it would be a good idea to attend. The President hadn't come, but he'd sent along a statement and my long overdue pardon.

That might come in handy down the road, I thought.

Aphrodite had released her own statement before the funeral, separate from the one made by her team, that was both kind and gracious. I figured that meant she hadn't read the book yet. It also lacked anything that indicated her memories had returned.

I did have to laugh at the shitstorm my memoirs had kicked up. It was an international bestseller already. Promethia's stock was at an all-time low and there was talk that they might even change their name, the way the tobacco companies did.

The next person to take the stage made me gulp involuntarily. Wendy looked like she hadn't slept since my armor blew up, and I immediately felt bad.

"I can't help but wonder what Cal would think if he were here," she began. "He'd say something completely inappropriate, I'm certain. I don't honestly know if I taught him anything about being a hero, but I can say that he taught me how to be a better leader, just by trying to keep up with him. He was a handful and a hot mess. He had this unfiltered personality that never failed to let you know what was on his mind. Cal could walk into a room and ten minutes later, everyone would be ready to strangle him. If this sounds like I'm insulting him, I'm not. Anyone who spent time with him knows this. In his book, he lamented that he had no real power to call his own. From my perspective, he had the ability to wield the truth in such a caustic and brutal manner that it angered you to hear what he said. When my child is old enough to ask about his or her father, I will say that he was a poor role model, who made a never ending series of bad decisions, but there was no one better to have at my back when I needed someone, because that was the kind of person Cal Stringel was. My child will grow up knowing that Cal died saving the city of Los Angeles, and was the primary reason the world was rescued from the control of the bugs. One could never accuse him of having noble intentions, but he did these things regardless, and that says everything you'd ever want to know about him. Thank you."

Bobby passes me a beer and says, "If she ever finds out you're alive, she's gonna kill you!"

Nodding, I didn't exactly relish the thought of telling her. "Hopefully, she never finds out."

"So, how long do you think it's gonna take you to build that new set of armor?"

I picked up the schematics I'd been working on ever since we'd gotten back inside, and removed what little contamination and irradiated materials there had been from the downstairs.

"I've got enough synth stockpiled to wire it, but I'll need some extra. I'm a little short on armor plating and that'll eat up a chunk of the remaining cash, but I still have a decent amount here of what Wendy loaned me, to get new armor. We shouldn't have to worry about money for a bit. I'm guessing three months for construction, since I don't really have much else going on."

"So," he said. "You okay with me going out on more jobs?"

My immediate reaction was to say no, but then I started thinking. "Actually, I guess there isn't a reason not to. No one knows the location of this base except for you and me. Hell, Aphrodite doesn't even remember where it is. I don't see why not. Go for it."

He looks all smug. "Guess I'm not the idiot you said I was in your book."

"You're not going to let that go, are you?"

"No. Are you surprised I could read?"

"I said that on purpose to make sure people think that I really didn't like you. You have to believe me. I was just covering all the bases."

"I suppose you're right," he said, not looking completely convinced. "So, you really have that sex tape of you and Aphrodite in your room here?"

With a groan, I replied. "No, you can't see it. Do you really want to see me having sex? Weren't you just accusing me of some kind of relationship with the Bugler? Are you jealous or something?"

That dig really got Bobby's hackles up, which made me feel better as he launched into a long and descriptive, profane rant.

But it did remind me that I needed to find a different hiding place for the drive containing that video. I wouldn't put it past Bobby to crack open my safe like a coconut, to get it.

• • •

Even a technohermit like me could get cabin fever. When I opened the safe to hide the only copy of my meaningful encounter with a love goddess, I dug out one of my old fake identities—Jason Durso. After dying my hair black and not using my shaver, I looked more like Jason and less like Cal.

With my new armor about forty percent complete, I decided to head down to the Gulf Coast and take in the sea air. Inevitably, I found myself drawn to the spot where I'd spread the ashes of Vicky and the clone of Joe Ducie. The last time I'd been here had been just before the bugs, when I still had a base a short distance away, where that little crater now sat.

I'd liked that base. I saw a homemade sign where one of my neighbors was selling Mechani-CAL memorabilia. I had to laugh. I had a gift shop and had put this little spot of Pascagoula on the map. Vicky would have laughed her ass off.

Either my base self-destruct or a lightning strike had damaged the tree. The old oak had been battered, but had somehow survived. It was a fitting comparison to my life. I'd endured so much since the last time I stood in this spot.

"Hey, guys," I said. "Look who came back? I'd have come back sooner, but I've been busy. Who would've thought that being dead would tie a person up so much? Since I've been gone, I've saved the world, became a poor excuse for a superhero, got the girl, lost the girl, fathered a kid with another girl, succeeded in knocking Lazarus Patterson from his perch, and faked the most epic death scene in history!"

Sitting down on a rock, I stared out over the water, talking to and joking with, a pair of dead people for close to two hours. The last time I was here, I'd hit what I thought was rock bottom and had been close to going insane, or was that even more insane? Tough to tell. I was in a better place now and not hearing any imagined voices. I was also at a crossroads. In roughly two months, the most powerful suit of armor in the history of this planet would be ready... and I hadn't the foggiest idea of what to do with it!

"Sure," I said, wishing either was here to give me advice. "I could go back to robbing places. Odds are no one could stop me. I could do the hero thing again, but it turns out that being a hero is more tedious than extraordinary. Monitor duty stinks, patrols stink, and it's more cliquish than any high school ever! That's the thing, rolling around in a pile of cash with everyone praising my name used to be the dream. People's opinions don't really mean anything to me anymore, and a villain's life is usually about the money, but it just doesn't cut it now. I guess I need to figure out where I'm going and what I want to be when I grow up, but that's on me... or whoever I'm pretending to be now that I'm dead. Maybe I should just pack it all up and move to Costa Rica, like we always talked about, huh, Vicky?"

The sun was close to setting as I stood and said my goodbyes to my fallen friends, wondering what either of them would do in my shoes. Joseph, the clone, would have likely overthrown his master and would be halfway to world domination. Vicky, naturally, would have already conquered the world and would be having the best time, ever, doing it.

Me? I'd always prided myself with being the idea guy. Unfortunately, I was out of those at the moment. Starting down the hill, I saw a car moving at an excessive rate of speed for the bumpy access road. The tires spit gravel when the red sedan braked hard and came to a stop, nearly hitting Bobby's truck. The driver threw open the door and came barreling out, staring at the cellphone in his hand.

Thankful there hadn't actually been a collision, and trying to think what this chump's problem could be, I was surprised when the man started running up the hill toward me. My pulse pistol was under the seat in the truck, so I became more than a little apprehensive. I stopped moving down the hill and waited for him to get closer.

"Hey!" he called, panting his way up the last half of the few hundred feet. The guy looked younger than I, late twenties I hazarded a guess, and was a bit on the overweight side.

"Yeah?" I replied.

"Were you just up there?" he asked pointing to the top of the hill.

"Yes."

"Was anyone else up there with you for, like, the last hour?"

"No. Just me. Are you looking for someone?"

He seemed to relax and slowed his frantic pace. "I guess I'm looking for you then. I was supposed to be here forty-five minutes ago, but got a damned flat; bet he saw that coming too!"

"What? What do you want?"

"To give you a postcard and ask you two questions."

A postcard? Who runs around giving people postcards? I let the stranger get closer. He didn't appear armed, and I was confident I could outrun the slob. "Okay," I said, very cautious now.

The man pulled out a postcard, folded in half, that'd been stuffed into his back pocket, and finished closing the distance between us. He had this giddy look on his face that was more than a little creepy. "I can't believe it's finally over! This is the last one!"

"What're you talking about?"

"Oh, sorry man. First thing's first, here you go."

I looked down at the bent postcard he hands me. It showed the Grand Canyon with the stylized phrase, "Wish You Were Here!" scrawled across it in blue ink. Looking at the back, it had a date almost a year from now, and some words below:

On the above date, you should be in San Francisco with the most powerful people you can recruit.

130

It was signed, Jeffrey Dunlap. The name sounded vaguely familiar and alarm bells began ringing in the distant corner of my mind.

"What is this?"

"What city were you born in, and what's your birthday?"

"Huh? Why should I tell you that?"

"C'mon man, I've been sending out these cards from Mr. Dunlap for over half my life, and this is the last one! Just tell me!"

"Who's this Dunlap guy?"

"You mean, you never heard of Prophiseer?"

Yeah, I had heard of him—some kind of psychic who saw the future, but he'd been captured and killed by the Overlord a long time ago. The memory of the HORDES battle came to mind, where the Overlord had taunted Lazarus Patterson with the knowledge that he'd be killed by a man in a suit of armor. It was followed by another one of Bo saying he knew to be in Biloxi the night he caught me because he'd gotten a similar post card.

People had speculated about those postcards with vague and mysterious warnings. They hadn't come from Dunlap's widow, or anyone else he'd been connected with.

"Yes. Who are you?"

The guy looked perturbed. "Does it matter? Just tell me what I want to know and I'm outta here!"

"Well, I'm curious how you knew Prophiseer?"

"Fine! You want to know? I'll tell you. We lived on the same street and he bought lemonade from the stand I ran when I was a kid. When my family got ready to move, he came over and gave me a box filled with these postcards and an envelope with five grand in it and told me to mail them out in order. This last one just had a map coordinates on it and said to use the GPS on my smartphone. They didn't even have those when he gave me the box!"

"Wow," Was all I could say. "Why didn't you just keep the money and pitch the post cards?"

He must've been ten at the time. The idea of some preteen holding on to all these little prophecies and mailing them out like a dutiful worker bee seemed slightly absurd, but if Matthew hadn't been my middle name Slightly Absurd probably could have been it.

"Tell me where you were born and what your birthday is first."

"Lincoln, Nebraska and August twenty-fifth." I didn't really hesitate. He could probably use that and maybe put together that I was really

Calvin Matthew Stringel, but Prophiseer could have just told him that. Plus, he really didn't look like he cared.

He scribbled it down on a piece of paper. "All through this, he's been leaving me pieces of a puzzle along the way. That's the last bit I need to solve where he hid my final payoff. Now, I just have to put it together with the rest of the clues and go find my three million dollars. If you'll excuse me, I've got a date with a pile of cash hidden somewhere out there."

My head was still spinning from all of this as he ran off like the white rabbit from Alice in Wonderland, leaving me staring at the note on the postcard. I'd gone up that hill looking for a little direction, and fate had responded by sending me a note from a guy who's been dead for years, telling me where I needed to be.

I've had plenty of odd stuff happen to me, in my life. This was definitely in the top five.

• • •

"You got a card? The last one?" Stacy asks. "Why didn't you say something when that came up earlier?"

"It's right there," I say and point at the workbench. Prophiseer's warning is pinned to the wall. My girlfriend went over and inspected the item with her critical eye. "I was getting to it. Besides, I like a little dramatic flair."

"So, it was a kid with a lemonade stand and a three million dollar golden ticket? One of life's mysteries just got solved."

"Pretty much," I reply, while she scans the still bent postcard.

"You could have come to me with this," she says. "Even if we weren't together, I would have taken this seriously."

"Except that I was dead and, if we're being honest, I was still a little ticked at you. If I had, how would you have handled me showing up?"

Frowning, she pins it back to the corkboard. "Good point."

"Wendy and I talked it over, and as soon as we realized that was Patterson's sentencing date, she put a bug in Bolt Action's ear to have all the available Guardians in town. Your team was already there, so telling you wasn't really important."

Bringing the audio up from Wendy's interview, I listen in.

"Actually, Gayle," Wendy says. "I find it the height of hypocrisy that they accuse me of child endangerment when these same people had no problem asking me, when I was seven months pregnant, to fly out into Hurricane Ishmael and spend hours fighting a hurricane. Now, the only thing that has changed is that I'm not toeing the company line anymore."

"Your hurt feelings are understandable," the interviewer replied. "However, from an outsider's standpoint, you've all but walked away from the Guardians and you're working with a pair of unknown superhumans who, by all accounts, are every bit as powerful as you are. You can understand how that might be troubling to the general public. Especially when two of the federal agents were taken to the hospital with injuries."

"Oh, I've heard what people are saying, Gayle – that this is a rebellious phase and I'm lashing out. Rubbish! The government, and not just my father, is more concerned about controlling the superhuman population than protecting the public. The idiot politicians think they can legislate the villains away! They want you to believe that they have everything under control. Instead of apprehending real villains, they come after a mom holding her child. Way to keep it classy, Federal Marshalls service. As for any injuries, I don't recall doing anything other than using a concentrated wind blast to keep them away from my daughter, after they drew stunners. Ever wonder what a taser, designed to take out a superhuman, would do to a seven month old? I didn't really care to find out. Every agent had a body camera on them, why hasn't the video footage been released, yet? The answer is that they're still editing it, I'm just as curious as you to see what they concocted."

I laugh at her verbal barb and the way she plants seeds of doubt about the official story as Gayle switches topics and asks about her "new" team.

"I'm not here to talk about them," Wendy says. "They have their own stories and I am going to respect their privacy. Megasuit and Red aren't interested in becoming a brand or doing appearances. I support their decision one hundred percent. They joined me for one reason, to make the world a better place. I will never know what it's like to have a secret identity. From the moment my powers surfaced, I've been a public figure, and I'm okay with that, but if my new teammates don't crave that kind of life, I completely understand. What I will say about them is that they are dedicated and committed to doing what is right."

Looking over at Stacy, I shrug and say, "She might be overestimating me."

"I don't think she is," my girlfriend comments.

"Not you, too!"

"Shush! I'm trying to hear what Wendy is saying."

A cynical thought crossed my mind that we sounded like a real couple now, but I let it slide, rather than say it aloud. There was no need to pick a fight that she'd probably end up winning.

"Still, there is the matter of the fugitive warrant that is out for you. Do you plan to surrender peacefully?"

"Gayle, I have done absolutely nothing wrong and I have no intention of being paraded around to satisfy my father's political ambitions."

There's a momentary pause while the interviewer prepares her next line of questioning. "Those are some very strong words, Wendy. Are you prepared for the backlash from the superhero community as well?"

"I've fought for justice all over the globe, alongside some of the most devoted and self-sacrificing heroes out there. Those heroes know who I am and what I stand for. I respect them for all that they do and I hope they can understand and respect what my team is trying to accomplish."

"Then you won't mind me asking what exactly is your team trying to accomplish?"

"When the bugs took over, it wasn't the government or the hero teams that saved us. It was a truly gifted engineer with a powersuit and a lot of dumb luck. Cal isn't here to save us from ourselves, and I don't think I'll ever have the kind of luck he had, so I'm going to rely on preparation and a pair of the strongest heroes on the planet. We're not going to let the next global catastrophe happen. We will stop it in its tracks."

"Can I ask the name of your team, Wendy?"

"Up until today, we were going to call ourselves the Reinforcements. Though I haven't had a chance to sit down and discuss it with the others, after today's events, you can call us the New Renegades. Don't look for us at a parade or some kind of event. Look for us when things are bad and you need someone to come and save the day. That's when we will be there. We don't want the glory or the gratitude. We're like that fire extinguisher over on that wall, with the 'in case of emergency, break glass' painted on it. The bad guys have had an advantage all this time. They know what teams they might be dealing with if they are in this part of the country, or that part of the country. They know where Mount Olympus is and where all the other public teams have headquarters. There are fan and gossip websites that make their living off of telling the world where the teams are. I'm here to warn them to start looking over their shoulders, because we're out there watching and we're constantly on the move."

Wendy pauses and looks directly at the camera. "I also have a message for the villains out there. If we show up, it doesn't matter what power you possess or how hardcore you think you are. We will pound you into submission and let someone else scrape you off the pavement and take you to the hospital and then jail."

"Nailed it!" I shout, throwing my arms into the air. "She stuck the landing and the crowd goes wild!"

Stacy appears pensive. "You three are plenty powerful; I'll give you that, but might doesn't always make right."

"Excuse me," Andy interrupts the likely start of an argument. "Calvin, I detected a change in the air traffic patterns in the Phoenix airspace. Based on the pattern, it appears that a flight has been granted priority clearance and their new approach will have them flying over the television station in two hundred and eighteen seconds."

I flip to the transmitter and let Wendy know we might have some company coming. At the same time, the fire alarm goes off in the building. It seems like they've got some help on the inside.

From my "behind the dumpster" vantage point, I see the low flying jet and a group of heroes deploy from it. Andy uses my video to lock in and identify each of the people descending: the Protector Armor, most likely operated by a woman who can see seven seconds into the future, First Aid in his shiny new Promethia provided First Responder armor, Mystigal, Grande Vizier, the shapechanging monk Rakshasa, and their new addition, some psychokinetic named Mindcracker. The West Coast Guardians are here.

"Larry!" I holler upstairs. "Get to the poop chute. Wendy, might want to wrap it up, the West Coasters have finally tracked us down."

"Yeah, I saw them on the screen upstairs," Larry answers, bounding down the steps in his red costume.

"Which do you like better, New Renegades or Reinforcements?"

"Renegades. Not even close," Larry says and uses his telekinesis to rise into the air and go feet first down the slide. I start my suit forward shoving the dumpster out into the parking lot like an empty cardboard box, giving Larry the space he needs to exit the portal in my armor.

"Bobby isn't around, so three votes carry the motion, unless you have a really good counter argument, Andy."

"The name is acceptable to me, Calvin, but I suggest we deal with more pressing matters."

My back monitor catches Larry dropping out Mega's ass and into a crouch.

"Damn!" he swears. "You could've picked a less smelly spot to hide in."

"Whatever, Red," I say and switch away from calling him Larry, in case our transmissions become decrypted by the two sets of Guardian armor. "Be wary of Mystigal. She's probably got the best chance of hurting either one of us with her magic."

"Got it, Ul... sorry, Megasuit."

I chuckle and say, "We should settle on names, soon, shouldn't we? You want to stick with Red or go with Extraordinary?"

"Big Red, like the chewing gum."

"Okay, be ready to take a bite out of them, then."

Larry's energy form swells and he rises into the center of the twenty foot tall mass.

"Wendy! Watch yourself! I lost track of their shapechanger. Andy, find him! He may be inside already. Better blow out a window and get into the air. You're at a disadvantage in there."

"Copy that, Mega. I'm on my... shit!"

"You're coming with us, WhirlWendy!" On the monitor, I catch a human form lunging at her.

Wendy blasts the monk off her, who then transforms into something larger and more difficult to brush aside. She's staggering, but still manages to keep the shapeshifter away.

"Wendy? Are you okay?"

She destroys a window and takes flight while mumbling, "Stuck me with something."

"Andy, don't lose sight of her! Wendy, stay close to the ground."

The rest of the Guardians hadn't made a hostile move... yet.

First Aid kicks on his armor's speakers. "Wendy, we have orders to bring you into custody. Let's not make this any more difficult than it is already."

Checking the monitor, Wendy doesn't look like she's up for any kind of conversation. Larry lacks any real world experience at dealing with people, much less superhumans.

That leaves me. I dial up the synthesizer to prevent anyone recognizing me and activate my external sound system.

"Considering Rakshasa already assaulted her, I think we're beyond that now. She's not going with you and if you think otherwise, you're sadly mistaken."

My weapons systems are now online, except the railgun. Flipping over to the private channel, I ask Wendy if she's okay. Her reply is barely intelligible. Larry expands his energy form's hands and slides them under where she's floating. Seconds later, she drops into them.

Rakshasa joins their side in the form of a wolf. They're running at full strength, and we're pretty much down one and one of us will need to watch her.

First Aid continues, "It would be best for everyone if she comes with us. Let justice run its course."

"Justice has nothing to do with this and you know it. Funny how you got here so fast, almost like you were heading down to where I'd been working on that fire break."

"We just wanted to talk," the man with the healing touch says.

"I doubt it. If you were, you wouldn't have drugged up the one person who is interested in talking, but I do have a question for all you Guardians—where were you when Patterson was attacking San Francisco?"

"We'd been told to stay away," First Aid's response comes a bit too fast, and I know I've hit a sore spot.

"And like a good little group of flunkies, you always do what you're told," I say, and have the suit extend a foot. "It's not a boot, but you can lick it if you want."

The arrogant Mystigal snaps first, "I've had enough of you!"

Her magebolt slams into my shielding as First Aid yells for her to stand down. At first I want to laugh and tell them to remember who fired first, but then notice the shard with my left arm's weaponry just went dark. The tip of the pulse cannon and the grenade launcher's barrel drop onto the ground next to the suit.

Shit! The crystals are susceptible to magic! I hadn't considered that.

There's a hollow feeling in my stomach as I realize my invincible suit of armor isn't nearly as invincible as I thought it was, only seconds before. I fire before she gets another opportunity.

"Red, give me Wendy. Take out the mystics. Magic screws with my armor!"

Larry puts our unconscious leader onto the hood of someone's truck and leaps over me as all the Guardians attack. I move by the truck to protect Wendy, and draw a bead on First Aid's suit. He dodges most of my initial barrage, but I still clip him. Larry thrashes about like a bear being attacked by a pack of wolves, and the parking lot of the TV station becomes a warzone.

Rakshasa's giant serpent tries to wrap up Larry, but he dashes him into a brick wall. Everyone ignores me for a moment and concentrates their firepower on Larry's energy form, causing him to stagger.

We aren't doing nearly as well as we had against Patterson's robots!

"Red, take out Mystigal and I'll be able to fully engage!"

"No," Stacy says and points at the monitor from over my shoulder. "Tape Delay's running the battle. She's the one you need to neutralize."

"What?" I demand and look at the hero in the Protector armor. So far, she is hanging back and only offering fire support.

"She's using her seven second foresight to tell the others when to evade."

"Damn, you're right! She's coordinating their side. Andy! Run a broad spectrum burst of white noise through the suit. If Tape Delay can't communicate with them, she can only help herself."

The way all of them discarded their ear pieces before I jammed their communications, told me that Stacy had guessed correctly. Unfortunately, my tactic knocked out Larry's earpiece as well and he hadn't thought to imitate our opponents.

The only thing I can think, seeing our Keystone Cops level of ineptness on display, is that I'm glad Wendy isn't awake to see this, because she'd be yelling at us for blowing off the training sessions.

Larry shared a few of his own four letter sentiments as he yanked his headset off and renewed his assault on them. I could only do so much and stay beside Wendy.

"I need to get her back through the poop chute. Andy, get ready to take control of the..."

"No, I'll do it," Stacy says. "Give me a minute to get a hoodie from your closet."

I'm stunned, to say the least. "There's a ski mask in there, too."

I wouldn't be me if I didn't have a moment of worry that she'd throw in with the West Coasters and sell us all down the river, but I realize that is a stupid idea. She could just take me out now, put Andy out of action and the fight would be over.

That's when I knew my problem won't be loving her; that's easy. My problem is going to be getting past all my trust issues and paranoia.

Now seating—insecurity party of one.

I take out the frustration at my personal shortcomings on Tape Delay, and treat the surrounding city blocks to an ultraviolent light show. Amanda Rae What'sherface probably doesn't deserve my ire, but I keep her fully on the defensive and unable to help her teammates while the rest of Patterson's former team gets to do the live version of the Imaginary Larry test. A jade bolt of energy called down from the sky above smashes into Red and drives him to his knees at the same time Mindcracker, First Aid, and Grand Vizier hit him with everything they've got.

Even my shields would suffer under that bombardment, but Larry forces himself up like the main character in one of those giant monster movies, and smacks the charging bull elephant form of Rakshasa aside like the shapechanger was nothing to him.

Stacy returns in my blue sweatshirt with the giant "Have a Nice Day!" smiley face on the back and a full face black ski mask. I make a mental note to tell her that she can pull off the hot terrorist look.

"Go feet first," I tell her. "Grab Wendy and push her back through. Andy, will help you. Wait for my signal; I'll lay down a blanket of smoke. She'll be on the hood of the truck, just to your right."

"Got it!" She says and climbs up on the slide, like a bobsledder waiting for the green light.

I flip a few buttons and the shard spins around inside the bottom of the suit. The thick bottom plate slides open and I chuck for smoke grenades through it.

Pausing, I wait precious seconds before saying, "Switching to infrared. We're obscured and go, go go!"

At my yell, Stacy pushes herself forward as I spread Mega's legs and pop the armor plate up and out of the way. Seconds later, Mega shits out a disguised Olympian. She rolls up against the front wheel of the truck and snatches up Wendy like she weighs nothing. It's so easy to forget how strong Stacy is as Aphrodite. She and Hestia rate as two of the weakest on her team in terms of physical strength, but even so, the Love Goddess can easily lift as much as Bobby.

Wendy's lolling head emerges from the large chunk of mirror, bringing a thick cloud of smoke with her. Andydroid finishes pulling her through and lifts the team leader out of the way. Stacy scampers back through and I reseal the opening in Mega's armor after making certain my girlfriend is clear.

When the board shows that the suit is airtight, I have Mega step through the wall of smoke. The West Coasties are barely holding their own against Larry, and it's high time I join the party. The way Protector circles my buddy, who is holding Mindcracker in one of his hands, reminds me strangely of King Kong against the biplanes, except Fay Wray never tried blowing the big ape to pieces with her mind like this dude is attempting.

Accelerating to a full run, I open up with my remaining weapons. First Aid still isn't comfortable in his new armor. He's still on the ground fighting in the manner he's used to. My opening salvo gives him a little extra practice being airborne and announces to everyone that I'm back in action.

As I unload everything against the difficult to hit Protector before she can successfully reengage, the pistol magnetically locked to Mega's hip becomes more tempting with each passing second. *To charge the railgun or not to charge the railgun? Billy Shakespeare asked the wrong question.*

Activating my propulsion system, I fly toward Red and his energy beast and zap Mindcracker with a taser pulse. Now they are the ones who need to be careful to avoid hurting their teammate. I keep Larry's energy beast between me and Mystigal.

Using my left hand, I hit the big red button with the Donkey Kong sticker on it and watch the lights dim around us as the capacitors begin drawing power to charge the railgun.

"You're not going to…?" Stacy whispers urgently.

"No, not in the middle of a city." Of course, my reluctance is more about how badly it would reflect on my team's current situation than out of concern for the population of Phoenix. Mostly, I just didn't want to get yelled at by Wendy when she wakes up.

After all, it's about keeping your priorities in order.

Toggling on the external speakers, I address the circling heroes, "We are withdrawing outside of the city limits. If you want to follow, we can continue this where innocents are less likely to get hurt. We'll wait ten minutes. If you don't come, we'll leave Prince Charming to get his beauty rest and go on our merry way. This is your one freebie. You attacked us first, and we have taken your best shot."

For effect, I draw the pistol from my side and continue, "But you haven't experienced what we're capable of, yet."

"You're in our jurisdiction!" Rakshasa protests.

"I recognize no one's jurisdiction on this planet, save perhaps for the exiled Rigellian Prince," I say and draw a surprised look from Stacy.

"Are you an alien?" The Vizier asks.

"I see no need to answer your question," I reply, avoiding the answer. To Larry I say, "Come, friend human. Let us depart."

• • •

"I think Vizier about shit himself when you said you were from outer space."

Thirty minutes later, Larry is still laughing it up on the couch as I emerge from Wendy's room with Gabosaurus Rex in my arms. Andy is constantly monitoring our leader's vitals after isolating the brand of sedative Rakshasa used.

Wendy probably needs the long nap anyway.

"I don't mind spreading a little misinformation, and that will get them thinking alien superscience instead of magic. I'm cool with that while I come up with a way to shield my crystals against magical energy. It's the big lie all over again. The Internet is already on fire with all kinds of new rumors. I, personally, like the one that the suit is an alien bonded to a human pilot."

Stacy doesn't seem nearly as happy. In fact she seems really angry. "They'll go talk to Gravmatar, Cal. What do you think the Rigellian is going to tell them? What if he wants to come up here and fight you in some kind of honor combat? I wish you had mentioned to me you were thinking about using that as a cover story. I would have talked you out of it."

"I came up with this on the fly and went with it. Besides, Gravmatar is strong, but Larry beat him a long time ago and I'm sure Mega could take him. What gives?"

"Holy shit!" Larry says recalling the memory. "I did beat Gravmatar! I can't believe I forgot that."

Ignoring my friend's revelation, I focus on the look on Stacy's face. It is practically screaming that I screwed up again.

"You don't joke about aliens, Cal. Ever! Now, the government isn't just going to treat you like a rogue super. They're going to consider you an operative of an alien race. Cal, they're going to send me, and my team, after you. You just guaranteed that!"

"Guess I need to change my name to Captain Unintended Consequences."

"Ya think?" Stacy adds. "They're also going to start tossing alien collaborator charges at Wendy. How do you think that's going to play out?"

It's tempting to ask Andy if he can put Wendy in a medically induced coma for a few days. Maybe there was still time to give her to the West Coasters?

Looking at my daughter, blissfully ignorant of the situation, I adopt that certain tone all parents get with their infant children and say, "Mommy's going to call Daddy a bunch of bad names when she wakes up. That's right, isn't she? She sure is!"

Gabby smiles and laughs while I consider that living to see my daughter's first birthday might require faking my death a second time.

Chapter Eleven

They Saved Andydroid's Brain

"So in summary, Stacy says I screwed the pooch royally by implying the Megasuit is an alien. The good news is that less than half the opinion polls online are saying that you're an alien collaborator. The bad news is that of the half who don't believe, some of those think you're under alien mind control."

Wendy sighs loudly and sips at the coffee I brought her; one cream and one sugar—just the way she likes it. The profane outburst hasn't happened yet, and I'm wondering if we can't get more of that drug they shot her up with.

"Cal," she says, and seems to be gathering her strength for an epic ass reaming. "You know what your problem is? You're too clever."

I'm still expecting the backhand instead of the backhanded compliment, but I'll take what I can get.

"Look," I offer. "If you think it's necessary, I'll go ahead and reveal myself. It's not like I'm running around the countryside."

Wendy shakes her hand dismissively, and her power swirls the air around where the two of us are sitting on her bed. "No. I meant what I said in that interview. You and Larry want your privacy and I don't want to take that from you. We'll figure a way through this. What are you going to do about your suit's vulnerability?"

I'd spent as much time on that problem as I had on practicing how I'd tell Wendy about this mess.

"I'm going to build a case and lay some protective runes on it, and run some tests to see if that will fix it. The other option is to run them through cold iron which in most cases is magically inert. I'm going to use a couple of the small shards and run a control experiment to test out my hypothesis."

Wendy looks at me with a blank expression on her face before saying, "I still must be a little stoned from that junk they injected me with. I only understood about half of that."

"Guess we better make sure Gabby doesn't get any boob juice until that garbage gets out of your system."

"I stopped breastfeeding a month ago, Cal." *Hey! There's that irritated tone I know and love!*

"Sorry," I say, feeling more stupid than I had before I started bringing her up to speed. "I should have noticed that."

"Well, you've been using formula when she's here with you, and you already know how difficult things were getting on the outside world. Where is your girlfriend anyway?"

"Normally, this'd be where I joke that I wore her out because I'm that much of a man, but she had to go. Apparently, the Olympians are training ahead of investigating this new alien menace. She's in her armor and I pushed a private comm circuit through the crystal shard into her suit. She should be installing it right now. I figured that when we have our eventual run in, I'll be able to help coordinate whatever we decide to do."

"Did the interview get broadcast?"

"Yes, and no. The government seized it, but Andy and I were recording it. So, we released it on social media in other countries, so that makes the government look even more suspicious. You're a viral sensation now."

"Yay, me!" she replies. "Good move on releasing it. We have that working for us."

"Yeah, it doesn't exactly paint the West Coaster's in a favorable light. They assaulted you and they fired first."

"Were there any civilian casualties?"

"No fatalities, but there are several in the hospital, and the property damage is estimated around eight mil. You sure you're not pissed?"

Ms. LaGuardia looks up at her ceiling. "I am, but not at you. You did what you needed to do to get the team out of there safely. I'm angrier at myself for being taken out of the fight so easily. They were going to send the Olympians at some point. You just forced their hand."

"So, we're good?"

She half-laughs and says, "I should probably have you rig up a switch for me that shuts off your external speakers when I'm not conscious, but we're good. I knew what I was getting into when I let you recruit me to be the head of this team. You do amazing things, Cal. Sometimes they're amazingly stupid and other times they're amazingly brilliant. It's one extreme or the other with you."

She's pretty good at this whole backhanded compliment thing.

"You up for company? I know a little girl who misses her mommy. Andy just isn't a good substitute. I recommended he try entertaining her with poetry. Thirty minutes later, he was doing this street poetry riff on being a superhero. Definitely not Little Miss Muffett."

"Yeah, go get the munchkin. I'll stick to raising her. You're on your own with Andy."

• • •

"So, she didn't blow a gasket? Guess you got all worked up over that for nothing," Stacy says over the private channel in her armor.

"I must've mastered the whole alien mind control thing. So, what're you up to?" I ask, lamenting that I don't have a tap on her video feed... yet.

Have to remember that for next time.

"Waiting for Apollo and Hera to finish sparring. I've got the winner, but Zeus and Athena are up next. I'm definitely liking the armor more and more. I didn't break a sweat taking down Tia, and before you got on, I was catching up on my neverending pile of emails."

"Aw, I'm telling!"

She laughs. "Just because I'm better at you than multitasking, don't be jealous. Besides, you're always nagging me to be in the armor."

"Did you ever tell Hera about the hacked video game?"

"Yes, she went and got a copy just so she could see the scenes herself. It was good for a laugh. Where's Mega today?"

"South of the Border. Decided to add illegal border crossings to my list of questionable activities. Considered taking him to one of the beaches and going through the poop chute and hitting the beach, but decided against it."

"Gravmatar is coming up from South America to help locate you," Stacy adds.

"Guess he didn't like the idea of being the only resident alien on the planet. Unless there's something you're not telling me."

"There is Cal, but this is something I need to talk to you about in person, and I'm not sure I'll be able to slip away anytime soon."

The yellow and magenta skinned Rigellians are the only race Earth has had contact with, after their Prince-in-Exile arrived on our planet several years ago. Supposedly, there are others out there, and despite the efforts of the various governments to open up more formal relations with Rigel, they've ignored us and let our planet be Gravmatar's private little Elba on the Milky Way.

Most assume that the aliens are waiting for us to "grow up," but now my girlfriend is hinting that it goes a little deeper.

"Well, if you don't want to talk about that, what would you like to talk about? More story time?"

"Sure, why not?"

• • •

"You gonna let me be on your team?" Bobby asked, after I'd explained the card, and he'd berated me for letting an easy three mil get away.

"I might have to recruit from the other side of the fence, Bobby. You up for that?"

"You got to bump nasty with two super hotties and you're butt ugly. Doesn't seem so bad to me."

He had a way of reducing very complex life choices into two sentences. It was admirable, but short-sighted. Sadly, life shouldn't be measured by who happened to be sharing a bed with me at the time.

Then again, I couldn't quite dismiss his wild speculations. With the exception of Hillbilly Bobby, I didn't have much of a team available to me.

"It had its moments," I answered. "But I won't get any recruiting done until I finish my new suit."

The now empty lower level was where I was assembling the new suit. At the moment, I had two pulse cannons and a pair of grenade launchers pushed through shards. There was plans for two more pulse cannons. It was symmetrical, but somewhat uninspired. I needed something more powerful, but was at a loss as to what. That could wait; I had both arms needing synthmuscle.

"Hey, Andy," I greeted the statue, and got to work running the spools of muscle through the autowinder. To the uninitiated, it looked a lot like making pasta. Taking the individual strands, I slid them into the winding collar and dialed up the mechanism. The eight strands wrapped around each other and became a single, thicker strand. When I got six of them, they were wrapped into a larger bundle and later six became four. All this became a single piece of the musculature.

For the Ultraweapon suit, Patterson employed two guys named Ettin. They were conjoined twins with superstrength, who didn't mind spending twelve hours a day winding synth.

My cynical side said that Promethia was also getting credit for employing people with disabilities.

Sometimes I could get Bobby to do this, but invariably he'd start drinking, and quality control suffered. My little banner saying, "Don't Drink and Wind," wasn't appreciated by my roommate.

It was tedious work that reinforces the mantra that armor building is a hobby for the rich or the obsessive.

But even the obsessive can get bored, so I slid another one of the spell plates into the holder and started translating. Even with the magic necklace giving me the ability to read languages, I was still having a problem understanding the context, especially when the text of the spells goes on to a second one of the tablets.

Rex's indexing system made absolutely no sense to a human like me. His math system appeared to be a base six instead of a base ten. The written language lacked any punctuation, and used very few words to describe anything other than a dinomage; and most of those words described how they tasted. It was a carnivorous dialect. This particular tablet was part of a set, with three others. Several words jumped out at me about materials and manipulation.

Last week, I pieced together the spell Rex had used to make his lizard hybrids out of Kim and the other townspeople of that Louisiana parish. Bobby bought a ferret for me to test the spell on, but became too attached to it to let me experiment with it.

The ferret didn't like me.

The feeling was mutual, but when Bobby goes to his room to "feed the ferret," it isn't a sexual innuendo.

Instead, I used a fish Bobby caught and the totem containing Rex's finger. The spell made the fish grow an extra tail. Bobby wanted to eat it anyway, but I talked him out of it.

Hey! Wait just a damned minute. What was this passage saying?

Materials can be altered in composition. It requires focus and fine control to make this change. You must feel the change, using your blood, and "will" the effect into existence.

Blood? Oh great! I'd found that most of these lizard spells required cold blood.

"Sorry, Andy," I said to him. "To cast this spell, I'd have to be..."

And there it was. I'd have to do a partial transformation and become something like Kimodo. To do that, I was going to need a ridiculous amount of practice.

"Bobby! Want to go fishing?"

• • •

All in all, I like lizard magic better than human magic. It has almost a computer language to it; where you can script components together to make a spell, almost like putting together an old batch file, albeit one that usually requires blood. Human magic is chanting with motion, runes, and other shit.

Of course, standing in front of a mirror wearing a swimsuit and the claw of dead dinomage like a belt buckle, in a crude ring drawn in my blood mixed with that of several dead geckos and an iguana, I was more nervous than enamored. That last fish had grown clawed feet and was able to survive on land until I undid the transformation. I'd kept it in a tank for a week and checked it on a daily basis.

"Remember," I said to Bobby. "If something goes wrong, pour that liquid on me. It should reverse the transformation. If it doesn't; stun me and contact Swamplord. He should be able to find someone who might be able to undo it."

"I still think this is a stupid idea," Bobby said. "I reckon that if Swamplord can't fix you, I'll sell you to one of those sideshows."

His crass words were oddly comforting. He made statements like that when he was nervous.

Because I wasn't starting from a lizard, I needed the ring of blood to kind of kickstart things. PETA would join the line of groups wanting a piece of my ass if they ever discovered what I was doing here.

However, no ferrets were harmed during the preparations for this spell.

Gripping the augment with my left hand, I started to cast the first section of the spell. Even with my previous successes, I was still a little skeptical.

"Ahhhhhhh!" I screamed, the fish hadn't seemed to hurt this much.

"Are you okay? Cal, are you okay?"

"It's working, but it hurts!"

An itch burned across the surface of my skin, and I could feel my muscles cramping up as the transformation took hold. My fingers were melding together and I could see the nails lengthening and curling. The food I'd eaten revolted and was summarily expelled. It was maybe thirty seconds of agony that felt like hours, as I collapsed in my own vomit and had a minor seizure.

The pain stopped and I pushed my tired body off the stone floor. There was a chill in the air that I hadn't noticed before.

"Dude," Bobby said. "You look hideous. Not that you ever looked all that good, but damn!"

"Funny," I replied with a distinct hiss in my voice. Looking in the mirror, I saw patches of my skin had been replaced with scales. My face was thicker, and my nose had flattened. My notoriously greasy hair was missing in spots, like I'd gotten into a fight with my barber and lost.

Thinking back to Kimodo, she'd kept short black hair, but her face had been way closer to reptilian than my spell had left me.

"All right, let me try this spell. Damn! Feels like it's freezing in here."

On the bench was a hunk of my old petrified armor—a roughly six inch square chunk that used to be part of the chest plating. I'd picked it because it was mostly homogenous; composed of metal and the cracked chest light.

My connection with the augment didn't just feel stronger; it was stronger. That was a bit scary—like there was a taste of power, something similar to holding a baseball bat with the wrong grip and knowing that if I could choke up on the bat a little more I'd be able to swing harder.

And I hate baseball analogies, especially ones that involve me becoming less human than I already was.

Of course, I felt much stronger. Kimodo could lift around a thousand pounds. She wasn't in Bobby's league, but the clawed hands and speed might have made a difference if Kim had been a real fighter and not some mind controlled puppet.

No bitterness there, Cal! It's not like you have trust issues or anything right?

So far, my sarcastic inner monologue was intact, so that boded well for my mental state, such that it was. My thought processes didn't really seem any different.

Gesturing with a claw, I concentrated on the energy flowing through my body. Strangely, the blood traveling near the augment was crackling with energy. I pulled that energy and directed it into the claw.

At the tip of my claw there was a weak glow, it started at about the brightness of your average Christmas tree light. I could somehow sense the fingerprints, or was that claw marks, of the magic that had transformed the piece. As the Grand Vizier had said when he and Mystigal tried to revert Andy, they had no grounding in this magic. Now I did, and my transformation wasn't so much about reversing the change as it was about unraveling the magic that had done this in the first place.

The elements of magic left in my chest plate fought back against what I attempted. It had been several months, and from what little I'd been able to glean from the silver rectangles containing Rex's spells, I'd need to overcome the inertia of the spell permeating the material.

There was also the small matter that I wasn't nearly in Rex's league. I was so far beneath him that it was a joke. Rex's spell was master craftsmanship; I would have to spend years working at this before I could cast it. Fortunately, for me, the guy ripping out the beautiful set of cabinets in the kitchen doesn't have to know how to do what the carpenter did. He only needs to know how to use a sledgehammer and a crowbar to take them out.

My feeble magic started chipping away at the enchantment on the material and it became something of a test of will. A magical tug of war, if you will, as the minutes passed.

"Hey," Bobby exclaimed. "It's starting to look metallic."

Naturally, that blew my concentration and I lost my mental grip on the spell.

Bobby grunted and said, "Nope, looks like it is back to being stone."

"All right," I said with my newfound raspy accent. "Get one of the smaller pieces from a storage tub under the workbench—labelled old armor. I'll try it on a smaller chunk and work my way up to this one."

Bobby complied with my request and a minute later, I was looking at a finger from one of the gauntlets.

"Will that do, Cal?"

I answered, and asked him to set it on the table just outside my blood circle. This time, I threw everything I had against the fragment, because if this didn't work, there was no point in trying more, and Andy was doomed to be a cool looking coat rack.

Centimeter by centimeter, the material changed from the coarse stone to the sheen of metal. It crept down the length of the finger like it had all the time in the world, but I was tiring quickly from the earlier effort. Seconds became minutes and I could sense that the original magic was becoming weaker, squeezed out of existence. Five minutes passed before that resilient sliver of magic was finally pushed out, and I saw a tiny flash of light that told me I'd managed to do it!

Spent, I took a deep breath and stepped out of the transformation circle. The spell changing me was locked into that spot, and my body began returning to normal. It wasn't nearly as painful as when I'd made the change, probably because my body was going back to its natural state.

Bobby looked at me and reached into the cooler. Instead of a beer, he passed me a bottle of water. "Drink up man, you look like death warmed over."

Wow! I must look really bad.

I felt warm again, shook off my short time as a cold blooded critter, and took a couple of measured sips to quell the civil war being fought in my gastrointestinal tract. I scooped up the finger and took it to the equipment on the table. Under the microscope, it sure looked like the metal alloy I'd used to make the hands of the Screaming Cyclops suit. The small bit of synth appeared to be intact.

"Looks good," I said to Bobby and gave him the thumbs up. "I think I'm going to go take a nap and check it over again in three or four hours. If everything's still good, I'll try a slightly bigger piece tomorrow. I think, as my body gets used to Rex's magic, that the transformation will be easier."

• • •

After two weeks of daily practice, I'd gotten to the point where the shapechanging only left me queasy and not "spewing my guts" nauseous. I'd also run out of material from my old Mark III armor to change back and wished I'd grabbed the two knock off suits that had been petrified with mine. There was even a few bits of useful salvage here and there.

The largest piece I'd managed to revert was the right knee assembly, and that had been a beast! Even with the augment, I just didn't have enough magic in me to do Andy's whole body. Like any good engineer, I examined my process and tweaked it where I could to maximize my performance. The first step was to use the blood from the lizard/bass hybrids I'd made, infusing my transformation circle with magic to start— the equivalent of priming a pump.

It also had the benefit of cutting down on Bobby's trips to pet stores. We were up to three ferrets and a chinchilla. With his career as a low-level criminal in a lull, he'd been picking up hobbies and it was beginning to annoy me.

Whenever I brought up the notion that he was turning our base into a damn zoo, he retorted that he didn't approve of what I was doing to "perfectly good eatin' fish."

On the things improving front, my lizard transformation was closer to something usable, and I looked closer at what Rex had done to those people, other than turn them into a bad extra in a low budget lizard people horror movie. I had a tail! That's an experience in itself. Naturally, when you get something, you invariably have to give something—it was a good thing I didn't have a girlfriend at that time—she would have been very disappointed.

Giving in to a whim, I'd tested my strength and could press four hundred and fifty pounds with relative ease, which was much better than what I could do as a human. Sadly, I couldn't even get close to Kimodo's league in terms of strength.

Naturally, I had some thoughts about how to miniaturize the casting circle into some type of a belt that I could use to transform into this form without being confined in a space.

Engineers gotta tinker and all that. Just doing what comes naturally to me... even if it creates an unnatural result.

It was time for a calculated risk. After determining the maximum mass I'd been able to revert at one time, I had sawed off Andy's head just below his chin. Even so, it was still fifteen percent greater than what I'd been able to do so far. From what I knew of my friend's schematics, his important functions were contained inside.

Here's hoping I didn't just screw the pooch... again.

I had to roll the dice here, but maybe I needed to back myself into a corner to try and get this done. I looked over at the wall where I'd stuck the postcard that said I needed a team. More importantly, I needed Andydroid on that team. He was a genius in logistics and communications.

The transformation was complete. Beside me sat a small Tupperware dish filled with fish/lizard hybrid blood. I knew it was required, but wasn't sure if I'd passed the point where it was being helpful. Other than making me squeamish, I didn't think it could hurt and went ahead and dipped my claws in it, smeared a clawful onto his head, and then gripped the augment strapped to the belt.

My connection to the magic was as good as it was going to get; it was a fifty-six kilobit dialup compared to the high-speed internet all the "real" magical folks have access to. I'd made a living working with less than all the others, because I'm an obstinate little so-and-so. All the extra tricks and amplifications I'd jury-rigged around me gave me a boost. I was cheating again, but if I was being honest, when wasn't I cheating?

The magic surged and began enveloping Andy's head. The dark mud-colored stone began changing back into titanium. In the times that I'd failed, I would hit a wall of exhaustion and the magic would falter and the tap would cut off. When it happened, the spell would spread back down and turn it right back.

Instinctively, I spread my legs and balanced with that ridiculous tail. The augment located at what could be considered the core of my being, glowed, and I grabbed on to Andy's head with one clawed hand while the other gripped the crystal containing Rex's finger. I threw myself against one of the dinosaur mage's final spells. Someone else looking at this would probably have said I was trying to justify humanity's rise after the reptiles had been driven to extinction. I wouldn't go that far. I just hated Rex and wanted to beat his ass one more time.

When the magic started to run out, I shoved anger into the breach and screamed my way through it. Dropping to the ground and marshalling all of whatever might be left, I released it all and collapsed onto the ground. For at least a minute, I could only shake and thrash on the ground, unable to rise. Bobby started toward me, but I managed to wave him off. Reaching up, I managed to grab Andy's noggin on the third attempt. Pulling it down to my level, I turned it over and over, searching the shiny metal surface for a spot that I'd missed, and hoping my spell had penetrated the inside and gotten all the way through.

Minutes passed and the surface remained metal. Flipping it around to stare up at the loose wiring inside the exposed neck, I was already guessing where I'd have to make repairs and where power needed to go.

"Did it work?" Bobby asked.

"Looks like it," I hissed, rolling onto my back, and holding up Andy's cranium like a wide receiver who'd just caught the game clinching pass in the Superbowl.

Lizard-boy for the win! Should I call myself Repti-CAL?

Using one of my claws, I awkwardly unhooked the belt with Rex's finger in it and pushed it off me. My connection to the magic snapped faster than Wendy discovering another one of my get rich schemes, and a fresh wave of exhaustion broke over me as I returned to being human once more.

It took another five minutes for me to stand up and carry my prize to the workbench. Despite wanting to crawl into my bed, or make it as far as the couch just up the stairs, and sleep for two days, I tugged at my toolkit and began rooting through it to find the connectors I'd need to splice the power cables back together.

Andy had waited this long; he probably could wait a little longer, but I couldn't.

• • •

"System Fault... sequencing error... motor systems offline... diagnostics unavailable... suppressing repeat errors... external sensors at five percent... limiting input... recovering from fatal stop... polling active systems... Andydroid Organic Lifeform Emulator is three percent operational. System firmware version is eleven point six, build four seven three. Automated distress beacon cannot be located or activated."

After a considerable amount of time wiring him to a power regulator and a Class B powercell, I was forced to sit through a solid ten minutes of Andy trying and failing to bring his missing body online. It was pretty boring actually, and I was nervous that he'd get partially up and then crash again. All I could do was wait, stifle my yawns, and pound another energy drink.

Just when I was about to break down and go look for some porn to pass the time, the endless monologue trailed off.

"Hello, Calvin Stringel," Andy said. "I appear to have suffered a major catastrophe."

"You could say that," I replied. "It's good to hear your voice. You've been out of commission for almost a full year now. What is the last thing you remember?"

"We were on a mission to rescue Kimodo, and discovered a tribe of what appeared to be humans transformed into reptilians."

"Good. You aren't missing any memories."

"Query, my creator should have been able to recreate my body. Why am I in this condition, in what appears to be your Alabama base?"

"It's a slightly longer story," I said and began to fill him in. When that seemed like it was taking too long, I uploaded my book to him.

When he finished, Andy had a tough to read expression on his face. "I have been replaced."

"The magic wasn't something anyone thought they would be able to reverse."

"You obviously thought differently," he said.

"Even a blind squirrel will occasionally find a nut," I said dismissively. "Besides, we got word that Doctor Albright would restore the new Andy from an old backup that predated the bug invasion. That new Andy wouldn't know me; I don't want to make friends with him."

His confused look remained. "A blind squirrel would still have a sense of smell. If you were such a creature, you could use that to locate a nut. Please tell me why you are laughing, Calvin?"

"Essentially, you just said I could smell my nuts. That just means I'm tired."

"Before you rest, may I ask two questions?"

"Sure."

"Why did you fake your death?"

"Seemed like a good idea at the time. I can build my new set of armor in peace and don't have to worry about meetings, briefings, and patrols. I was tired of them dangling a pardon over my head like a carrot; demanding that I be a good little boy. But I do have a problem."

"What problem would that be, Cal?"

I stand and go get the postcard. "Prophiseer's messenger brought me this when I was near my old base, taking in the sights. It says something bad is going to happen in San Francisco nine months from now and that I need a team to stop it."

"Do you have any idea what the event will be?"

"Could be a big fire like before. Earthquake, Tsunami, supervillains, aliens! Hell! I don't know. You're one of the most advanced artificial intelligences ever created, so, I wanted you to be on my team. Left to me, I'd end up making the wrong guess, but you... you'll figure it out way before I do and tell me who else we should recruit."

Andydroid smiled, or made a close approximation of what one would look like. "I am pleased that you hold my skill in such regard. I will do my best to vindicate your belief in my abilities."

"You're welcome," I said and stood. "Well, I'm going to go... oh wait, you wanted to ask something else?"

"Yes. When will I get a replacement body?"

"I've got an old Type A robot frame in one of storage rooms and will see what else I can get my hands on, but I promise it won't be too long."

• • •

"You're lucky, he's the patient sort," Stacy says.

"Yeah, it's still on my list. I was holding out to see if I could get one of those Type E frames, or even a warbot."

"He who waits is lost," she admonishes.

"I've been lost for so long now I've considered registering that as my place of birth."

She laughs and says, "Cute Cal, very cute."

"I thought it was. So anyway..."

She cuts me off. "Hold that thought! They're almost done, and I'm on deck to spar now. After I make short work out of my prey, I'll be eager for more!"

"Yeah, I'll bet you're eager," I say. She's too easy.

"Hardy har har. So, does your winky completely disappear when you turn into a lizard, or what?"

"Aww, man! Why'd you have to go there, Stacy?"

"I figured I'd go there before you use that lame 'Do you want to see my lizard?' line. Going offline for a few minutes to kick some ass."

She does give as good as she gets. At least I have time to think up a decent retort.

Walking over to the workbench, I pick up the hollow tree branch I'm carving protective runes into, hopefully to shield Mega from suffering another magic related outage. Something organic and unworked by man should serve best. My gut tells me that Rex's magic probably responds best to blood and sacrifice, but I'll start with wood, my own blood, and maybe wrapping it in snakeskin or alligator hide... yeah the second one will probably work best.

"Cal? Am I interrupting?" Wendy calls out from the top of the steps.

"No, come on down."

She descends, with Gabolicious in her arms, and I smile automatically at seeing my little girl.

"What's up?"

"Well, I was thinking about a way to get us out of this alien mess without tipping everyone off that you're still alive. Also, I've determined a suitable punishment for you."

Now completely curious, I ask, "Which do I get to hear first?"

"The punishment," Wendy replies and hands me the little stinkbug. "She needs a change... big time, and since I have to put up with your shit all the time, I figured I should start returning the favor."

"Language, Wendy. You're supposed to be her role model. Unless you want her taking after me? Yeah, didn't think so. All right boss lady, what's your plan?"

The tiny tornado maker flashes an evil smile as I'm assaulted by Gabby's foul odor. "I guess I've been hanging around with you too long, because I'm pretty sure this will meet your approval."

"Well, in that case, let's hear what you've got in mind. The Cal Stringel seal of approval doesn't come easily, so you'd better impress me."

Chapter Twelve

WWCSD

"You okay, Larry? I can slow down if you want?" Mega is cruising at two hundred-fifty miles per hour over the rolling landscape of the western part of Virginia, staying fairly close to the ground to avoid showing up on radar. Two minutes ago, I'd brought him through the poop chute, but he wasn't holding up well with the landscape zipping past him.

"Yeah, I'm good. Just a little nauseous. Still getting used to all this flying around stuff."

One of the most powerful people on the planet and he gets airsick.

"Sorry we couldn't just let Mega land and use the poop chute when we get there. I don't want to lose that advantage. We're probably close enough to go higher."

"Sure, go ahead."

Flipping over to my private channel to Stacy's armor, I contact her. "Hey, Stacy, are you monitoring this channel?"

There're a few seconds of dead air before she comes on. "What's going on? I rigged a light on my HUD for when this channel is active."

"Good idea! But, you're not hanging on my every word? I'm hurt."

"I can hurt you worse if you'd like," she offers.

"I'll pass. Larry is getting motion sick, so I'm going to go ahead and get some altitude. We're probably going to show up on some radar system shortly, and we'll be making a beeline for Mount Olympus. Looks like the show is going to start a few minutes early. Are you ready? Who else is there?"

"Athena, Ares, Hermes, Hestia, and me."

"Ares all healed up?" I'm hedging my bets. I doubt there is going to be a fight, Stacy isn't about to let me pound on her friends. I'm not really looking forward to seeing Holly Crenshaw again, but it might make our little ruse easier to sell.

"He's still limping a little, but he could go if need be. Hera and Apollo are in DC. Gravmatar is with them, so they can be here very quickly. Don't be surprised if they are."

"Well, let's make sure this doesn't spiral out of control. See you in a few minutes, I'd have brought flowers, but that would seem odd."

"Nice try," she says.

"Besides, any flowers, no matter how beautiful, would pale next to you."

"Laying it on thick now, aren't you?"

I am, but that's not the point. She brings out the need for witty banter. "How's your mom and dad?"

"I went to their house for dinner the other night, Mom is wondering when I'm going to start dating again."

"I'm not exactly her favorite person, am I?" My inkblot comment in the book probably should have been cut, but in my defense, it was one of the most hilarious lines.

"You have to ask?"

"No, but I figured I would anyway," I quip. "As long as I'm your favorite person, I'm good."

"Aw," she says. "Rest assured; you're in my top five."

"Serious burn!" Wendy says sitting down on the couch by the workbench.

"No comments from the peanut gallery," I say and check my instrumentation. "Someone's picking me up. Might be that regional airport near Winchester. Roll out the welcome mat, Stacy. We'll be there shortly."

"If only it were that easy."

Turning to Wendy, I say, "So far so good. Do you think this is going to work?"

The fiery tempered brunette nods. "You were the one who introduced the world to how gullible heroes are when it comes to The Big Lie. As much as I hate to admit it, you're right."

"You need to warn me when you're going to give me a compliment. Things like that need to be recorded for posterity."

She waves her hand dismissively. "Whatever, Cal. Just remember, we wouldn't be doing this if you would just keep your big mouth shut."

If this had been a card game, she would be holding the trump card right now.

"Person who got taken out by a sedative says what?"

Yeah, I went there.

"You're so childish, Cal. It's not one of your better traits. Do you know how many times I've looked in the mirror and asked myself why I signed on for this?"

Stacy asks a question. "Who did you recruit first, Cal? Wendy or Larry?"

"You want more storytime?"

"I've got a few minutes to kill, at least until some jerk shows up to ruin my day."

"I might resemble that jerk," I reply, and feign hurt. "If you must know, it was Larry."

• • •

"What are you doing, Cal?"

Andydroid's head didn't quite fit on the old Type A frame I'd put him on. His cranium was a little too small for the broad shoulders of the chassis. He looked like one of those people who'd ticked off a voodoo priestess and gotten their head partially shrunken. I'd get to his new body soon.

"Just trying to create another list of who else we could recruit."

"I've also been compiling a roster of candidates," Andy said.

"You probably have a more complete list than I do," I confess. "Let me hear what you got."

"Have you devised a suitable method for contacting WhirlWendy?"

Helplessly, I shrugged. A plethora of scenarios played out in my mind, with none of them ending well for me, plus she had her bodyguard with her day and night now.

"I think it might go better if I already had some other people on the team before I approach her."

"Have you considered your history with Edward Paulson?"

"Eddie is a jackass," I responded. "He is more trouble than he is worth; decent enough in a fight, but thinks way too much of himself. I'd end up babysitting him."

Andy processed my answer. "Very well. I will remove him from the list of possible members."

"So far, Bobby, you, and I won't exactly frighten people into surrendering."

My robotic companion didn't really bat an eye at Bobby's inclusion. "Our problem appears to be that most of the significant heroes are aligned with the various teams already; and revealing your identity to the world at large would be counterproductive, and provide Ultraweapon's defense lawyers with additional avenues to pursue Lazarus Patterson's freedom."

"No kidding," I practically growled. "No one wants that."

"Next, there is the matter of trust for individuals who are either villains or those not aligned with a team."

Wendy was someone I felt I could trust, but I had the advantage of her being pregnant with my child. Unless I suddenly became sperm donor to the supers, I didn't see that being a draw for any other person.

"What if I build you a second suit of armor?" I ask. "I'm just about finished with my set."

"The base's powerplant is currently incapable of supporting a second set of the Mark IV Mechani-CAL armor. We would need to either increase our current capacity or reduce the effectiveness of both sets of armor."

Anyone who knows me will understand that reducing the effectiveness of a set of powered armor is the rough equivalent of making a sexual reference to a person's sister in front of them.

Obviously, that wasn't going to happen.

"I could maybe build you a set based on the Mark III design. We could integrate you into the design and use the extra space for additional B and C powercells. It wouldn't quite match the performance parameters of the new suit, but it would still be a significant upgrade."

"I would consider it, but you will recall that I am programmed to not take human life except under extraordinary circumstances. I suspect this would not be an optimal result."

I started to say that maybe I could figure out a way to bypass Andy's morality programming, but thought better of it. Somehow, I doubted he'd appreciate me trying to turn him into something no better than Patterson's death machines.

Instead, I went with, "You're right, and we can't exactly create our own superhumans."

"Technically, we can make one," Andy said. When I appeared confused, he continued, "You still possess the necklace belonging to the deceased life partner of Chain Charmer. It gives the wearer superpowers."

"Yeah, I guess we could hold some kind of audition and see who gets the most useful powers from it, like Sheila had wanted to do, but it would be kind of difficult to keep something like that quiet." I didn't really need it anymore. With Andy's assistance, I'd read all the plates into the base's computer while he scanned them, and together we had built a human to dinosaur dictionary. Also, after so much practice, I'd gotten pretty good at reading all those reptoscratchings. I wasn't about to translate Shakespeare or even Heinlein into it, but I could pretty much decipher things without the dictionary, with roughly eighty percent accuracy.

Not too shabby for a dude who struggled with Italian in high school.

Racking my mind for normal human acquaintances, I was a little short on normal people. The only names that came to mind were my college roommate Joey Hazelwood, and the woman who helped me write my "screw you all" memoir. Considering how Megan Bostic felt about the superhuman community in general, I discarded her because I was afraid of what I might unleash. As for Joey, he was an overweight pawn broker I hadn't seen since before the bug invasion. He'd done a couple of interviews as someone who'd known the infamous Cal Stringel, after my run in with a fusion power core. To be honest, he'd seemed a little too eager to cash in on his fifteen minutes of fame and said a few surprisingly harsh things about yours truly. Mom? Dad? Not a chance.

"I guess it doesn't speak well of me that I can't think of a single person I know who really deserves superpowers."

Andydroid doesn't judge my lack of normal friends. "In my time as a solo hero in the Atlanta, Georgia area, I encountered several individuals who would benefit from superpowers. Would you like me to tell you about them?"

I was feeling frustrated. "Sure. Why not? The necklaces only other use would be to halve a person's powers and I don't know how cutting someone's powers in half would help us build a better super team, do you?"

Andy's head snapped up, almost breaking free from the chassis. "Cal, you may have stumbled onto the solution. There is, in fact, one superhuman who is too powerful, and he is unaffiliated with any group of superhumans."

It took a second to figure out who he was talking about, but the realization hit me harder than a telekinetic construct. "Holy shit! You're right!"

There was silence for a minute, who knows what Andy spent those processor cycles doing. I, on the other hand, wondered if this would work. I'd seen an insane Imaginary Larry beat Wendy in Charlotte. That kind of power... even only half that kind of power, wielded by someone in control of their faculties... it boggled the mind.

"Andy," I said, wondering if this was what The Prophiseer wanted me to do, and deciding it didn't matter anyway because I was going to do it regardless. "We need to finish the armor and get it op checked. We'll need it if we're going to go up against Imaginary Larry."

• • •

"There it is," I say to Larry, cutting off Stacy's storytime. "Mount Olympus in all its pretentious glory. Last time I fought here, I lost the battle, but won the war... I think."

Aphrodite's previous interruptions of my thrilling retelling of how I decided to use the necklace on Larry let me know that the Olympians were on high alert. Hera, Apollo, and the Rigellian prince-in-exile had high tailed it back from DC using the Chariot, and were awaiting our arrival with the others. Apollo's Chariot is some kind of self-repairing, high-speed construct that is able to cross great distances in short periods of time and can even reach escape velocity.

How long would it take to recover from a hit with my railgun?

I'm actually happier with the Olympian's leader beating us here, because it meant I'd be dealing with her rather than Holly Crenshaw. Athena irritates the hell out of me. The alien and the Olympians, along with a dozen Type B gyroscopic ball robots and their two Type D warbots waited for us.

The Mount was a manmade hill with a Greek style building atop it. People were scurrying down the four staircases like rats abandoning a sinking ship and I felt a pang of sorrow for what was once the premier super team in the world. The guard is changing and they haven't figured it out yet.

We set down at the flat end of prefabricated plateau. I want to give Larry a chance to get his feet under him before we mosey on over.

"Nervous?" I ask.

"Maybe, a little," Larry confesses.

"Me, too," I say. "Let me do the talking and remember this; you've handed all of them their asses at some point in time. If for some reason, things go all stupid, you and I will take the opportunity to do it again, with interest. Push comes to shove, we shove real hard."

I know Stacy is listening on this channel and the warning is partly for her as well. Larry straightens up and nods with new-found resolve. Maybe I do have a future as a motivational speaker.

We walk side by side toward the group. Hera and Gravmatar detach to meet us twenty feet away from the others. Her powers generate strong forcefields and his super dense gravity warping beams and near invulnerability made for a good opening shot.

The attractive sandy-brown haired leader of the Olympians spoke first. "Welcome to Mount Olympus. I understand you are called Red and you are the Megasuit. How is WhirlWendy?"

"Thank you for the reception," I reply through my external speakers. "A short time ago, one of your subordinate super teams attempted to bring our leader into custody based on the flimsiest of excuses, resulting in a fight in the middle of a highly populated area. We decided to come speak with you to ensure that something like that does not occur again, and to issue a warning that if it does, there will be consequences. Our leader has recovered from the attack and is monitoring this conversation. If she makes an appearance, it will not be for a social call."

Hera nods. "We had nothing to do with that confrontation. It was something the government was pushing and the West Coast team was all too eager to pursue. They had a long history with Ultraweapon, and reacted poorly to his demise."

"We acted with restraint to minimize the potential for civilian casualties. They were the ones who initiated a fight in the middle of a major city."

The stocky, yellow and magenta Rigellian slapped all four of his seven-fingered hands together, causing twin pulses of energies to engulf them and says, "This posturing bores me. We already know who that one is. All that remains is to determine if the other is an alien."

The people of Columbia elected Gravmatar their President for Life after he pretty much single handedly, or is that four handedly as it were, wiped out all the local rebels. According to Gravmatar, Rigellians have an average life-span of three hundred and twenty-five years, so they'll have an opportunity to enjoy their decision for some time to come. They didn't appoint him for his patience.

The engineer in me wondered whether his gravity warping abilities could stop my railgun.

Maybe I obsess about the railgun too much? Nah.

"Gravmatar! Please!" Hera exclaims. "My apologies, Mr. Hitt."

Some of my instruments pick up a surge around Larry as he says, "Everyone seems to think they know me. Considering I barely know who I am, perhaps you should be less anxious to jump to conclusions."

"He has a point," I interject. It didn't take a rocket scientist to take Larry's disappearance from his prison and mental facility and the arrival of Big Red on the scene and come up with something. The Brits, who bet on virtually everything, had stopped taking wagers on his identity. "If he is who you think he is, then you might be a bit more concerned about pissing him off. That's just my opinion, but I'm not the one who will get their ass kicked six ways from Sunday, so by all means keep irritating him."

"No one wants a fight, today!" Hera shouts. "We're simply having a discussion."

"The Rigellian culture is based around ritual combat," I say, before deciding to throw her a bone. "If it helps progress this discussion we are supposed to be having, I am not an alien."

"Then why did you claim to be?"

"I implied it because it stopped a fight in downtown Phoenix, with dozens of innocent people around. I acted under the assumption that this is what the good guys are supposed to do, prevent civilian casualties and property damage where possible. Is it not one of your bylaws, or do your own rules mean so little to you, Hera? If it sounds repetitive then perhaps, you idiot humans should try comprehension and not just listening!"

Back in our headquarters, Wendy gives me a sideways glance. I shrug.

"You said humans," Hera comments. "Like you're not one of us."

"Bring over Aphrodite. I will lower my shields and allow her to scan me."

Hera motions for Stacy to come over in her gold and silver armor. The outer shell now has a centurion motif, no doubt approved by their Public Relations overlords. Her faceplate splits down the middle and the seam spreads apart to reveal the Love Goddess.

"I'm not receiving anything," Stacy says and I can see the fake confusion on her face. "Even Rigellians give off some kind of emotional response. It's almost like he is ..."

"A machine," I offer and pop the seal on my helmet.

"Andydroid?" Hera gasps.

"Indeed," I say using Andy's head to transmit my voice. "I'm the original. The one turned to stone."

"Wait a second!" Athena jumps in. "Andydroid is programmed not to kill. If that's the case how do you explain killing Ultraweapon?"

"When I awoke, I discovered my friend, and the only one who'd tried to save me, was dead. Fortunately, I had been doing experiments with Calvin Stringel to determine why he was so effective in comparison to your recent string of failures."

"What are you saying, Andy?"

"I had an extensive library of brainwave patterns belonging to Cal Stringel. I merged them with my existing program. And so, in any situation, I simply ask myself what would Calvin Stringel do?"

And there it is, the Big Lie, coming to our rescue once more. Let's see if they bite.

"I'm having a problem accepting this," Stacy says, playing her part.

"Of course you are; I will use smaller words to make it easier for you to follow, Aphrodite. Strange, despite Athena never doing anything to me personally, I feel the odd compulsion to create a detailed list of your failings. The late Calvin Stringel truly did not like you. In fairness, your leadership record is only slightly below average and not an abject failure."

Wiping that shit eating grin off my face is going to be a tough job, but for now, I'm enjoying it. *That was actually rather fun, although I'm sure Andy is going to give me hell for making him say that.*

"While I'm thinking of it, you might as well have this," I say and toss the thumb drive with our sexual escapades on it. "I don't exactly have a need for it anymore."

Technically, that is true. Stacy let me make another copy and I have the real thing, which is much better.

"So, you're using your base in Alabama?" Stacy asks.

"Nice try, but no. I cannot risk you getting your memory back, Barbie Doll. Besides, I think that idiot Bobby is using it again. We've got a nicer place now, but depending on how your paymasters continue to treat Wendy, we might be looking to relocate. The Caribbean is nice and I bet Havana would welcome us with open arms. They like WhirlWendy. The only people who do not appear to adore her are criminals and the United States government. Actually, since Columbia's president is right here, we could discuss relocating down there."

The look on Hera's face is worth adding to my screensaver rotation, and unless my assumptions are off, Gravmatar would never want anyone more powerful than he is hanging around. Returning the USB drive would put an end to the occasional porn prospectors coming into the area.

Hera regroups. "You must understand that the government's wary of a team of your caliber operating with no oversight."

"They only deal in control," I reply. "But it is you who need to be concerned. Patterson had you outclassed and you were getting beaten. My analysis of the footage indicates half your team would have been killed if we had not intervened. You did not perform well against the bugs and seem to lack the ability to adapt to your opponents' increasing capabilities. The Olympians are in danger of becoming stagnant, so, I submit that you need to get your house in order rather than worry about what the New Renegades are doing."

"Are we done here, Mega?" Larry asks. "I'm ready to get out of here."

"That really depends on Hera and Gravmatar. Do you need any other questions answered for the politicians, or feel the need to have some kind of asinine fight?"

Gravmatar still looks like he wants to throw down, but Hera doesn't. Back in the cave, I'm leaning over to give Wendy a fist bump when Stacy interrupts. "Radar detects a launch. Looks like fifty drones, five miles out!"

"It's got to be the Overlord!" Wendy hisses and jumps up, heading to the poop chute.

I have to cut off the external speakers. "Don't! Larry and I can handle this."

She looks like she wants to argue, but I'm being pulled in different directions; dealing with her and listening to Hera bark orders.

Bringing up my shields, I begin looking for the wave of missiles. Of course the Overlord would have Mount Olympus under surveillance! I'd been so worried about the stupid Olympians that I forgot about the real villains.

"Hera? Do I stay or go? If it is the Overlord behind this, I am the target."

"Stay," she says, as the humans inside of Mount Olympus activate all the defenses. Gun emplacements, rebuilt after I destroyed them, activate and begin tracking the skies. This many attackers are beyond Hera's forcefields.

Megasuit's pulse cannons cycle up to full charge and I get a visual on the first wave of drones coming. It's about ten, carrying an unspecified payload. This, naturally, creates a dilemma for the hero types on whether to shoot them down, risking the civilian population, or wait until the weaponry reaches the three mile "clear zone" surrounding Mount Olympus before engaging, which would only give us a short time to destroy fifty drones and their munitions.

The drones deploy their weapons, two missiles per, and suddenly the number of targets triples from fifty to one hundred and fifty.

"Red, can you throw up a barrier? Keep it close, so their defenses can stop as much as possible. Hera, throw your shield up behind it. One group of missiles is traveling faster than the other. That means we have three waves, if the drones themselves are on a suicide run."

Hera agrees and shows Red where to put his energy wall up. The air defense cannons open up as Mount Olympus attempts to defend itself. Twenty-three missiles are destroyed and I begin firing, using four pulse cannons available. My railgun is useless in this case. The nice part is my power systems can support continuous firing for over two minutes, until the heat load becomes too much for the individual weapons to handle.

Gravmatar emits a field of energy, causing several of the missiles to drop short and impact against the side of the mountain.

Stacy joins me with her pair of force blasters, while Athena hurls energy spears that detonate like proximity charges—never knew she could do that. Only five of the initial fifty strike Larry's telekinetic barrier, but we shot our wad and will have to suffer the consequences.

Well over thirty missiles from the second wave hit, and Larry collapses under the strain, as his barrier snaps. Hera fills the gap adequately, but several strike the decorative stonework because the Olympian isn't nearly as powerful as Larry Hitt.

Shards of imported marble spray against my shields as I move the suit over the prone form of my friend.

I start looking for the drones and see that half have changed their approach vector, but are still headed in our direction. The remaining ones begin firing darts of plasma energy at us. It isn't especially effective and I'm beginning to believe that the Overlord is losing his touch, when the remaining twenty-five detonate simultaneously. Hera's faltering shield keeps most of the shockwave from us, and to her credit, she's still standing; even if it looks like a stiff breeze would knock her over.

Like that, the battle is over, but something doesn't make sense. Those drones should have detonated much closer to us.

Andy contacts me on our private channel. "I am detecting increased levels of background radiation."

"Stacy, rad alert!" I link her in. "Andy, what is it?"

"Anaylzing," the robot responds. "It appears to be a cloud of highly refined particles containing a significant amount of radium-226."

"That's an alpha emitter, "I say. "Stacy, warn your team against breathing it in."

"Larry's mask should filter most of it out. What's the threat level to the rest?"

"Minimal. The Olympians heal very quickly. Whatever sickness they experience should not be prolonged."

"Then why do it?"

There's a long pause before Andy replies. "The clothing and the surface of your armor will require decontamination. The likely scenario is that the mastermind behind this plot is going to use the alpha radiation emitted in an attempt to track his enemies. There is also another problem."

Before I could ask, Gravmatar collapses and begins having some kind of violent seizure.

"High concentrations are known to affect Rigellian physiology."

Hera shouts for Ares to wade through the fluctuating gravity fields and get Gravmatar inside.

"Oh, that's sneaky," Stacy says via our private link. "He's after you, Cal. Obviously; he already knows where we are."

"Tell the others, Stacy. I'm getting Larry out of here!" Scooping up the barely conscious Larry, I fire up my jetpack to leave while my girlfriend updates the remaining members of her team.

"Where are you going?" Stacy asks with her external speakers.

"The Overlord wants to know my location. I will make it easier for him to find me."

"Then you're going to need backup, Andydroid. You might not be the real Cal Stringel, but I can at least try to square the books with you."

"If you really feel it is necessary, Aphrodite. I guess I will never understand you hero types."

"Hera, I'm going with him."

"Understood, Aphrodite. We'll check out the launch site. Help is only a chariot ride away."

Lifting off, I switch over to the private channel and ask, "What's going on?"

"Well, you're going to need someone to shove Larry up your butt. Where're we going?"

"I've always wanted a woman to talk about shoving something up my ass. As to where I'm headed, it's back to the location where we had our first date. Add it to the list of reasons to attack Branson, Missouri. A week ago, I saw Paul West there on a satellite image. I think I'm going to go pay him a visit and say hello. Are you sure you want to come along. I might just be going there to see what he'll give up before I kill him."

"Which do you want, Cal? His blood or a lead on the Overlord?"

"He'll break one way or the other," I reply.

"I can break him," she says.

"Really?" I stammer. I didn't expect that.

"Cal," she says and gives a rather throaty laugh. "I'm not going to beat him up. He's a man; I'm the incarnation of the Goddess of Love. The only thing I will break is Mr. West's dark, twisted, little, heart."

Having had my heart broken by her once before, I think Paul would be better off letting me kill him. It is less cruel.

Chapter Thirteen

Evicting Peter Pan from Neverland

We land briefly in a farmer's field about sixty miles from Mount Olympus and I drag Larry into the barn. Stacy's Centurion armor follows, and she helps get Red back up the poop chute.

On the other end, I wear some protective gloves and arm-sleeves to help pull him through. The strong radioisotope wouldn't stand a chance of getting up to the surface, so our base remains secure, but I think it is a good idea to get him out of those contaminated clothes and into his spare costume while we bag up his other one. I worry about the radium exposure if it got into his lungs, but maybe his telekinetic powers shielded him, or can be used to remove it from his body.

"How should we clean our armor?" Stacy asks as Wendy and I drag Larry to the couch.

"They sometimes use a paste-like plastic substance that is applied then peeled off during decontamination, but I was thinking that we take a dip in that pool at the Overlord's Branson estate. If that doesn't work, you can lean on your Uncle Sam to get you the right decon equipment. Do you still have a watertight seal?"

"I'm good," she answers.

"Any word on Gravmatar?"

"Our medical team is working on him, and Robin has sent the chariot to Columbia to bring his personal physicians. Even if he is imprisoned on our planet, I don't like the idea of what the Rigellians would do if they find out he's been killed. I was going to ask Apollo to pick us up after we got Larry back to you, but Gravmatar's health takes precedence."

"Did they find anything at the launch site?" I ask, and begin unsnapping Larry's costume. No doubt, if Bobby was here he'd be doing his best rendition of a porn soundtrack and irritating the hell out of me. Wendy's holding a bag wide open for me to roll the costume into. "Andy? Can you interface with the environmental controls and shut off the vents to this area, and to where Gabby is sleeping? Best not to even chance exposing her to this."

"All they found is more traps left by the Overlord. Everything okay back at the base, Cal?"

"Larry's a bit heavier than I recalled, but we're managing."

Wendy attaches some monitoring sensors to him and activates a handheld. Her small fortune significantly upgraded our medical capabilities beyond the old wall mounted first aid kits and assorted eyewash stations.

"Pulse is good. Blood pressure is slightly elevated," she reads off the results.

"All things considered," I say, and bag up his mask and shirt; followed by dumping my arm-sleeves and gloves into the thick biohazard bag. "He's in pretty good shape for taking thirty-five missile hits in such a short span. I'm not sure that even with all the extra shield emitters Mega could've stopped that onslaught."

"Do we move him up to his room or just let him stay here?"

"Carrying him over here was enough for me," I say. "Besides, he's going to want to take several showers to get anything we missed. I'm already going to have to pitch this couch. There's no need to crap up anywhere else. In fact, why don't you go take a long shower and remind me to take one before I handle Gabba Gabba Do?"

"Got it. Since you've got a long flight ahead of you, why don't you let Andy run the suit, and you get cleaned up yourself? Oh, don't start with that frown Stringel. Andy won't take the suit into combat without you."

I just don't like anyone else, even my best android friend, controlling the armor. Possessive and insecure? That would be yes and yes.

Even so, I bow to Wendy's sensibility and run down the checklist to surrender control of my pride and joy to someone who isn't me. I also patch the scanner monitoring Larry's vitals into Andy's circuit so he can alert me if anything changes for the worse.

"Hurry back, Cal," Stacy says. "You can finish your story as soon as you're done showering."

"Actually, if I patch the audio up to my bathroom, I can talk and shower at the same time."

"Two things at once?" she mocks. "I wouldn't want you to stress yourself."

"Ha, ha. Funny. Too bad you aren't here. It would make showering more fun. It's a damned shame I don't have a shard big enough to use as an escape hatch from your armor. Actually, I can start by transmitting you the video from my suit on the night I went to liberate Larry."

"Do you have any idea how much panic that created when everyone found out he was missing?"

Knowing she can't see my smile, I laugh and say, "Watching people run around in a panic is something of a hobby of mine. Even when I'm shallow, I try to be deep."

"Or full of shit," Stacy's zinger follows me up the steps.

"That too," I acknowledge.

• • •

There wasn't much to be said about the area surrounding Asheville, North Carolina. It was as scenic as any other part of Appalachia, and looked to be more exciting as the flat portions of Nebraska that dominated my childhood and became the motivating factor for me to do well in school, so that I could leave and never return. Even so, twenty miles northwest of the largest city in the western part of North Carolina was mostly mountains, the Appalachian Trail, and one really special facility.

It had been a strange ride since I got my acceptance and scholarship to UCLA. If I could go back and tell that wet behind his ears kid something, I wasn't sure if I'd have him swallow the red pill or the blue one.

The green tint from my night vision gear gave everything an unearthly glow. This was also my first real time out in the armor rather than sitting in the control chair.

Imaginary Larry was a world class telekinetic, and I had no idea if his powers could somehow muck with the armor. Plus, there was something about being in the suit that made the heart pump a little faster, and provided an extra edge that remoting sometimes lacked.

Sometimes being a "hands on kind of guy" is a good thing. Unless that crushes my ubersuit like a beer can; then it was a really bad idea.

Then again, I have that big shard installed in the tail section. I should be able to pull my legs up and slide right back through into the base if my suit gets a failing grade on the Imaginary Larry test.

Larry's high school was more like a complex. Part of it is an actual old high school that's been repurposed into a personal sanitarium. The nearby middle school, or at least that's what Larry thought it to be, was an always manned, National Guard Armory.

I actually wasn't too concerned with those dudes. It was three in the morning, and Larry was situated far enough away from any major population centers that the Olympians, and whatever reinforcements they could scrounge up, could recapture him before he got too far. He simply wasn't worth the effort for the bad guys to control and transport to wherever they planned to unleash him. A few had tried and failed miserably, most notably General Devious who thought her own mental powers could soothe the savage beast.

Momentarily regaining his faculties didn't sit well with him, and the General ordered a tactical withdrawal, with my old pal Maxine carrying her away at super speed, while Larry destroyed her floating throne chair and beat the snot out of her minions. The General's catastrophic failure firmly established that only an idiot would ever try and free Larry from his padded cell.

Perhaps nature actually does abhor a vacuum, because it produced me—a bigger, better, idiot. A montage played in my mind of everyone I'd known who had, at one time or another, called me the "I" word, and it didn't calm me.

"Is something wrong, Calvin?" Andy asked. The android was the only one I could recall who'd never accused me of being mentally challenged in some way, shape, or form.

"Just thinking of all the ways this can go wrong," I replied.

"I am confident you will succeed. Based on the capabilities of your new Mechani-CAL suit, I estimate that you have a sixty-three percent chance of victory should you be forced to defend yourself from him."

"Thanks for the vote of confidence. Although, I'm not sure I want to call this armor, Mechani-CAL. It seems like it is so much more."

"What name would you choose for it? In almost all categories, it outclasses the performance parameters of the Ultraweapon armor."

"With him going to prison, I guess I could start calling myself the new Ultraweapon. What do you think, pal?"

"It seems like an acceptable name for now. Perhaps you will come up with one that is more suitable, in the future."

Andy doesn't really understand human pettiness. I, on the other hand, am all too familiar with it. Taking Patterson's name would be the icing on the cake! That's right! I'm the new Ultraweapon and one badass mofo! What the hell? If a nuke couldn't kill me, what's the worst a forty-year old teenager could do?

Larry and the therapist playing his "dad" lived in a two-story farmhouse within walking distance from the school. Supposedly, he'd have his telekinetic construct "friends" over for sleepovers and study sessions. The therapist was a cousin to that Mather bastard I waxed at Mount Olympus, and also a projecting empath, but on a much weaker scale than MindOver.

While Andy disabled the alarm systems, I planned to use the hose that replaced one of my grenade launchers. It was hooked to a tank of knockout gas. The plan was to get in, snatch Larry while he dreamed, and take him somewhere else to meet his new world.

It was a good plan, which was precisely why I felt it was doomed to failure.

• • •

To the credit of my armor's builder, namely me, it survived being dashed into the ground from one hundred and fifty feet in the air. One minute I'd been flying along with the sleeping prince on his twin-sized bed, and the next thing I experienced was the telekinetic pile driver.

The shields protested, losing forty percent and frying one emitter outright, but they held. Already, they were recovering as I pushed the suit into an upright position and brought my weapons online.

Larry's bed was smashed into the ground and he stood next to it, flaring with his power. A small army of telekinetic constructs surrounded him.

When Wendy and I had fought him, she said that the Olympians usually wore him down until he dropped. That might take some time, but I didn't have much to do anyway.

"Looks like we're doing this the hard way," I said, and opened up with the four pulse cannons. There were cases and cases of grenades and fifty caliber machine guns also available to me, but I still lamented not having some kind of unstoppable weapon yet.

His constructs swarmed over me, but the large number he created actually worked to my advantage. My shields were repowering faster than the constructs could wear them down. If he focused his attack into bolts like the one that had knocked me down, or into a couple of giant sized energy forms, I'd be in trouble.

With cannons blazing, I walked toward him like one of those stupid TV weathermen in a hurricane, trying not to let the band members climbing onto my back and beating at me with their instruments bother me. We'd crashed into the side of a mountain and he held the high ground, so it was a foot-by-foot struggle to break through the energy barring my way.

A construct in the form of a pole-vaulter slammed into me and I responded by turning on the fifty calibers and added something physical that he'd have to deal with. I also kicked on the sonics built into the thorax, thank you Bo Carr.

For the first time in my life, I actually was the unstoppable force, breaking through wave after wave of constructs. Though it slowed me, I cut off the steady stream of bullets. I didn't want to injure the man if I could avoid it. I also eventually turned off the sonics.

The tide started to turn in my favor, and maybe on a subconscious level he was starting to panic. Detecting an energy anomaly ahead, I angled my shields forward and seconds later a powerful bolt smashed into them. The wedge of power I'd created in front of me turned white against the exertion, but stayed active. Larry's bolts came at the expense of his constructs, which dwindled in number.

Seeing that wasn't working, he spun and fled. Some of Larry's "friends" tried to help him run, but I closed the gap and brushed them aside.

Finally, it was he and I. "Take it easy, Larry. I'm just here to give you your medal. Don't you want your medal?"

"What medal?"

"The state championship basketball game in Charlotte; don't you remember? You were the MVP."

His medal might have once belonged to Chain Charmer's husband, but that was beside the point.

"Who are you?"

"I'm Coach Cal. The basketball coach. Remember?"

"Uhhh, what are you wearing?"

"This? Oh, this is one of those suits they make for you to help you walk. I got in a bad car accident after you won the game and they only let me out of the hospital last week. When I found out you didn't have your medal, I came to give it to you."

Lying to someone not fully in possession of his faculties turned out to be really easy for me. I'd prepared this whole lie earlier with Andy and Bobby, but even so, it just flowed out of me as natural as could be.

I guess that doesn't speak very well about me, but what's a guy gonna do?

"Where's my watch?" Larry asked in a panic. "Dad said he'd never forgive me if I lost it! It's a priceless family heirloom."

He was referring to the GPS unit they made him wear. It had taken Andy two minutes to override the damn thing and make it fall off Larry's hand. I was going to have to check him for other tracking devices, but that could wait.

Needing a quick answer, I said, "I think your dad took it into town to have a repair shop put a new battery in it. Don't worry. So, are you ready to get your medal?"

He seemed a little skeptical, but straightened up. Some of his remaining constructs came to his side and appeared to be cheering him on.

Opening a small compartment in my armor, I slid out the necklace and felt a pang of regret. If this worked, the boy who never grew up was about to be evicted from Neverland. I don't normally face moral dilemmas, well that's not true; I usually just don't let them bother me that much.

Letting it drop over his head and onto his neck, I took two steps back and held my breath.

Larry grabbed his forehead with his right hand and sank to the ground. A couple of his constructs reached to help him, but they disappeared; followed quickly by all the other shapes that had been milling about.

"Mister Hitt? Can you understand me?"

"What's... what's going on...? I don't... what."

"Take it easy for a minute. Focus on my voice if that helps. You are a superhuman with incredible telekinetic powers. Those powers have been out of control for years. The necklace I just gave you dampens that power. Hopefully, you can think straight now. Do you understand this?"

Thrusting his left hand out, he screamed, "No!"

His energy became an extension of his hand and it was as large as I was. It crashed into me and sent the suit hurtling backward and I was reminded that I hadn't been concerned about so many constructs before and was glad he didn't just focus on just a single attack.

I wasn't glad anymore.

The energy swelled around him, becoming a full body some twenty-feet tall, with him hovering in the center of it. Spending a good chunk of my life dealing with criminal lowlifes, I recognized the look of murderous rage on his face. Whatever was going on in his mind at that time wasn't my problem. *He* was my problem!

"No!" he shouted again. "It's not true!"

Both his transparent arms reached for me, but I used my jetpack and went skyward. He responded by ripping chunks of earth from the ground and throwing them at me.

It took all of one hit and the loss of a second shield emitter to break me out of my funk.

"Round two it is!" Four pulse cannons lanced downward and struck one of the arms he used to shield himself.

He ripped whole trees out and chucked them at me. I responded by flying higher and that's when I knew he didn't know how to effectively wield his powers. He doubled in size to forty feet, but I didn't detect a corresponding change in energy output. Sure, he was bigger, but the power was less defined.

If he survives this, maybe I can help him with that, I thought, and then let him have it.

Sustained fire from the pulse cannons rained down on him like a sleet storm and drove the telekinetic version of King Kong to his knees. When he curled into a fetal ball, I stopped and waited for thirty seconds before descending next to the giant head.

"Mind telling me what that was about?" I demanded, my voice booming over my external speakers.

The energy-being dissipated, and all that was left was a forty year old man, sobbing in the middle of what used to be the side of a mountain that now looked like it had taken a dozen missile strikes.

He mumbled something about his mom and I said, "What?"

"I killed her! My powers went out of control right before I graduated high school and I killed her! Don't you understand! I killed my own mother!"

Guess that explains why they never had a "mom" living with him. Also, why he never graduated, and always reset to a ninth grader every time he was about to get his diploma.

"Damn," I said, not expecting that. "For what it's worth, I'm sorry, Larry. But you've been torturing yourself over this for over twenty years, and it sounds like it was beyond your control."

"Cal," Andy said. "I recommend you keep him talking. If you get him to confront the issue, it may defuse the situation."

"Copy that," I said.

"Who're you talking to?" Larry asked. I hadn't switched off the microphone.

"You ever hear of Andydroid? He's on my team and wants to meet you. But before that, tell me more about your mom."

My inquiry pushed him back into a funk and he said, "She had the power too, but nothing like mine," he babbled. "Mom was always on me about control and not hurting anyone. We got into an argument... she didn't... want me to go to college until she said I was... ready... and I... I..."

I guess I've gotten better with the pop psychologist bit. "Anyone with powers has made mistakes. I've made enough of my own to know that.

There's plenty of blood on my hands too, Larry. If you let us, we can help."

"I don't want your help! I should die for what I did!"

Okay, maybe I still suck monkeyballs at head games. How about this, then?

In response I turn toward one of the trees that'd been knocked over and had the root ball exposed and fired all my weapons at it. Satisfied with the destruction, I turned back to him. "You've got three choices, Larry. Number one, take off the necklace and go back to being the ninth grader worried about oversleeping for your morning class and if Peggy Sue likes you. A few more decades and you can use social security to pay for your lunch money. Number two, I leave this mountain with your blood on my hands. I'm sure if you learned how to use your powers better, you might be able to stop me from killing you, but you haven't. If you really want your ticket punched, I'll be your huckleberry! Or, you can pick what's behind door number three, which means you accept what happened twenty years ago and man the hell up! Obviously, your mom was right, and you weren't ready for college, but the only school I'm offering is the school of hard knocks. You'll be around a few other misfits of the superhuman world and you can figure out your powers, and figure out what kind of man you want to be. Take a few minutes and think it over, Hitt. This is the biggest decision you'll ever make, maybe the last one too, so think long and hard."

Activating my jetpack, I gave the guy some space. Andy immediately asked me, "Calvin, I fail to see how eliminating Imaginary Larry would advance our cause?"

"Can't make a person who doesn't want to live, want to, Andy. If he wants a mercy killing, I can't think of a good reason to deny it."

"You were able to coax Aphrodite out of suicidal depression during the bug crisis," he replied.

"Not the same, in my eyes. Aphrodite was a functioning hero before the bugs. This guy's a train wreck. The only person who can get him out of this mess is himself. They've had an army of specialists try to help him through the years. Other than the necklace, I've got nothing to offer him when it comes to how to live your life. In case you haven't noticed, I'm pretending to be dead to the world at the moment."

"Not quite knowing what it is like to be alive makes it hard to fathom why someone would want to abandon it so quickly."

The robot had a point, but I wasn't really the person to debate deep issues like that. Instead, I went for something we could both grasp. "Did you get the readings on his energy levels? He was pumping out megajoules even with the necklace on. You could power a whole city with what he's capable of!"

"Quite true, Calvin."

"Yeah, if he'd compressed those rocks into a tiny missile and shot it at me, it'd be like one of those railguns the Navy keeps working on. Even with my extra shielding I wouldn't have stood a second hit from something like that unless I was really, really lucky."

Holy shit! That's it!

"Andy! Andy! I know what we should make for this suit's ultimate weapon!"

"Based on your level of excitement, I am guessing you would like to make a railgun. Is this correct?"

"You bet your ass it is!"

"It is difficult to imagine a reason why wagering an integral part of your anatomy is justified. As to your proposition, we will require an additional power supply for this base in order to charge the weapon, but the space in this area should be sufficient. However, the cost of the materials would be a problem."

"I was already trying to figure out how to approach Wendy, this just gives me another reason."

I did see an interview where she said she'd be happy to see me one more time. The question is would she be happy enough to buy me the parts to make a hypersonic railgun?

For the next few minutes, I went over the possibilities of what we could fit into the area. That went on until Andy reminded me that it had been twelve minutes and I should go check on Larry.

I'm OCD, not ADD, but who wouldn't get distracted by the prospect of their very own megaweapon?

"I was beginning to think you weren't coming back for me." Larry said, sounding a bit defeated.

"Sorry," I replied. "I got held up with another issue. Did you decide what you want to do?"

"I remembered that woman, she got into my mind and said that she'd help me make everyone pay. I didn't like that."

"Oh, General Devious," I said. "Yeah, she's a megabitch. As I recall, you sent her packing with her tail between her legs."

"What do you want from me?"

"A dead guy, who could see the future, sent me a warning that something is gonna happen in San Francisco in a few months. His warning said I needed the most powerful people I could find. Most supers would lose half their powers with that necklace on. On you, that's a good thing, but even with it, you're still one of the most powerful people on this planet. I want you on that team, at least for whatever is going down in California. You wanna walk after that, I won't stop you. In the meantime, you can lay low at my base and figure out what you want to do with your life; or you can take either of the other options tonight."

The manboy thought it over. He didn't strike me as the suicidal type. If he was, he'd have done himself in already.

Finally he said, "Dying's like giving up, and Mom only wanted me to be the best person I was able to be. I don't want to go back to thinking I'm some thirteen year old, so I guess I'll go with you. Maybe if I work real hard at being a hero, it'll make her proud of me."

Guess he's been upgraded from Neverland, to the Island of Misfit Toys. There I go again, mixing metaphors.

"Fair enough, Mister Hitt. We got the one government tracking device off of you, but Andy needs to scan you to see if there are any others. We've spent too much time here, so let's put some distance between us and here and then meet up with him."

"You weren't really going to kill me," Larry stated, rather than asked.

"Why would you think I wouldn't?" I answered.

"Well, you're a superhero. You wouldn't do that. Hey, why are you laughing?"

"Get to know me a little and you'll understand. Now use your telekinesis and grab onto my arm. I'll fly us deeper into the mountains and Andy will meet us when we land."

The dude didn't make it a hundred feet before he started blowing chunks all over the suit. *Airsickness! Add that to his list of problems... and mine too.*

• • •

"I don't think you would have killed him," Stacy says.

"I agree with your assessment," Andy adds.

Hesitating before I toss the towel into the hamper, I instead set it on the sink. I'd need to check it for contamination before deciding its fate.

Glad they seem so certain, I think. Wish I could say the same.

"I'm just happy I didn't have to make the decision. Larry's a decent guy who was dealt a pretty raw deal. Except for being a decent guy, he's a lot like me."

Chapter Fourteen

Oz Against the World

As I finish telling Stacy about how I recruited Larry, Wendy marches in with a fussy Gabolicious in her arms and holds her out to me. She's got her "I'm annoyed face" on. I'm pretty used to it at this point.

"Naked here!" I protest.

"If you spent less time running your trap, you'd have some clothes on. Your daughter wants you and won't take no for an answer. Besides, been there done that, and she's the proof. I'm going to finish getting into costume. Andy, what's the ETA?"

With Stacy's stifled laughter crackling on the channel, Andy replies, "We are currently ninety minutes out. Larry is awake, but I have told him to remain on the couch until one of you can provide protective clothing so that he may access the showers."

When Wendy looks at me, I smile and hold up the Gabster. "Can't watch her, get dressed and help Larry at the same time. Booties and coveralls are in the utility closet. Yell, if you need anything. You're really good at that. If he's up for it, he'll be able to put it on with his powers."

"You blow chunks, Stringel. You know that?"

Smiling at my daughter I say, "Mommy doesn't like to lose arguments. That's right! No, she doesn't."

"Get over yourself," she retorts.

I point at the speaker and say, "They were just saying what a decent guy I am."

The brunette baby mama gives a derisive snort and says, "You keep saving Andy's life, and as for Aphrodite, it's a known fact that gorgeous women have questionable choices in men. If she's the most gorgeous in the world, that makes you the biggest questionable choice in history! Compared to her last boyfriend, you might actually be a decent guy, but I know better."

At least she admits I'm an upgrade over Lazarus Patterson, may he never rest in peace.

As Wendy vacates my suite and my girlfriend openly cackles across the radio link, I grab a fresh towel and carry my daughter out to her playpen. She fusses when I set her in it, but I give her Mr. Quackers and hope the plushy duck buys me enough time to get changed. The way she is yanking at him makes me wonder if this will be the stuffed animal's last stand. *This isn't a playpen! This is Sparta!*

"I hope you don't get your mom's temper," I say to my daughter as I note the gleeful look of destruction on her otherwise angelic face. "Then again, my temper usually ends up with people dead, so here's hoping you get your disposition from someone else in the family."

Pulling on a fresh set of undies, I grab a pair of shorts and one of my many Biz Markie concert shirts. To the speaker I say, "Where'd we leave off before I was so rudely interrupted by a washed up TV starlet?"

Wendy chimes in from downstairs, "The speaker is on down here, I heard that!"

Of course, I knew that already. "You just washed up, you were a TV starlet, and were pretty rude about interrupting us. Tell me what part of that is untrue?"

Her angry growl is so worth it. If Shakespeare wrote a play about us, it would be *The Taunting of the Shrew.* I would probably be killed at the end of the play, but I've learned that death is what you make of, or perhaps fake of, it.

"Larry was yakking all over your armor," Stacy says. "I'm guessing that irritated you."

"I can't help it if I don't like to fly!" Larry says defensively.

"No harm done," I reply to him. "Anyway, Larry came here, started mastering his powers, got season tickets to the Panther's games, met Bobby and learned the high art of watching porn on one screen while playing video games on the other—and the judge at Bobby's sentencing hearing said he'd never have anything to offer society!"

"Hey, that's harsh," Larry protests.

"In defense of Mr. Hitt," Andydroid states. "He is also taking college level courses from me and is a very capable student."

"He also cleans up after himself, and his cooking is worlds beyond what you are capable of!" Wendy fires back.

I start to teasingly ask how many times Larry took home economics and stop myself. That's a low blow that I'm not willing to throw.

Instead I go with, "I build robots to clean up after me and give me time to raise a beautiful little butt kicker. And you're not one to point fingers, Ms. Laguardia or should I say Ms. 'Where's the catering truck?' Your cooking isn't much better than mine."

"Many of our culinary problems would be solved if you would prioritize building a new body for me," Andy comments. "I am able to emulate master chefs when properly outfitted."

"You know how busy I've been, Andy," I protest. It's kind of a hollow one. I've been keeping my friend on the back burner for way too long, and if I'm being honest, Andy is more like a sculpture than a robot. I'm afraid that nothing I build will be up to the genius of his creator. Albright is a DaVinci, and I'm a guy who makes stuff go boom.

"I can give you a detailed breakdown on the amount of time you've spent in the past week fornicating, if you would like?" Andy deadpans. Clearly, he thinks working on the new chassis is more important than sleeping with Stacy. He's very wrong in this instance.

"Well, this just proves you all are as dysfunctional as any team I've been around. Say, Andy?" Stacy interrupts our banter. "Why can't you build your own body?"

"I can repair an existing body, but my programing prohibits creation of a brand new body. Doctor Albright specifically encoded this in his robots to prevent them from self-replication."

"That might be a problem," she says.

"What are you thinking, Stacy?" I say.

"Well, I know Robin will go to Doctor A. and find out if there are any things our team can do, if we are forced to fight the Megasuit. If you know of any other backdoors in your code Andy, you might want to consider how to defend against them."

"The lady has a point," Wendy says. "Since Cal is the best qualified to help you, and it's his fault to begin with, he's going to check your code for any Easter eggs after he finishes your new body."

By the end of that, Wendy sounds rather smug. "Sometimes I regret asking you to be the leader, La Guardia."

"Not as often as I do," Wendy says in a sing-song voice. "Go ahead and tell her, Cal. You're pretty much up to that part anyway."

• • •

It was a miserable day for a reunion. All the credit in the world goes to those folks who fly out into hurricanes to take measurements, but gusts of wind up to one hundred and twenty miles per hour kicked the suit around as I approached the eyewall of Hurricane Ishmael.

Sixty miles north, the southeastern part of Cuba was already taking a pounding from the storm, and a certain pregnant superheroine was out in the middle of it all, trying to weaken it. This was the chance I'd been waiting for to get her alone. Her mother had hired Paper Tiger to be her bodyguard and he rarely left Wendy's side. There was even a rumor of a budding romance between the two of them. I wouldn't say I was jealous, but she could do better.

She's done worse!

Using logic, I was able to narrow my search area. She had to be on the northern side of the storm, near the center. I tapped into weather buoys to try to find any area where the barometric pressure was significantly higher than the rest, but that came up empty. There were bursts of radio transmissions from her, garbled in static, which I used in a "getting warmer/getting colder fashion."

Essentially, she was a five foot three inch needle in the haystack of a dark and angry sky. It took me exactly one hundred and twenty-seven minutes of searching before I finally located her, or more appropriately, the six hundred foot tall waterspout, rotating counter to the direction of the hurricane, which was what caught my eye. She was chipping away at it, and had been for hours—all in the name of improving relations between the US and it's considerably smaller neighbor.

I don't think it really does a damn bit of good for international relations, but Wendy is the most popular hero in Cuba who isn't a national, so bully for her. Even if she'd clearly like to be somewhere else.

My baby mama was seven months along, and past the point where doctors would advise against a normal human flying in airplanes. Several people were questioning whether even a superhero should be out in this, given how far along she was. I happened to be one of them. Her leadership of the Gulf Coast Guardians was spotty at best, because her condition somewhat limited her ability to fight crime. I was certain that very much annoyed her, because I knew she wanted to lead a team, and not simply bankroll it. Sheila didn't seem to mind, because it left her in charge most of the time.

Approaching the waterspout, I had Andy begin jamming the Guardian's frequencies and hoped it would be seen as just a random atmospheric disruption occurring in a monstrous Category Five hurricane.

The windspeed picked up as I approached Wendy's funnel cloud. If Larry was here, he'd be spewing vomit everywhere. As it was, I wasn't doing so hot when I broke through the outer rim.

My worries about how much longer it would take to find her were pushed aside in a near fit of hysterical laughter. She had this neon orange vest thing on. I didn't know whether to take a picture, or mindwipe the image from my brain before it became trapped in there.

She didn't notice me because she was fiddling with her headset and looking angry, so, I drew to within twenty feet of her and activated the floodlights attached to my armor's shoulders.

Startled, the headset fell from her hands and was swept away by the currents of air swirling around us. Guess I didn't have to worry about her calling for backup.

Her mouth was moving, but it's not exactly like we could carry on a conversation in the middle of her smaller storm, which sat in the middle of a much larger storm. So, I held my hands up in what I hoped to be a peaceful gesture and beckoned her to come closer. I would have moved toward her, but I was having a hard enough time staying level.

Wendy waited for a few seconds; no doubt evaluating how much of a threat I was, before drifting to within five feet.

"What do you want?" she screamed.

"Sorry for the scare, but I wanted to come talk to you in private," I used my external microphones to let the suit answer for me.

"I don't recognize you!"

"I'm still working on a name, how does the new Ultraweapon sound?"

"Retarded!" she replies. "Well, you went to all the trouble to find me, what's so fucking important?"

"I hope you can rein in that mouth of yours when you're raising our daughter!"

"What did you say?"

"I said our daughter! Or am I that easy to forget? I'd open the helmet to prove it, but there's no way I'm letting that much moisture into the suit."

"Cal Stringel is dead! And trying to make me think he's alive is only going to make me kick your ass even harder!"

"Here I didn't think you cared, Wendy. It's good to see you, too! What's with the stupid vest? I know it's not your idea."

"If you really are Cal Stringel, you could tell me something that wasn't in the book. Something only the two of us would know."

"I sanitized most of your dialogue in the book to cut out the foul language."

"Not good enough! Anyone who knows me knows that I have a New York City mouth."

"Okay," I say going over my mental list of things I could tell her that I didn't choose to publish. "After I'd asked if you wanted me to get down on one knee, and you shot me down, I joked with you in private the next day that we should at least sleep with each other again and see if we liked it. You kicked me in the shin, hard. I asked why you couldn't just slap me across the face like a normal woman, and then you kicked me in the other shin—just as hard."

Small wonder that incident didn't make it to publication, isn't it?

The waterspout began collapsing, as a cocoon of air enveloped us. It was dead calm inside, no driving rain or anything else.

"All right, open up! If you're really Cal, I want to see it, and then I want to hear what you have to say for yourself."

I pop open the helmet, which spreads on a vertical line and look at her large, vest covered stomach. "How's little Gabby doing?"

"You look like Cal and sound like him, but shape changers do exist, so how about you tell me how in the fuck you managed to survive a nuclear explosion?"

"Remotely operated armor, Wendy. Those pieces of that dinosaur's magic mirror are a functioning two way portal. After I got it finished, I went back to my little hideout in Alabama and ran it from there. When that armor was destroyed, it took me awhile to build this new set. I was just going to stay retired, but I was visiting the site of my old base that I blew up to flee from the Olympians, when I got a postcard from Prophiseer. I could have it passed through one of the portals in my armor if you want to see it, or I can just show you a hologram of it, your choice."

She opted for the hologram and I projected it. "That's in four months! If this is legit, you should have fucking come to me earlier!"

"Didn't want to blow my secret, and didn't have a suit ready. My team needs a leader, and you're the best one I know."

"Your team? You have a fucking team! Who else is on it? I'm barely leading my team as it is!"

"I broke the spell on Andydroid, so there's him, but he needs a complete body. From the villain side, I've got my old pal, Hillbilly Bobby..."

"That's all? You'd be hard pressed to fight a Guardian team!"

"You haven't seen this armor yet. My railgun is almost finished. But, you cut me off before I got to the best part."

"Fine!" the ill-tempered tornado queen growls. "Impress me."

"Imaginary Larry, your bitchiness. Fully aware and working to control his powers, Imaginary Larry! What've you got to say about that?"

That did the trick, and she closed her slack jaw and asked, "How?"

"The Logger's necklace," I answered. "Remember that? His power is cut in half, but he can think clearly. So what if he can only move half a mountain instead of the whole damned thing?"

"You're the insane, son of a bitch who kidnapped Larry?"

"I prefer the term liberated," I said.

"I've got a few terms I'd like to use right now," she said, menacingly.

"Just save the name calling," I stated.

"What makes you think I want to lead another team? Much less one with you on it?"

That actually stung. "Because I know you're not happy, even with the Gulf Coasters. Jin was arguably the most effective person on your roster besides you and he just went back out on his own. Who're you going to replace him with? All the best go to the East and West Coast teams leaving you and the idiots in Montreal fighting over the sloppy seconds."

"I've talked Paper Tiger into coming onboard," she said defensively.

"Your bodyguard? Yeah, he seems okay and maybe a notch below Chain Charmer, but dammit Wendy, you're a powerhouse! You deserve a team of people in your league; a team that takes no shit from anyone, even the Olympians!"

"And you're suddenly in my league? Did your death come with those delusions of grandeur or did they come after the fact?"

"In this armor," I said. "Yeah, I am. I've got a nearly unlimited power supply and the firepower of an entire base at my disposal. Did I just mention that I'm building a damn railgun? Besides, Larry didn't just up and come with me. We had ourselves a little fight first and wrecked the side of a mountain in the process. I won. He didn't. Andy's done the simulations and has me beating Patterson's last suit or even his nuclear robot nine times out of ten."

Of course, that was with the not yet completed railgun, but she didn't need to know that at the moment.

She's still not convinced, I could tell.

"Look at it this way," I said. "You hate the bureaucracy. I know you do! Your dad is even using my book to try and clamp down on people with super powers. I just..."

Wendy cut me off. "Yeah let's talk about the book, you miserable fucking bastard! Do you have the slightest idea of how much damage you caused? Do you?"

"It's only going to cause problems for the people who let it! The question is – are you letting it cause problems for you and what're you going to do about it? The truth hurts, Wendy! And that book was pretty damn close to the truth. You told me you went to the Gulf Coast team because you were going to walk and fund your own squad if they didn't let you. Is New Orleans everything you dreamed it would be? My team has

187

no plans of getting Uncle Sam's or the UN's stamp of approval. Everyone seems to think the only time I'm worth a damn is when the world needs saving, so that's what Larry and I are going to do. We're going into the kick ass and take names business with no government oversight, no public relations people, no mission reports and patrols. I've had my share of the limelight and it sucked donkey balls."

"So if your suit is all that," Wendy challenged. "How come you haven't broken into Patterson's cell and do what you did to Mather?"

"I figure the best revenge is letting him rot in prison while he tries to figure out how my suit works. Since magic won't occur to him, it's going to drive him insane. Of course, if he somehow walks free, I'll make sure he doesn't get very far."

"You're serious about this team," Wendy said. It was half a question and half a statement.

"You bet! But I'm not the person to be in charge. That's where I need you. C'mon Wendy, if anyone can keep me and Larry on the straight and narrow, it's you."

"Let me think this over," she said. I took it as a good sign.

"So, what's with the stupid orange vest? Thinking of finishing the day off with some deer hunting?"

"They made me put it on in order to come out here. If I faint, this thing is supposed to inflate and become some kind of survival bubble to protect me."

"That must annoy you to no end," I said. "Do you want to slip through the portal piece in my armor and take a look at my base, meet Larry for yourself, or get a cup of coffee?"

"Had to give up coffee, for a few more months. About the only substitute I can stomach is peppermint tea, but I could really go for some pizza right about now. Got any of that?"

"It's frozen, does that matter?"

"Normally, I would say yes, but right now, no. So, this teleportal thing? Is it safe?"

"Andy doesn't believe it will harm the baby, but I'll understand if you don't want to go through it. It's a shortcut through another dimension, not some dematerialization process, just like walking through a door to the next room."

"Okay. I'm in. How do I get to your portal?"

I laughed and told her.

"Crawl up your ass? I guess that proves you're Cal Stringel!"

I didn't know why she thought that and wasn't certain I wanted to, but opened the rear doors and let her go through to the base.

Five minutes into introductions, karma paid Wendy back, and her high tech safety vest inflated. It was on some kind of timer that'd been tripped by her being out of communication with the Gulf Coasters for too long. It was like my lost dream of putting Hermes in a giant plastic ball had finally come true! The amount of profanity Wendy began to hurl made me wonder if she didn't possess some super speed as well.

Needless to say, everyone, except Wendy, got a good laugh out of that.

• • •

"Bobby wanted to play piñata, but I had to remind him that there was a pregnant and highly irritated woman inside," I add.

"Yeah," Wendy says. "It was great. Given how my involvement in this team started, it was a bad omen. First thing jackass here did was hit me up for a loan to buy all the things for his railgun."

"Oh, you love us, and you know it," I say.

"I like Andy and Larry," she replies. "I tolerate Bobby, and I'm stuck with you."

I laugh at her while I crawl up inside of Megasuit, retrieve Andy's head, and transfer him back onto the Type A frame so he can finish removing the contaminated material and I could reassume control of Mega. Settling into the control chair, I bring up the datastream and assess the situation.

"We're ten minutes out," I announce. "Any sign of activity at the estate?"

"The satellite we had borrowed passed out of range sixteen minutes ago. The next one we can use will not be available until seven minutes after we have arrived."

"All right, team," Wendy says. "Cal, flip the portal around. I'll go now. Larry, can you be ready in five?"

"I'm good."

"Game faces, people. Let's cut the stupid shit and pretend we know what we're doing. Cal's knowledge of the defenses is a few years old, so expect that they have been upgraded."

Reversing the shard, I roll the suit over so Wendy has a downward exit vector. "You're clear, bosslady."

She slides out the suit's exit and immediately the wind speed increases and wraps around her slim figure, turning her into a tiny blue and silver dart soaring next to my armor.

At the five-minute mark, Larry goes through. We try to minimize his flight time where possible. It's easier than listening to him complain or vomit.

The incredibly powerful telekinetic slingshots himself out, spins and latches onto the back of my suit like an electromagnet and he literally holds on for dear life.

Minutes later, we descend on the estate. A dozen Type B robots roll out the welcome wagon, spitting plasma energy at us. A sudden squall sends them careening away with their gyroscopes straining to correct their course. Stacy and I fire our weapons while Larry's energy form crushes two underfoot, and fields a third like a grounder to second. The robot crumples in his hand like an overripe tomato.

His tactic seems wasteful to a salvager like me, but it's hard to argue with the results.

The fight was over before it had even started.

Heading to the front door, I ask. "Do you think we should knock?"

"Just kick the fucking door in!" Wendy shouts.

"As you wish," I answer and comply. Over the private channel, I ask Stacy, "You picking up any emotions?"

"No," she answers. "I think your man, West, is gone."

"They could have added an escape tunnel," I say and turn to Andy. "Hey Andy, is the satellite in position yet?"

"Not yet."

"When it gets into position, start checking the surrounding area to see if you can find West."

Standing in the foyer a sculpture, really a cosmetically enhanced Type A, waits for us.

In a poorly rendered mechanical voice, the robot says, "The Overlord will greet you in the conference room. This way please."

"Trap?" Larry asks aloud.

"I would be disappointed if it was not," I say, using my Andy voice and trying not to use any contractions. The earlier encounter with the West Coasters could come back to haunt our lie, but there's nothing I can do about that. "I will go in alone with full shields. Even if he has a self-destruct, it will not get through. I will transmit our conversation."

"Be careful what you say to him." Wendy warns.

The question is whether his truth detection powers had a range limit.

The others remain outside while I march down the hallway to the conference room. A hologram of the Overlord floats just above the center of the long table. Jerimiah Orlin is in his early fifties with a full head of black hair and a goatee that gives off that whole Ming the Merciless vibe. He radiates contempt for everyone.

There was a time when that would have intimidated me. The last time I'd seen him was during the whole HORDES nonsense. Since then, I'd saved the world twice, and drunk from the cup of badassedness. Now, his act just keeps me on my guard.

"I see only one of you decided to accept my kind offer," he begins.

"I figured that I was the one you wished to speak with, Jerimiah. Given your obsession with being the one to terminate Lazarus Patterson's existence. I suspect I will be having a similar conversation with Elaine in the near future."

"Such an interesting group you've surrounded yourself with little, Andydroid."

"I see news travels fast." *Impressive, but it makes the lie easier.*

"There are so many people out there with talents similar to mine. I specialize in helping these people realize their gift. A person who can hear conversations from miles away can be just as much of an asset as someone who can shoot fire from their hands. I learned your secrets and it was child's play to deduce your destination. Paul left well before you arrived, if you were looking for him. But now, what to do with you? You are the Tin Man, robot. You now have a heart, such that Stringel could be said to possess one. Perhaps it would be better to say you now have self-interest and it becomes something I can use against you."

"Starting a vendetta with me will only decrease your life expectancy, Overlord. My allies possess the kind of power you can only covet. You couldn't keep up with Patterson. What makes you believe you can succeed where he failed?"

Damn! Used a contraction!

"Ah, yes," he continues, unfazed by my threat. "Your team of merry adventurers. Perhaps I should be worried Tin Man, but then again, Wendy could be a stand in for Dorothy, so young and eager to prove herself. Goading her is no herculean task as Mr. Mather proved. And Mr. Hitt makes a suitable Cowardly Lion. He certainly looks impressive, destroying non-living opponents, but can you trust him against a living foe. I can promise you that he will be tested. You even completed the metaphor by bringing your own token Scarecrow—Aphrodite has been trying to prove she has a brain since she first was given her powers. The world remains sadly unconvinced."

"You mention Mather, but should be mindful of his fate. In your analogy, that makes you either the Wicked Witch or the Wizard. One dies and the other is proven a harmless fraud. Your best option is to walk away from this and find the darkest hole to hide in, but we both know that will not happen. Enjoy each sunrise because it may be the last one, so bring forth your flying monkeys and see how they fail."

Does that make Bobby Toto?

"Brave talk, you almost sounded human there for a second. The late Stringel didn't appear to care much for his parents, perhaps you will care about their fate more, or even the venerable Doctor Albright. Do not believe for a second that you don't have a weakness that can be exploited, Tin Man. Many battles are won before the forces take the field."

"Going after any of those would guarantee you would not survive our encounter."

He laughs. "The world blames me for the premature release of my bioengineered insects. In their eyes, I am guilty of genocide on the levels that make the likes of Pol Pot and Hitler look like rank amateurs. I know I will never go to prison. There is either death or the number of people I must destroy on my path to domination. Shall we see if I am up to the challenge?"

"I will have them put that speech on your tombstone."

"How considerate," the Overlord says, spreading his transparent hands wide. "Since you've squandered your first move, it is black's turn now. Pawn to Queen four."

The house is engulfed in a fierce, upward blast of plasma energy as the self-destruct mechanism activates. Megasuit's shields take it, and I ride the wave while trying to figure out his stupid chess metaphor.

Working the jetpack and stabilizers, I get the suit under control and see that it knocked the shields down to eighty-five percent—more powerful than expected, but still lame! Unfortunately, I know this is just the beginning... the best he could come up with at a moment's notice. He's already planning the next encounter.

Two can play at that game!

"Is the suit okay, Cal?" Stacy asks over our private channel, as her suit races up next to me. "How about you?"

"Yeah, we're both good."

"I'm going to personally kick his ass for that Scarecrow comment!"

Laughing, we rejoin the others while continuing our private conversation, "You'll get your chance. If it helps, I know you have a brain. Want to know why?"

"Let's hear it," the Olympian replies.

"Simple, you're with me."

"Some would argue differently," she says with a chuckle of her own.

"Before it gets crazy, I want to tell you something Stacy," I say, marshalling more courage than I needed to walk in and speak with the Overlord. I would be face to face with her much sooner.

"What's that?" she asks, with just a hint of quaver in her voice.

"It's easy for me to say I am in love with you, and I am, but you have heard that from virtually every guy you've ever given the time of day to, and I'm willing to bet a few women along the way. I want you to know beyond that, I respect you and I trust you."

She's quiet for a good five seconds and it is cause for a little concern. "Sorry, you caught me speechless for a moment. I've said those words before to men I didn't feel half as much of what I feel for you, Cal. I love you, too."

"The Overlord and others are going to try and stop our happily ever after."

I can almost hear the smile on her face. "Let them try!"

If I had empathy to spare, I'd feel sorry for our enemies.

But, I'm Cal Stringel, the original D-List Supervillain, so don't expect any pity or quarter from me. My origin is common knowledge. My confessions are a matter of public record. My secrets are shared with those I trust. Now, it's time for me to rise to the challenges ahead. Get in my way and you'll end up as roadkill on the yellow brick road. Consider yourself warned.

• • •

Cal Stringel and the New Renegades will return in *Rise of a D-List Supervillain.*

About the Author

Jim Bernheimer is the author of several novels and the publisher and editor of three anthologies. He lives in Chesapeake, Virginia with his wife and two daughters while writing whatever four out of the five voices in his head agree on. Visit his website at www.jimbernheimer.com

Other Books by the Author

Horror, Humor, and Heroes Volume I

Horror, Humor, and Heroes Volume II

Horror, Humor, and Heroes Volume III

Dead Eye: Pennies for the Ferryman

Dead Eye 2: The Skinwalker Conspiracies

Spirals of Destiny Book One: Rider

Spirals of Destiny Book Two: Sorceress

Prime Suspects: A Clone Detective Mystery

Origins of a D-List Supervillain

and

Confessions of a D-List Supervillain

The best is yet to come!

CPSIA information can be obtained at www.ICGtesting.com
Printed in the USA
LVOW10s1109091215

466106LV00015B/244/P